ONE STEP CLOSER

"What can I do to help?" He swore to himself he would do anything she asked, right down to murdering the bastard who had dared to touch her. He was shaking with fury, as close to exploding as he had felt in years.

"You can—you can—oh, God," she stammered, then dropped what she was holding into his outstretched palm. Something metallic jingled as it fell. "Take this. Take it, please."

He stared down at the blue loop, at first not comprehending. Then he realized it was Peavy's collar.

"Look at it," she demanded. "At first, I missed it, too. I thought it was the tags I heard, and then..."

She swayed and draped her arms over his shoulders. Helpless against the impulse, he embraced her tightly.

"The ring," she whispered in his ear. "Look at it—the ring."

That was when he saw the thick, gold band that hung between the rabies and ID tags. Still holding her, he turned it to stare at the three diamonds—diamonds he remembered winking on his brother's hand.

FATAL ERROR

COLLEEN THOMPSON

LEISURE BOOKS NEW YORK CITY

A LEISURE BOOK®

November 2004

Published by

Dorchester Publishing Co., Inc.
200 Madison Avenue
New York, NY 10016

ISBN 0-8439-5421-3

Printed in the United States of America.

Visit us on the web at www.dorchesterpub.com.

ACKNOWLEDGMENTS

Every book needs people to believe in it before it can become real. I'd like to thank some of those who had faith in *Fatal Error* from its earliest stages: critique partners Patricia Kay, Wanda Dionne, Linda Helman, Betty Joffrion, and Barbara Taylor Sissel; friend and mentor Kathleen Miller Y'Barbo; agent Meredith Bernstein; editor Alicia Condon and all the fine people at Dorchester Publishing. Thanks, too, to my husband Michael and son Andrew for giving me the peace and support needed to focus on this project.

I'd also like to express my sincere appreciation to William Simon of Abberline Investigations for sharing his expertise in the field of computer forensics and Ken DeHoff of Intel Corporation for his helpful comments regarding data recovery. Sheriff Ronny Dodson of Brewster County, Texas, served as a generous source of information on certain details of West Texas law enforcement. Any errors or omissions contained herein are my own. Finally, Ocotillo County, Texas, and its inhabitants are fictional creations. Any resemblance to real people and places is purely coincidental.

FATAL ERROR

Prologue

It is an uncomfortable fact that human remains are sacred only to the human race. To the scavengers, our dead are a food source only, no better or worse than the carrion of other species.

In the rugged backcountry of Southwest Texas, the margin for survival is thinner than in most places. The gaunt coyotes can no more afford to stand on ceremony than the turkey vultures or the badgers, the flies or stinging ants.

Yet even the hungriest leave something: a bone too hard for jaws to shatter, an indigestible mass of matted hair, a scrap of bloodstained denim. The scattered remnants linger, bearing witness to an ending as inexplicable as it was inhumane.

But not inhuman, no matter how vile the circumstances. And not unmourned, however lonely and remote the grave. For no heart should be defined by the fatal errors that lead it down the path to stillness, but rather by what drives it while it beats.

1

Chapter One

When Susan took a seat at one of the barbecue joint's tables, the rancher parents of one of her ex-students stood up and walked out of the place. But not before the graying redhead who had been one of her high school's most fervent volunteers shot her a world-class go-to-hell look. And not before the pain of it had the chance to seep into Susan's soul.

She ought to be used to it by now: the dark looks and the whispers, the speculation about whether she was getting away with murder. Somehow, though, it never ceased to shock her; it never ceased to hurt.

As the Harrises' pickup left the parking lot, Susan made out a dust devil working its way across the arid valley. When the smoky plume resolved itself into a motorcycle, her breath caught in her throat.

Let him help me out of family loyalty, or guilt over his brother's bad behavior, or, I don't care, even that one night we've tried so long to forget. Just let him say he'll do it.

Not the most orthodox of prayers, she knew, but

3

maybe she'd earn points for desperation. She had a perfect right to worry, because after an hour-long bounce from Clementine across a ranch road that saw more lizards, tumbleweeds, and roadrunners than car traffic, Luke was bound to be long on sweat and short on temper.

Worse yet, he was a Maddox, the last person she should trust.

"You take that box and turn it in to the . . ." Her mom had leaned on her walker, searching her mind for the elusive word. Frustration glittered in her brown eyes before she'd wrestled the damaged speech center of her brain into obedience. *"To the* sheriff, *like you ought to. If you give it to one of them Maddoxes, he'll just make . . . just make you more trouble. Or haven't you learned yet?"*

Susan had learned, all right. A person learned a hell of a lot when her husband of six years ran off with the local banker's wife, a fortune in false loans, and God knows how much stolen from the family business.

But the toughest lessons in the world couldn't keep her from concluding that her husband's brother was her and her mother's only chance. Even if he'd be furious when he learned she'd lied to get him to drive out to a third-rate barbecue joint at the intersection of the ranch road that connected Clementine, the county seat, with busy Highway 90.

Susan might be in a foul mood herself—she'd spent most of the eight months since Brian vanished mad as hell—but she wasn't stupid. If ever there was a time to play nice, this was it.

Despite her resolution, when all six feet, four inches of Luke blew in through the front door, his expression did nothing to ease the tension knotted in her stomach. With his helmet tucked beneath his arm and his dark hair damp with sweat, he strode directly toward her, a scowl plastered across his face. A puff of dust rose from his jeans with every step.

After pulling off his sunglasses, he glared down at her, clearly not fooled by her red lipstick or the wide-brimmed hat that hid her shoulder-length brown hair. But then, even seated, Susan couldn't hide her athletic, six-foot frame.

"That's your red Jeep parked outside, right? The one you called about?" His tone warned he already knew the answer. "Tires look fine to me."

At least they were now the only customers. She had the feeling this was going to get loud, and the last thing she needed was a public scene.

"Have a seat—please," she suggested, trying the same note of calm she used to defuse her biology students' daily dramas. She faked a halfhearted smile. "Wash some of the bugs out of those teeth."

He didn't smile back. "It's ninety-three degrees out there. The bugs are all at home enjoying their air-conditioning."

"So why didn't you grab one of the demos and crank up the AC?"

After all, she'd called him at the dealership—the same dealership that had been her husband Brian's second home—with a story about frozen lug nuts on a flat. But it shouldn't surprise her that he'd ridden his motorcycle instead of a demo car. Luke had never been the Maddox brother known for sanity. That brother was probably in Mexico by now, soaking up the sun on some beach and grinning over what a naïve fool his wife had been.

And nobody seemed to give a damn about finding

5

him but she herself—and maybe Hal Beecher, whose wife had disappeared at the same time.

"Because those cars don't belong to me, or my family either," Luke said. "Not since the meeting your call interrupted."

"Meeting?"

"Corporate came to seize the dealership this morning. Mom couldn't bear to turn it over—not after all the years Dad sank into that place. She asked me to take care of it for her."

Susan winced at the reminder that she hadn't been the only one hurt by her husband's betrayal. Apparently, he'd been ordering and selling vehicles but had failed to pay the automakers or properly clear the titles. What he'd done with the hundreds of thousands of dollars owed, no one could say. So now the dealership his late father had worked a lifetime to establish was gone.

"Sorry." Susan fought the urge to add that she was even sorrier for not guessing what her own husband had been up to, for not paying more attention to his behavior in the months leading to his disappearance.

If she hadn't been distracted by her mother's stroke, would she have noticed? Ruthlessly she thrust the thought aside and imagined jabbing yet another pin into the Brian voodoo doll she kept tucked inside a mental pocket.

She fought back a smile as she fantasized that somewhere on that Mexican beach, a man's severed penis had just dropped out of the leg of his swim trunks. She hoped Jessica Beecher had brought along a vibrator. . . .

"I'm sorry too." Luke dropped into the seat across from Susan. "Sorry my mother trusted Brian with the business in the first place."

Susan shrugged a shoulder. "How could she have predicted? How could any of us?"

"Sometimes people choose not to see what's too painful. Sort of like hysterical blindness. You ever hear of that?"

Heat suffused her face, and she felt her temper rising. Still, she measured her words, mindful of her need—and the narrow box inside her purse.

"You imagine you would have done better if you'd been around?" she said carefully.

He shook his head. "I'm not saying that at all. We talked on the phone every now and then, but Brian and I weren't really close. You know that. But I *am* around now. I'll be doing some long-distance telecommuting for at least a month or so. That eight-hundred-mile round-trip between here and Austin got old really fast."

She wasn't too surprised that the facts differed from the version she'd heard—that he'd been fired from his computer-security firm because of all the time he'd spent dealing with the fallout of Brian's disappearance. She'd learned the hard way that West Texas gossip painted every story a more interesting shade.

"Nice of your boss to let you do that," she said.

He gave a shrug. "I hate dealing with bosses—so I bought him out a while back."

Susan was surprised she hadn't heard this through the grapevine. But, knowing Luke, he'd kept it to himself.

The moment Luke's attention turned to his empty glass, the waitress materialized, though she had been steadfastly ignoring Susan's presence for nearly fifteen minutes. A hard-looking blonde on the verge of middle age, the woman bore a pitcher of caramel-colored tea and a tar-stained smile. Susan made note of her name tag, which read *Cyndee,* and laid a mental bet the woman had changed the spelling back in junior high.

"Would you like some?" Cyndee asked, her heavily made-up gaze a compass needle to the lodestone of Luke Maddox and his killer hazel eyes.

At his nod, she poured without once glancing in Susan's direction. After setting the pitcher on the table, the waitress stretched provocatively toward the controls of a wall-mounted window unit. Still staring at Luke, she added, "Thought I'd turn that up for you. You look awfully *hot.*"

Susan rolled her eyes. Fifteen years past their high-school graduation, and Luke's broad shoulders and chiseled features were still turning females into fools. She ought to know; once upon a time, she'd been the president of that club. Thank God, her mom had put a stop to that.

She filled her own glass before asking the blonde, "How about leaving the pitcher and bringing us two specials?"

Cyndee blinked at Susan. "What?" she asked, her tone annoyed.

Susan had to repeat the order twice before the woman beat a retreat into the kitchen. Probably to spit into Susan's sandwich.

Luke drained half his tea, then said, "Now tell me why you lied to get me here. It's sure as hell not for the service."

"I picked this place because it's private," she explained. "No one from Clementine ever darkens the door."

No one except the Harrises, anyway. But at least they hadn't seen her here with Luke.

"Why all the secrecy?" he asked. "Surely you aren't that intimidated by my mother."

Her laughter sounded brittle.

"Maybe not yours," she lied, realizing she was stalling. "But mine scares me half to death."

Her mother was so adamant on the subject, Susan had had to say that she was going to the sheriff. She couldn't recall the last day she had played so fast and loose with truth.

"How *is* Maggie?" Luke asked.

Real interest softened his expression, and she couldn't help feeling grateful. Since Brian's disappearance, Susan had almost forgotten what it felt like to see eyes that didn't teem with unvoiced questions.

Could you have done it? Did *you?*

Friends and neighbors, coworkers, and parents of her students might look directly at her, but Susan knew they were seeing her picture in the paper. Right next to photos of the missing Jessica Beecher, Brian, and her husband's burned-out car smoldering in a remote arroyo in the desert.

She still couldn't believe the jerk had been heartless enough to create such a cruel diversion. Mentally she stuck another pin into his eye.

"Mom's doing so much better," she told Luke. "The therapy's made a big difference, with her speech especially. But she's still weak on her right side, and mentally—well, let's just say I can't see her living on her own."

"So you two are roommates now?"

"Yeah, can you believe it? After all the grief I gave her raising me, now I get to be the responsible party. But it's been good for me, having someone to look after. It takes my mind off everything. Well," she said with a shrug, "that's a lie, but it does give me someone to pretend for."

A span of silence stretched between them as she searched his gaze. No suspicion there, thank God; only troubled comprehension.

The polite thing would be to ask about his mother now, but even though the woman had been through her own brand of hell, Susan couldn't make herself. Not without choking on the memory of the older woman's accusations.

Luke's voice jarred Susan out of the unpleasant thoughts. "Let's get to the point. Why'd you really bring me all the way out here?"

Her stomach crawled into her throat, but she forced the truth out past it. A truth she'd been keeping from her mother for a week. "The superintendent called me. He said . . . he said the board's decided to terminate my teaching contract."

The panic that had been building burst out in an unstoppable torrent. "I can't let them do this. If I can't teach this fall, I'll have to leave town to look for work and pack my mom off to my sister's. And you know Carol. She'll park Mom in some California nursing home the minute she gets inconvenient. And God, Luke, that would kill her. Mom's lived around Clementine her whole life. Her friends are here, and all her memories. I'm not about to let those bast—"

"Hold on. Let's back up a minute," Luke said. "Why would they fire you?"

"He says parents have been calling, saying they don't trust me with their kids. He says I've become a 'distraction to the learning process.'" Her laughter made a harsh sound. "It's funny. The last time Dr.

Winthrop called, it was to tell me I'd been named the district's teacher of the year. Spineless little weasel."

"What I don't get is, why would anyone complain?" Luke said. "Brian's *alive.* Hell, two witnesses saw him and Jessica Beecher at that New Mexico gas station a couple of days after the sheriff found his car. And didn't Jessica leave some kind of message on her answering machine?"

"A story that was buried on page seven. But I don't think it would matter anyway. It was that first article that did it." Her throat ached with the anger she had swallowed back. "No one's forgotten those pictures— especially the ones of the deputies hauling evidence out of my house. And I'm sure they've all been talking about what that ass Ramirez said."

Every word of the deputy's quote was seared into her memory: *"Susan Maddox claims she was hiking out around the national park the day her husband disappeared, but so far, we've found no witnesses to verify her story."*

Her *story*, as if she'd made up the whole thing—and if her photos of the park, stamped with the date, weren't evidence enough, what would be? She'd decided on the spot that she'd make room for Manuel Ramirez's picture next to Brian's on her dartboard.

"But the sheriff cleared you the next day," Luke argued. "He said neither you nor Hal Beecher was a suspect."

"Beecher's never had a problem." She could barely keep the resentment from her voice. While old friends turned their backs on her, Jessica Beecher's husband was being showered with casseroles and kindness. But then, on the day their spouses disappeared, Hal Beecher had been in a meeting in El Paso, with a dozen witnesses. Better yet, he'd gone there to raise money for a clinic for the indigent he wanted to establish in his late daughter's memory.

What sport would there be in suspecting the father of a little girl who'd died of leukemia two years before? And the stress of the Beechers' loss provided a perfectly plausible explanation as to why Jessica might have fled. As if grief excused the things she had done.

"Beecher's had a problem, all right," Luke said. "In case you've forgotten, his whole world has caved in. Brian not only stole his wife, he put a hell of a dent in his bank, too, with those loans. And now the guy has a four-year-old to raise alone—a kid who's lost his mother."

"I know, I know. Brian's been the son of a bitch, and it's everybody else who's paying. Not just me." She shut up when she saw the waitress coming with their orders.

With a smile for Luke, Cyndee put down both plates. Pretending not to hear Susan's request for ketchup, she stalked back to the kitchen. Susan began to wonder if the blonde's antagonism was more than simple rudeness. Did the woman also recognize her from the paper?

Susan told herself she must be getting paranoid. The Cyndees of this world skipped the front page and flipped straight to the Health and Beauty section. If they read at all.

Luke stood, and for one heart-stopping moment, Susan was certain he was walking out the door. Instead, he snagged a ketchup bottle from another table and came back to hand it to her.

"Here you go," he said, his fingers brushing hers. "I think we've seen the last of our waitress for a while."

Susan couldn't answer. She was too stunned by the impulse that had nearly driven her to grasp his hand

12

and hold it. If she'd been quick and bold enough, would he have held hers back?

What was happening to her? He'd barely swept his fingers past hers, and worse yet, he was Brian's brother. Not the boy she'd known back in high school, the troublemaker whose reputation for tinkering under the hoods of fast cars and faster girls had scared her into refusing him each time he'd asked her out. Until that one time, when he'd talked her into sneaking out for a ride in his convertible at night. The night the yucca blossoms had perfumed a star-drunk sky . . . the night she'd been fool enough to let him charm her out of her virginity. The next day, she'd been grounded for two weeks after Carol squealed that she'd seen the two of them by Susan's locker "leaning way too close." If Carol had known the whole of it, Susan figured she would still be grounded now.

Even as it was, by the time she'd managed to escape her mother's and sister's scrutiny, Luke had gone on to bigger and better B-cups—as if their time together hadn't meant a thing to him. Certainly, neither of them had brought up the incident again.

Thinking of Brian, Susan wondered if a short attention span was a genetic trait or simply something carved into the Y chromosome. Which would explain so much about remote controls and men . . .

"So what do you need?" Luke was asking. "A good lawyer? Seems to me you could sue the hell out of Dr. Winthrop, and the whole damned school board for that matter. They can't just fire a good teacher because a few hysterical parents complain."

"I'm not so certain all those callers were hysterical parents," Susan told him. "Dr. Winthrop mentioned a few names. Names you'd recognize from the roster of the CLC."

She let it sink in for a moment, the knowledge that school-board elections, along with several others, would be held this November. And that not one official had been elected without the CLC's endorsement in more than forty years. In Ocotillo County, the Conservative Ladies' Coalition ruled. And Luke and Brian's mother, Virginia Maddox, was the one who ruled *it*.

"Oh, hell," Luke said. "I know what you're thinking. And I know the two of you have had your problems, but you're still a Maddox. Mom would never—"

"I've filed for divorce, Luke—months ago. My attorney said I had to, to legally protect myself from everything Brian's done." She shrugged. "Of course, I would have filed anyway, but your mother didn't understand."

He grimaced. "She wouldn't. She's still saying Brian'll turn up with an explanation if we give him enough time. Either that or that you . . ."

He cut himself off abruptly.

"What?" Susan prompted, as if she couldn't guess.

He shook his head. "Let's just say that in her mind, it must be someone else's fault. Anyone's but Brian's."

Susan nodded, suddenly buried in a landslide of raw memories of Virginia Maddox's fury and frustration in those first awful days when they had waited together by the phone.

"He never would have left you," her mother-in-law would begin, *"if you'd only been . . ."*

More traditional. More pliant. More reasonable. Less stubborn. The attacks had gone on and on, each one a knife thrust, each one making Susan wonder if the older woman might be right. Until she'd finally gone too far and said, *"If you'd only given him a child."*

That had been the last straw, one that finally shocked Susan out of self-blame and started her blood boiling. She had given Virginia thirty seconds to grab her purse, climb on her broomstick, and get on the road back to her own place. They hadn't spoken since until her mother-in-law called to blast her about the filing. How the devil had she found out anyway?

"I'll talk to Mother," Luke said, "but I seriously doubt she's part of some conspiracy against you. For one thing, she hasn't been the CLC's president in years. I don't think she's even active anymore."

"Guess you've forgotten how things work around here," Susan said. "Of course, you're a Maddox. Maybe Maddoxes don't have to think about the rules."

"I've heard that sorry bullshit all my life," he fired back. "It never had a thing to do with me."

He started to get up, and her hand shot out to clamp down on his wrist.

"Please don't go," she begged. "I'm sorry. It's just that—"

"It's just that one—make that two—Maddoxes have already kicked you in the teeth," he finished for her.

As he spoke, he stared at his wrist so intently that she released him. And held her breath until she could be sure he wouldn't rise.

"The question is," he continued, looking in her eyes now, "what the hell would drive you to try your luck on a third?"

Her trembling hand found its way inside her purse and pulled out a box about the size of a standard paperback.

This was what she'd come for, the long shot she was betting could save her. As she passed the box to Luke, tightness gripped her chest, and perspiration boiled to the surface. Swallowing back her emotions, she tugged at the creeping hemline of her denim skirt, then crossed her bare legs to unstick them from the vinyl seat.

"Last night, I found this," Susan told him. "And I'm hoping—praying, really—that it might hold some answers."

Luke took it from her and glanced down at the packaging. "A hard drive? Brian's?" At her nod, he added, "I thought the sheriff's department confiscated his computer."

"They didn't get this part."

He raised his brows, an unmistakable invitation to explain.

"Our hard drive went belly-up about two weeks before Brian disappeared. He was really upset about it, said he had a bunch of tax stuff stored there that he didn't want to spend the next three months inputting."

Luke muttered, "I told him he needed a good backup routine. Some people never learn their lesson."

"Brian and half the computing world." *Including me,* thought Susan, though she certainly knew better.

"I shouldn't gripe. It's the same half that keeps a lot of us tech guys in business."

"He wanted it fixed right away," said Susan, "so he drove the computer all the way to an electronics superstore in El Paso. The guy ended up selling him a new drive. Said he couldn't fix the old one."

"Typical superstore-geek move," Luke said. "Installing a new hard drive's a lot simpler than trying to restore lost information—*if* the guy knew how. Real data-recovery specialists charge thousands, and they don't guarantee a thing."

"Afterwards," she said, "he gave Brian the box with the warranty information inside. I was packing away some of Brian's stuff when it fell off the top shelf of his closet. I picked it up and noticed the old drive was in there too. Then I got to thinking, maybe there's a chance that someone with your background could fix it, find a way into Brian's e-mail and financial records—"

Luke laid the box back on the table, outside the range of crumbs. And used the tops of his fingernails to slide it back to her.

"The state has experts trained to do that. You don't want me touching this."

"Why not?" The pitch of her voice climbed with her rising panic. "I know you're really good, with all those industry awards. You've been in high tech almost all your li—"

"Exactly," Luke said. "*And* I'm Brian's brother. Assuming I could get anything out of this old hard drive—and that's a huge assumption—the information would be tainted. Do you know how easy it would be for someone like me to falsify computer files?"

"But you wouldn't. And what would it matter anyway, if something in those files helped me track down Brian?"

He shook his head. "I want Brian back here just as much as you do. I want to hear from him what the hell he was thinking, and then I want to see the bastard pay."

"After we show everyone he's alive, we can—"

"*No.* I don't want him paying with some chickenshit family scolding that'll end up with my mom selling off the ranch to bail him out. I don't even want him paying with a good ass-kicking, which I would *happily* dispense. Brian needs to go to jail for what he's done. He's screwed up a lot of lives, and for once, he's going to have to face the music."

17

Resentment burned in Luke's expression, and Susan could guess the reason. How many times had she heard Virginia Maddox dismiss his job as "monkeying around with those fool contraptions," or call him "a tumbleweed, hardly better than oil-field trash" for his frequent job changes within the volatile technology sector? From personal experience, Susan knew that Brian had the market cornered on the rare commodity of that old bat's approval, but how much worse would it have been had Virginia Maddox been *her* mother?

Hot as the day was, she shuddered at the thought.

"You're going to have to take this to the sheriff," Luke said. "I can't understand why you didn't in the first place."

"The man's been in office since Sam Houston was in grade school," she erupted. "It would take me hours to explain to Hector Abbott exactly what a hard drive *is.*"

The last time she'd gone to see the white-haired grandfather, he'd been plunking away hunt-and-peck style on an old manual typewriter. He worked with his elbows locked straight so he could see what he was doing.

"He has younger deputies to call on, not to mention the resources of the Texas Rangers," Luke said. "Didn't they send your computer to the state lab at the Department of Motor Vehicles?"

"Ages ago. Sheriff Abbott tells me he's still waiting to hear back from the DMV about it," Susan explained. "But he doesn't seem to care much about their results—or anything else these last few months. Every time I talk to him, he just pats me on the hand and says, 'These things take time, Miz Maddox.' When I'd finally had enough of his patronizing garbage, he told

me that as far as he's concerned, this is more of a do-
mestic issue than a crime."

Luke frowned as he reached for a fry. "Maybe he just
wanted to get you off his back. Something tells me
you've been calling his office every day and pestering."

Susan thought about the days she'd phoned twice,
even three times, wanting to know what progress the
sheriff had made. "I *hate* sitting on my rear end waiting," she admitted. "I'm no damned good at it."

"Maybe not, but you have other talents. Aggravating
people and telling lies, for starters. I don't think you
should add obstructing justice to the list."

"I *don't* lie."

Luke hooked a thumb in the direction of her red
Jeep and its four perfectly inflated tires.

She grimaced, remembering, too, what she had told
her mother. And worse yet, what she hadn't. Sooner or
later, her mom would have to know of her dismissal
before she heard it elsewhere. Thank God the school
board hadn't leaked it yet. Legally, they couldn't discuss the personnel issue, since she'd told them she
planned to appeal. But in a small community, Susan
knew her secret would spread faster than cold sores
on prom night.

"Yeah, I did lie, but I had good reason. And I'm not
planning on getting in the way of justice. All I want to
do is hurry it along." Her eyes burned and her vision
wavered. She blinked, telling herself she would be
damned if she would cry. "I'm *going* to find my husband—and I have to do it in the next two weeks. That's
when the board will be hearing my appeal."

She pushed the hard drive back toward him. "Luke,
you have to help me, please. There isn't time to play

this game by their rules anymore. I'm already going to lose the house—Beecher has no choice but to fore-close—but once my paycheck's gone, I won't even be able to keep up the rent on Mom's apartment."

Luke didn't touch the box. "Take it in to Hector. This is his investigation, not ours. But if you need some money—"

This time, she was the one who stood and stared him down. "I don't need your damned money. Luke Maddox, I need *you*."

Chapter Two

Thanks in part to Susan, Luke nearly killed himself on the way home.

He should have seen it coming, should have remembered that no matter how dead the desert looked in the midafternoon glare, life waited out the sun in hidden pools of shadow, islands in reverse.

The accident occurred when his motorcycle startled a rodent from a crevice. Luke saw the small figure dart across the road. He veered to avoid it—and struck something that cracked against the bike's windshield, then flipped over it, glancing off his helmet and snapping his head back.

A pale cloud exploded in his vision as he fought to steer the Kawasaki. He felt himself losing control, sensed the bike sliding out from under him, the rutted shoulder rushing up toward his left side. But experience took hold, and somehow, miraculously, he righted himself and skidded to a stop.

All around him, brown and white feathers settled to

the ground as his heart tried to hammer its way through his chest wall.

"Holy shit." His voice shook as he spotted the limp bundle lying about ten feet away.

It had been a bird—a damned big one. Looked like a red-tailed hawk. Dead, from the angle of its neck.

His gaze flicked to the crack down the middle of his cycle's windshield, and his adrenaline-soaked brain groped for an explanation. Remembering the ratlike creature that had crossed his path, he decided that a hawk perched in one of the nearby mesquite trees must have seen the movement and plunged toward what it saw as dinner.

After shutting down the engine, Luke dismounted on legs that felt as flimsy as two blades of spring grass. If his head had taken the full impact instead of a glancing blow, he'd be lying on the road now too, every bit as dead as the huge bird.

And for what? Because for a single moment, the hawk had allowed hunger to distract it from the greater danger. Just as he'd allowed Susan Dalton Maddox to distract him from his ride.

Kicking a rock, he swore at the way that, even now, her image loomed like a mirage on the horizon. Her blue eyes shimmered with disappointment—until she turned her face away from him.

Get out of here if you won't help me, she had told him. *Go, and I won't bother you again.*

She'd been wrong in that, he realized. She'd bother him all right, every time he thought of the absolute faith he'd seen when she'd asked him to help her. And how broken she had looked when he had crushed out that belief.

He'd seen that hurt before, the first time he had let her down. And though his memories of high school were mostly a long blur, he'd never quite been able to leave that one behind him—or the evening he'd seduced her just to prove he could . . .

He warned himself to focus, to put regret out of his mind and pull himself together. With slow, deep breaths, he allowed the silent landscape to work what always felt to him like ancient magic, older than the Indians who had once called this place home.

His gaze rose to where, far above the sky-stretched arms of ocotillos, a buzzard floated kitelike on the breeze. The dark bird glided toward the distant purple smudge of foothills, its apparent aimlessness a study in deception. As soon as Luke left here, it would wheel back for the body of the hawk.

A puff of wind lifted a few of the loose feathers and sent them tumbling past his feet. Bending, Luke captured one and stroked it with a fingertip.

Moments later, he opened his hand and let the hot breeze carry it away. It skimmed along the sand until he lost sight of it among a thorny mass of cholla cactus.

"I was right," he told the desert. "I was right to tell her no."

The sound of an engine pulled his attention to the road behind him, where a cloud of dust was rising above a tiny speck of red. Susan's Jeep, he guessed, and she would be here soon.

Time to get moving, unless he wanted to get stuck explaining what had happened. More uncomfortable still was the thought that doing so would allow her another chance to start on him about the hard drive.

After remounting his cycle, he rode the gentle incline leading toward the greener hills near Clementine. This time, he was careful to keep his full attention on the journey.

He was careful, too, to keep his speed up, widening the gap between himself and his brother's wife.

By the time he turned off toward the ranch where he'd grown up, Luke's chalk-dry mouth had driven all else from his mind except the prospect of an ice-cold beer. He left his cycle in the designated car shed, then strode toward a rambling, dun-colored structure that looked as if it had grown out of the rocky soil. Behind the house, a windmill presided over an assortment of weathered outbuildings that formed the nucleus of what had once been a working cattle enterprise. Near one, an open shed, a pair of horses whickered, hoping for an early feeding.

Luke glanced at his watch. "Sorry, you beggars. You've got another couple hours."

He stepped inside through the back door—and decided he could kiss the guy who'd invented the swamp cooler, the Southwest's answer to central air-conditioning. Eager to slake his thirst, he started toward the kitchen but stopped dead at the low murmur of his mom's voice, no doubt talking on the phone.

She'd tack his hide to the nearest wall if he didn't take off his dusty boots before setting foot on her hardwood floors. As he collapsed into an old chair to do so, a fat black dog thumped its tail against the washing machine.

"Must—have—beer," Luke croaked. "Fetch, Duke. Fetch."

Unfortunately, reality bore no resemblance to the popular commercial. Instead of heeding his command, John Wayne's namesake merely thumped his tail against the mudroom floor and stretched his grizzled jaws into a yawn.

Luke could hardly blame the old Lab mix. The tile felt cool against his now-bare feet, and he'd be willing to bet that the side of the washing machine felt even better.

In the kitchen, Luke found his mother seated at the table. Her back was to him and, as he'd expected, she held the phone pressed to her ear. Outside the window near her, something iridescent flashed: a pair of hummingbirds competing for the crimson nectar in a feeder. Their battle grew heated, with the larger female diving at the ruby-throated male each time he drew too near.

Though she faced the war zone, his mother seemed oblivious to everything except her conversation. Silhouetted in the window's light, she looked thinner than he could remember, almost fragile.

The unsettling thought was banished by the cool flint of her voice.

"I don't care what the New Mexico policemen told you," she said into the receiver. "He didn't just decide to run off with that money. That Beecher woman had him over a barrel, so she tricked him into doing it. And now that he's realized what he's done to us, he's too embarrassed to come home."

As his mother spoke, her index finger tapped a sheaf of papers she'd spread across the old oak table's surface, documents she had gathered through an El Paso detective agency. The private eye, or whatever the guy called himself, had taken her for a ride, charging her a fortune for a bunch of paperwork Luke could have found himself in a couple hours on the Internet. The detective had tossed off terms any idiot could glean from an episode of *America's Most Wanted* to disguise the fact that he had no idea what had become of Brian. Yet Virginia Maddox pored over his "findings" daily, reading more into the doublespeak with every pass.

Luke hoped whoever she had on the line was reminding her that Jessica Beecher, a pretty, red-haired receptionist who'd worked at the dealership for three years, was nobody's pick for Criminal Mastermind of the Year. Quiet and supposedly devout in her Catholic faith, she was also a stretch in the role of Other Woman, but Luke figured that maybe she was using Brian as a distraction from her grief. Still, it made Luke sick to think of how her little boy would feel once he understood that his living presence had meant less to her than the memory of the child she had lost.

He pulled a beer from the refrigerator, clinking it deliberately against its fellows so his mother would know he was home. But she gave no sign that she heard him.

"It was that awful Dalton girl, then," she continued, calling Susan by her maiden name. "Perhaps she's . . . I think . . . well, it's possible she's done away with Brian, and now she's covering her tracks. She's certainly smart enough to hide the money somewhere, maybe offshore in the Caribbean."

Luke choked on his first mouthful of beer. Apparently, his mom thought that years of reading mysteries qualified her as Ocotillo County's answer to Miss Marple.

She started slightly at the sound, then frowned at him.

"Mom," he said, setting down the bottle. "We have to talk."

Her mouth tightened in irritation before she told the

caller, "I'm sorry for the interruption, Hector. Let me get back to you."

After a pause, she added, "I really do appreciate your . . . discretion. And I certainly won't forget it later, no matter what manner of ex-cop comes knocking at my door."

Luke was sure that by "later" she meant election time, and that the ex-cop she'd referred to was Steven Myers, a Dallas transplant who was running for Hector's long-uncontested job by appealing to the small but steady influx of newcomers to the area. No wonder Susan couldn't get the sheriff to do jack.

His mother placed the receiver in its cradle and turned toward him, peering above her narrow glasses. They'd slid down her nose again, making her look like a stern librarian—or a bespectacled bird of prey.

But she rubbed her back, and the illusion faded, revealing the thinness of her wrists, the slight stoop of her shoulders, the deep lines that had etched themselves into her sun-flecked face. At sixty-seven, she still dressed in jeans, invariably dark blue and ironed with a crease as straight as any ruler, and she kept her hair the same rich auburn that had highlighted her youthful beauty. Yet age was catching up to her, especially since his brother's disappearance.

"I don't smell any smoke," she said, a reminder of her old rule: Unless the house was burning, she was not to be disturbed while "conducting business" on the phone.

He refused to let her make him feel like a child, not after what he'd heard. "Are you trying to influence Hector Abbott's investigation?"

"Influence? I don't know what you mean."

"I mean an endorsement. Or do you work in campaign contributions now?"

She waved away his statement with a humorless smile. "Honestly, Luke, you make it sound as if I'm some sort of mob boss. I'm simply a concerned citizen, making observations on a case involving my own son."

"Tell me, were you *concerned* enough to phone the members of the school board about Susan? Or did you have your old friends from the CLC work on it?"

She glared at him as if he were an insect. "I see no need to answer such an insulting question."

Fortunately, he'd been treated to "the look" so many times before, he'd become immune. Almost.

"I'm sure you don't," he said. "You probably don't even remember the last time anybody made you. Answer, that is. For anything."

His mother turned away and settled her forehead into her hands, her elbows onto the kitchen table. Wondering, he imagined, why she had been left with the wrong son.

Moisture dripped onto the table. At first he didn't understand, it had been so long since he had seen her tears.

When he saw broken things, he fixed them; it was what he did. So automatically, he reached out to comfort her, but his hand froze only inches from her shoulder. In that moment of hesitation, he searched his memory, thinking that she must have wept when his father died, or in those first few days when they had all feared Brian was murdered. But all Luke could come up with was an image of her resolution, a strength that others envied. Something tightened in his chest at the thought that, despite promising Dad he'd always look after his mother, he had been the one to make her cry.

His palm settled on her back as gently as the dead

· hawk's feathers had settled on the rutted asphalt of the old ranch road.

"I'm not trying to buy anything," she said, her voice soft now, the way it had gone sometimes when she spoke to his brother. "I'm merely pointing out—"

"That it would be easier on everyone," he suggested, "if Brian never turned up."

She looked up sharply, her green eyes strange and shocking, with their dark fringe of wet lashes.

"You think I don't want my own son back?" Her gaze drifted to the paneled wall, where Brian's picture hung. He smiled confidently, dressed in full high-school-football-god regalia, his blond perfection a stark contrast to the unkempt look Luke had favored in the years he'd spent playing the disaffected youth. A look which had not, in point of fact, earned him a place beside his brother on the Maddox Wall of Fame.

His dad's picture hung there, and Luke couldn't help focusing on the shot of the huge man grinning beside a glossy pickup from the fifties, the first vehicle he'd ever sold, years before he'd built the dealership. Dad had a fifties-era haircut, too, a crew cut he'd stuck with until the bitter end. Luke had to look away, blindsided by a jolt of grief.

He struggled to focus on what his mother was saying.

"How could you say such a thing?" She rose to face his challenge.

"Because it's true," he answered, lowering his hand. "It's easier to remember Brian as the ideal son, maybe even easier to imagine he's been *murdered*, than to cope with the fact that he's an adulterer and a thief."

The color washed out of her face, and her mouth tightened, fracturing the skin around it into wrinkles. "I know your brother. Brian wouldn't steal, especially from me."

"I'm sorry, Mom. He has," Luke said, keeping his voice low, as if someone else might overhear. "Dad's dealership is gone because of all he took."

She closed her eyes and gripped the chair's back. "It might seem that way to you now, but Brian couldn't . . . *I* couldn't be so wrong."

How could anyone be so blind? Gritting his teeth, he reminded himself he'd come home to help his mother, not try to understand her. But that didn't mean he had to stand back and watch her ruin Susan's life.

"I know it's hard," he told her. "But blaming Susan's not the answer. We both know she's innocent."

"Luke Hale Maddox, don't you take that tone with me. And I wouldn't be so quick to vouch for any Dalton's innocence. Morals run in families—you know that."

She *would* bring up the old scandal about Susan's father. After the IRS discovered he hadn't filed a tax return in years, he'd been hit with enough fines to force the sale of his small ranch. To George Maddox, Luke and Brian's father.

The dealership was located on the section where the family's house had been before their second daughter, Susan, had been born. The same dealership Luke's family had now lost.

It occurred to Luke that the land might be unlucky. A few years after Frank Dalton had lost it, lung cancer killed him, although some people still claimed it had been a broken heart.

"So tell me," he asked his mother, "are you ready to be judged by *Brian's* morals?"

"There is nothing wrong with him. *Nothing*," she insisted, a tear trail gleaming silver by the window's light.

"Mom." He awkwardly attempted an embrace. It had been so long since he'd dared to hug her that he scarcely knew how.

She stepped out of his reach, her nose wrinkling. "You're dirty, Luke, and sweating like an old cow pony. Next time, you should take the Cadillac to town or that jalopy you had trailered here—I'm presuming the thing runs."

He sighed. She was right, of course. He was a mess after spending most of the afternoon astride his cycle. But still . . .

"I give up." He shook his head. "I'll be in the shower."

She gave no sign she heard him. She had already turned back to her papers—and her compulsive search for someone besides Brian to blame.

It ought to make him furious, but what he really felt when he looked at her was sad.

And worried—that the phone call he'd make later would drive the last nails in the coffin of his once-proud old family.

By the time Susan stopped at her neighborhood's bank of mailboxes, clouds were building above the mountains to the west. Normally, the area's summer storms spat no more than a scant handful of raindrops, so it must have been her mood that shrouded the sky in somber tones. Even as it must have been her anger and frustration at Luke's refusal that summoned a memory of thunder.

Inside the hacienda-style home, Susan kicked off her sandals and crossed the cool, brick-colored tiles in

31

bare feet. Stopping at the granite counter that separated the kitchen from the breakfast nook, she tossed her mail onto the teetering stack that had collected this past week, since she'd learned of her dismissal. After today's meeting with Luke, she felt as if she might at any moment be buried in an avalanche of envelopes—and trouble.

Damn him anyway, for being so difficult. And curse him for a fool if he thought saying no was going to make her go away, no matter what she'd promised. She'd hammer his resistance flatter than a nail head if that was what it took to make him help her. Because with her mother's future and her own at stake, she understood that even a reluctant ally beat having none at all.

"Susan Lorraine Dalton, are you listening to me?"

She started at the sound.

"You scared me," she explained, turning toward her mother's voice. "I guess my mind was wandering."

Between the salt-and-pepper hair escaping the clasp behind her neck and the sunken pallor of her cheeks, Susan's mother looked faded, long past ready for a nap. Yet the fire burning in Maggie Dalton's dark brown eyes would have warned Susan of trouble even if her full name hadn't been invoked. Minus the Maddox, of course. Her mom had never acknowledged Susan's marriage, not even when the union had seemed blessed. She had boycotted their wedding, and for several years her relationship with Susan had been strained.

Until the first miscarriage, when Maggie had resolved to be the mother Susan needed.

Agnes Hoffman and Roberta Culberson sat near her at the breakfast table. Each woman had a glass of lemonade at her elbow, and each held a hand of cards. The three friends looked like a pastel rainbow, each in a Mexican cotton dress, colorfully embroidered and blissfully loose on a hot day.

"You remembered how to play?" Susan smiled at her mother and gestured toward the half deck lying face-down on the table. To the best of Susan's knowledge, Maggie's memory of most games had vanished with her stroke, though she and her friends had met to play cards and share lunch weekly for as long as Susan could recall. It was a relief to see them back at their routine.

Before anyone could answer, the realization dawned that her homecoming hadn't been heralded by the scrabbling of tiny toenails on the tile or the brain-rattling yapping of another of Brian's legacies.

"Where's Peavy?" Susan swiveled her head, looking around in case prayers had been answered and the dog had been struck mute. "Tell me you didn't forget the barking rat outside again."

One of these days, the long-haired Chihuahua was going to end up lining some predator's stomach. Not that it would be much of a loss, but she had enough headaches without getting the SPCA on her case too. Besides, Peavy—short for Pancho Villa—was sort of a cute little bugger, though she wouldn't admit she thought this under torture.

"The hateful little poop bared his teeth at Agnes," Mom said. "He . . . he was banished to the backyard just a . . . just a bit ago."

Susan hoped he was still there. When she'd mentioned to Brian two years earlier that she might like a dog, she'd been thinking of a German shepherd or maybe an Australian cattle dog, a rugged companion to bring with her on her hikes or those days the two of

Colleen Thompson

them went riding. Instead, her husband had surprised her with a tiny bit of tan fluff that would barely raise a lump in a full-grown rattler's belly. Worse yet, the damned thing was a force of nature—right up there with locust plagues and landslides for sheer destructive power.

"I know he's a brat, Mom, but you just can't leave the little guy out there unattended—" she began before her mother interrupted.

"St-stop trying to . . . distract me, Susan. I asked you how the meeting went, your meeting with the . . . with the . . ." She frowned, then swore and slapped down her cards. While the right word often failed to put in an appearance, Susan had noticed that Maggie never seemed to struggle for a curse.

"*Sheriff*," Agnes finally supplied. She held her hand close to her drooping double Ds, as if she were expecting acts of rummy espionage. "She wants to know if you stopped by to see the sheriff."

Beside Agnes, Roberta fanned her flushed face with her cards and looked anxious. Susan tried—and failed—to make eye contact with the retired postal clerk. Since Roberta detested confrontation, Susan figured that someone or something must have given away her true errand to Mom.

Agnes, on the other hand, looked eager, a worse sign still. The only thing the woman liked better than watching an argument was helping one along.

"I didn't actually get over to the sheriff's," Susan confessed. "I had some other errands, and I—"

"Hector stopped by here." Scowling, her mother laid a hand on the walker waiting beside her: her prelude, these days, to shuffling from the room.

"You didn't mention it to him, did you?" Susan

34

asked, not daring to bring up the hard drive specifically. She hoped like hell her mother hadn't discussed it with her friends.

But even as she thought it, Susan knew they'd long since hashed out the subject. She'd bet not one of them had kept a secret from the others since they'd met in second grade.

Susan didn't begrudge her mother's friendships; on the contrary, she thought of Agnes and Roberta as honorary aunts. Still, she cursed herself for blurting the news of her discovery to her mother yesterday. Even if Mom didn't pore over every aspect of her life with her best friends, she needed to concentrate on her recovery, not her daughter's problems.

"I'd rather Sheriff Abbott didn't hear of it until I brought it up," Susan added.

"We didn't say a word—" Roberta vowed before Susan's mother lost control.

"You'd r-rather keep a lot of things to yourself, wouldn't you?" Maggie accused Susan. "Such as the fact you've lost your . . . lost your . . ."

She pursed her mouth as if to swear before Agnes burst out, "Why didn't you tell us you'd been fired?"

With a barely audible groan, Susan dropped onto the one barstool not occupied by boxes of her kitchenware. Even so, she had to put her feet up on a box marked "blender." During the past weeks, she'd been packing a little at a time so that when the bank at last foreclosed, she would have a head start.

"Sheriff Abbott drove here to tell you that?" Susan didn't question how the man knew in the first place. The superintendent's secretary, one of the county's leading rumormongers, had a sister who was one of Abbott's dispatchers.

"Yes, he did," her mother told her. "Hec-Hector is a-a very thoughtful man. He wanted to see if you were . . . if *we* were holding up all right."

Agnes and Roberta exchanged a look and smiled. For years, the two of them had been convinced that Hector Abbott was enamored of Maggie. Back when she'd been waiting tables after Susan's father died, the widower had been her most faithful customer.

Maggie had always laughed off their intimations and said she'd never take up with a man who couldn't properly figure fifteen percent of a four-buck break-fast. But Susan knew for a fact her mom was fond of the old man.

Too bad he couldn't keep his gossip to himself. Su-san tried to think of some way to set her mother's mind at ease. "I'm not really fired," she began. "It's more like a sabbatical—"

Agnes smirked, Roberta looked sympathetic, and her mom . . . well, her mom's look stopped Susan mid-lie.

"All right," she admitted. "Right now, things look bad, but I'm appealing in two weeks. And by then, I'm going to fix this."

"Fix what?" her mother asked. "And how?"

"Fix *everything*," said Susan. "I mean to fix it all—if I can get the three of you to help me—and, even more important, keep what's said here in this house."

But even as she looked from one gray head to the next, the idea struck her as the longest of long shots.

With that uplifting thought, she grabbed her sandals, then headed for the backyard to rescue Peavy.

Beneath the spreading clouds, scarlet stained the west-ern sky in a swath like glowing blood. But though the sun had fled the foothills outside Clementine, the hard-packed earth still radiated heat.

Swearing to himself, the watcher lowered binoculars and wiped sweat from his forehead. Too many people in *her* house now—bunch of gray-haired grandmas playing cards around her kitchen table, probably gabbing about everybody's business, the way old ladies did.

Probably gab about him, too, if they were to catch sight of him crouching beside a juniper, his body half hidden by the base of an agave. Probably call some deputy to check him out. And if the law caught him . . . *no*. He damned well wouldn't think on that.

He once more aimed his binoculars toward the kitchen's sliding glass door. "Time to go home now," he whispered. "Get back in that big-ass Chrysler and head on down the road."

After all, it would be fully dark soon, and old ladies shouldn't drive at night. Anything might happen.

When they didn't leave, he knew that he should, but one of the old bitches had booted the fluffy drop-kick dog—*her* dog—outside a while ago. It had left the deck and was now trotting importantly around the unfenced backyard, its nose to the ground and its tiny brain oblivious to his presence. But he knew from that night last weekend that if he tried to move, the damned thing would yap its head off.

The dog's sniffing grew more purposeful, and it started ranging farther from the deck. As it approached, he felt the blood congealing in his veins, freezing as it always did before things went into slow motion, before things happened that he wouldn't want to think on later.

Removing the field glasses from his neck, he watched his hands make a loop out of its strap—a long, thin strip of leather strong enough to stop the tiny animal from barking.

Strong enough to stop its breathing too.

The dog ranged ever closer . . . almost close enough to grab it by the scruff and—

"Peavy."

The watcher's head jerked toward a voice, a voice that stole into his dreams so often, his body responded like one of Pavlov's dogs.

It was *her* voice, calling the damned animal—and, oh, God, she was walking right toward him.

Without conscious thought, his hands began pulling at the leather strap as if to test it for some even darker purpose. His mind glazed over, thick with the ice crystals his heart labored to pump . . . yet his every muscle coiled like a bowstring at the ready.

Thunder grumbled in the distance, and just that quickly, it was over.

The dog bounded to the woman, and he watched the way the fine curves of her bare legs reshaped themselves as she bent to pick it up. He couldn't hear what she was saying, but sweet sounds soothed the animal, and she laughed as it tried to lick her face.

Lucky little creature, to be held between her breasts. And even luckier that she had rescued it in time.

He watched her walk inside, watched the subtle sway of her hips and the way her loose hair fluttered at her shoulders. Funny, how her femininity manifested itself in her movements, how walking seemed to tumble her walls down.

The earth had cooled by the time he picked his way between the agave and a clump of prickly pear cactus, his progress slow and careful. He couldn't risk leaving a thread of clothing on the spines, much less a hair or drop of blood.

With keen precision, his mind recorded every step and every obstacle that might block his way when he returned. Because the next time, the watcher wouldn't have a lurid sky to light his path.

Next time, he'd have no better than the faint illumination of the moon.

Chapter Three

The stack of mail teetered when Susan's elbow bumped it. Before she could put down the knife she'd been using to chop a pepper, the pile tipped, and half a dozen pieces sailed onto the floor.

"Shoot," she said, grabbing a towel to wipe her damp hands. She was already late preparing dinner—Agnes and Roberta had dawdled a long time, trying to solve her life as if it were a crossword puzzle.

As she knelt to gather up the mess, she noticed a windowed envelope with the words "Invoice Enclosed" stamped in red ink. Picking it up, she saw the business name above the return address: "U-Store-All."

She frowned. It was bad enough receiving bills she couldn't pay, but she'd never rented any storage facility. Even if she wanted one, she certainly wouldn't pick a place on Rocky Rim, a hillside rural road lined with attached cinder-block houses the government had once constructed for the poor, then inexplicably abandoned. The last time she'd driven up there—to check on Jimmy Archer, one of the ragtag collection of truants who drifted through her ecology club—she'd found the place mostly abandoned, except for a handful of squatters living in deplorable conditions. When she'd mentioned her trip to Brian, he'd been mad as hell.

"Let the sheriff's department or the social workers pry the little delinquent out of that shit hole," he'd told her. "Anything could happen to a lone woman in a place like that. Hell, I wouldn't set foot in it myself."

Which was why, when she saw Brian's name above the address, she was even more perplexed.

She glanced into the family room, where her mom was calling out answers to a woman on a TV game show while Peavy yapped encouragement. Satisfied she wouldn't be giving her mother another juicy tidbit to chew over with her friends, Susan used her knife to slit open the envelope.

The bill appeared to have been produced by an old dot matrix printer, so she had to squint to read it. From what she could make out, it looked as if a nine-by-ten-foot room had been rented almost a year ago—four months before her husband's disappearance.

She chewed her lower lip, thinking that had been about the time he'd warned her away from Rocky Rim.

"So what were you hiding, you miserable worm?" she grumbled as she scanned the bill for a phone number.

Nothing. Forgetting dinner for the moment, she hurried to her bedroom and dug out the directory she kept in the top drawer of her nightstand. Neither the white pages nor the yellow yielded any listing.

Cursing in frustration, she slipped the folded bill inside her purse. First thing tomorrow morning, she would drive to Rocky Rim and find out what was there.

And best of all, she wouldn't need Luke's help—or any man's—to get inside.

"You should eat." The two voices spoke in unison, each woman directing her admonition toward the other.

Susan laughed, and, to her relief, her mom grinned back from across the table. Outside the sliding glass door leading to the deck, the moon peeped through a veil of clouds to cast a spotlight on their meal.

"Listen to us," Susan said. "Nagging in stereo. I'll tell you what. If we both finish dinner, I'll go pick up milk-shakes from Swenson's."

Interest glinted in Maggie's eyes. "Chocolate malts?"

"Is there any other kind?" Susan asked, feigning enthusiasm for her mother's sake.

Susan glanced down at the spill of colors in her bowl. She remembered loving the simple combination of crisp lettuce and cucumber, yellow pepper, and red tomato topped with a sliced chicken breast, remembered how she'd once enjoyed the play of crunchy vegetables against the tang of vinaigrette dressing. What she'd forgotten—once again—was how to eat. After Brian took off, a similar lapse had cost her the five pounds she'd always dreamed of losing—and then fifteen more, until she barely recognized the thin and rangy woman in her mirror. Over the last few months, she'd gained back enough to keep from looking like the poster child for famine, but this latest round of worries had dampened any interest in food.

Her mother started eating, though she looked almost too tired to lift her fork. Susan followed suit, spearing a chunk of chicken still warm from the grill. Finally awakened, her stomach growled as the aroma

43

reached her nose, so she ignored the Chihuahua's begging and popped the bite into her mouth.

After they'd finished about half their salads, her mom said, "When Carol called the other night, she said I needed to come and stay with her. She doesn't think you're 'up to the burden.' That was how she put it."

Susan loved her sister, but once in a while she could smack her into next week. Carol might know the Oakland housing market inside and out, but she was a hell of a long way from understanding the real estate of tact. "Mom, you're not a bur—"

Maggie waved off Susan's protest. "I told her I was cer-cert . . . I was *sure* you didn't feel that way. But maybe Carol has a point. Now that there's this trouble with your job, I think I should go see her, at least for a whi—"

"I need you, probably a lot more than you need me." It was true, too. For one thing, if she didn't have her mom to cook for, Susan knew she wouldn't bother.

Pleasure bloomed in Maggie's eyes, and for a moment, decades rolled away. And all it had taken was a reminder that she had another role to play besides that of recovering stroke patient.

"I told your sister this . . . this family's built of . . . of stern stuff," Susan's mom said as she straightened in her chair. "We've outlasted plenty of hard times."

"We have, thanks to you."

"I . . . I know it won't be easy. Never is." Her mother frowned. "Sometimes I wondered how I'd make it."

A lump thickened Susan's throat as she thought of all the years her mom had worked alone to feed them. Susan had never heard her complain about the backbreaking hours she put in at the café. Instead, she'd taught Susan that an honest day's labor was a proud achievement and that waitresses and housemaids had as much right to hold their heads high as a queen.

"More, in fact, than any queen I've known," Maggie had often added with a wink, leaving her younger daughter full of admiration for the mom who not only knew royalty but refused to bow before it.

But something about the thought jogged another memory, of a time she'd found her mother crying. When Susan badgered her, she'd finally confessed that an old friend had pretended not to know her when she'd gone to wait the woman's table. Susan hadn't thought about the incident in years.

"Was it Virginia Maddox?" Susan asked.

"Was—what?"

"Was she the one who snubbed you that day in the café? The one who made you cry?" Who else could be the Queen of Ocotillo County?

"You m-mean back when you were . . . What were you? Maybe *six*?" Her mom smiled and touched her temple. "And the doctor says *I'm* the one with problems. What brought . . . what brought that on?"

Susan shrugged and chewed another bite of salad. It *was* good. "Just wondering."

Her mother waved a hand. "That woman's not worth . . . not w-worth . . ." Her forehead furrowed and her lips pursed, but she recovered. "*Worrying*, that's the word. She's not worth worrying about. Now, see there? I *am* better."

"You're getting there," Susan agreed, even though Roberta had confided, before she'd left the house, that the rummy combinations Maggie laid down had been utterly at random. Her mother's friend had suggested, too, that Susan remove the knobs from the gas stove anytime she needed to take a shower or run an errand.

"Right after you left, she said she'd make some tea," Roberta had whispered. *"And the next thing you know, we heard this tick-tick-ticking at the stove, then WHOOSH! That flame shot up so high, it near to singed her eyebrows. Scared Agnes half out of her support hose, I can tell you."*

"Pretty soon," Susan's mother said, "I—I'll be back to w-work and taking care of us—like old times."

Susan had to look away so her mom wouldn't see the tears that threatened. Had Maggie forgotten the café had closed down years after her retirement, when the owner, Ernie Palmer, died? And did she really expect to get another job—*any* job—in her condition?

Before Susan could begin to formulate an answer, the phone rang. If it was Carol, she decided, she was going to chew her out royally for filling their mom's head with that "burden" crap.

"Mrs. . . . Miz Maddox?" The caller's voice shook, but she still recognized him.

"Marcus?" she asked, surprised to be hearing from one of her ecology-club students. Marcus Bingham wasn't the toughest of the lot by any means, but he sounded alarmingly somber for a happy-go-lucky kid known for his creative excuses for missing assignments and transparent attempts to cheat on exams. "Has something happened?"

"N-no. It's just that . . . well, some of us guys from the club . . . we heard . . . we heard you might not be coming back to school next month. And me and Jimmy and all, we were just wondering if there's anything . . . you know . . . anything we can do."

Susan's stomach dropped at the realization that the news was out already. Instant messaging and e-mail had nothing on the Ocotillo County rumor mill.

"It's just a little misunderstanding," Susan told him. "Don't worry. I'll have it ironed out soon. I wouldn't miss your senior year for anything. For one thing, I've got money riding that you're going to graduate."

He laughed at that. "Well, at least you weren't dumb enough to bet on Jimmy."

Susan couldn't bring herself to laugh at Jimmy's expense. Not when the memory of that hellhole where he lived loomed so large in her mind. With its stark cinder-block walls, cracked windows blocked by faded newspapers and duct tape, and jerry-rigged electricity pirated from the nearest power lines, the place attracted more flies than a stable. And though she'd seen a lot in her ten years teaching public high school, she would never forget how Jimmy's old man, a sallow drunk who reeked of piss, stale beer, and about a million cigarettes, had merely shrugged at her assertion that his son's truancy was closing a door on his potential. He'd closed the door on her that day, after he'd caught her noticing a collection of gleaming, mismatched hubcaps—probably stolen—leaning against the wall like trophies. Or the inventory of a small-time, illegal enterprise.

She'd called Children's Protective Services that same day about Jimmy, not that it had done a lick of good . . .

"You tell Jimmy I said, smart as he is, I was banking on him pulling your hopeless butt through, too."

"I'll tell him when I see him," Marcus said, clearly enjoying the abuse. "And, Mrs. Maddox?"

"I'm still here."

"You need any arms broken or anything, you be sure and let us know."

She laughed it off, though she had the distinct impression that Marcus and his troublemaking friends were more than half serious about the offer. Even so, she was touched by their devotion. At least some people in Clementine were in her corner, even if they were only what some of her fellow teachers dubbed the "PITAs" for their pain-in-the-ass qualities.

As she sat down at the table, her mom looked up from her dinner. "What was that about?"

Susan snatched a mouthful of salad in an attempt to delay explaining that word of her dismissal had leaked out. When she heard a car door close outside, she was grateful for the diversion.

"Sorry to keep jumping up," she told her mother, "but I think there's someone here."

She wiped her mouth just before the doorbell rang. But after racing the hysterically barking Chihuahua to the entryway and looking through the peephole, whatever relief she'd felt curled into a fetal ball.

A man stood on the other side of the door, smiling hopefully. Though Susan knew he was closing in on forty, Hal Beecher managed to look boyish in spite of his thinning, sandy-colored hair and country-club-casual combination of an expensive golf shirt and pressed khaki pants.

Oh, hell, she thought. Why couldn't it be a nice, friendly Jehovah's Witness or a vacuum-cleaner salesman—or anyone but Hal, here with the eviction notice?

As she scooped up Peavy and opened the door, Susan cursed her husband for the "buy local" philosophy that had placed their home mortgage in the banker's hands. If Brian was going to buy local, maybe he should have done his wife-stealing out of town.

This time, she didn't bother imagining a pin. She stretched out Voodoo Brian on the rack instead.

"Hey, Susan," Hal said, sounding uncertain, or maybe even nervous.

If he really had come with those papers, he damned well ought to be. Though she hadn't picked the house, she'd lived here for six years, more than long enough to come to love its skylights and the hills outside its huge windows, its Mexican tile work and the pretty little fountain in the desert garden. If she thought it would help, she'd hole up with her mom like Butch and Sundance making their last stand.

"Hi, Hal," she managed, though as usual she couldn't bring herself to meet his gaze. Between the mortgage and the situation with their spouses, the weird quotient of their relationship was off the charts.

He put a fingertip beneath her jaw to lift it. "Chin up, Suz. We have to stay strong."

Peavy growled. She shushed him, despite the fact that she was thinking, *my sentiments exactly.* She absolutely *hated* it when Hal called her "Suz."

Susan briefly considered dropping the still-snarling fuzz-ball down the front of Hal's pants. Opting for civility instead, she stepped back and gestured toward the family room.

"Come in, Hal," she invited, resigned to going through the motions of a grown-up. "Have a seat, please. We've just finished eating."

She led him past a row of photographs she loved, framed shots she had taken of desert dwellers starkly redefined in black and white: a tarantula caught marching, its every hair distinct; a jackrabbit on its hind legs nibbling a tree limb; and her favorite, a coyote mother leading a half-dozen pups, all seven of them sharply silhouetted by the dawn. How strange, she thought, that their lives remained in focus while hers had blurred with doubt.

Out of the corner of her eye, she saw her mother standing at her walker, trying to balance salad bowls. Turning her head, Susan called, "Don't you dare clean that. It's my turn, remember?"

It was always her turn, but her mom never caught on—or at least she was willing to pretend she didn't.

Maggie put down the bowls. "Good evening, Mr. Beecher. I hope you'll excuse me. I'm a little tired."

Normally, wild horses couldn't have kept her from coming to the family room to find out what brought Hal here. Susan cast a worried glance in her direction, only to be reassured when she saw her pick up the TV listings on her way to her bedroom.

Susan understood then. While at the rehab center, her mom had gotten hooked on those ridiculous reality shows. At least this evening's visit would save Susan from having to watch some smarmy, squeaky-clean host tormenting starved contestants in the jungle.

"Have a good rest, Miss Maggie," Hal called, but his smile flashed over so quickly, Susan couldn't be certain she had seen it. The sadness left in its wake made her wonder if she'd been wrong about his reason for coming. Was he here to tell her something new— something he'd learned about Jessica and Brian?

She hoped they'd been found rotting in some moldy Mexican prison, or better yet, the Turkish version. But she kept her thoughts to herself, suspecting that if his wife walked through the door, Hal would throw himself at her feet and beg forgiveness for whatever he had done to drive her off. And that if he'd learned she *was* incarcerated, he'd send her care packages in prison.

Personally, Susan found his devotion idiotic—after

all, the woman had not only left him but also their child—but according to her mother's grapevine, most of Clementine's female population seemed irresistibly drawn to the catnip of his tragic story. Or, more likely, to the fact that the guy was pleasant-looking, well-heeled, and, most importantly, available.

"So what brings you here?" she asked, pausing in front of a caramel-colored leather sofa. At his hesitation, she guessed, "Foreclosure, or . . ."

She'd meant to add *"or something new on the investigation,"* but at the last moment, she chickened out. "Or did you decide to take me up on my offer to give you Peavy in exchange for a clear title?"

As if on cue, the hairball bared its teeth.

Hal looked at her intently, his forehead crinkling in that earnest way he had. "Think I'll pass on that offer," he said, "but this *is* about the house."

Susan sat, then pressed the fingertips of her free hand to her forehead, where a killer headache loomed. She *so* didn't want to think about this now. In a last-ditch effort to stave off the inevitable, she changed the subject to his four-year-old. "How's Robby?"

Despair flickered across Hal's features, making him look more vulnerable than ever. For the first time, Susan saw what other women must. Somehow, calamity had made him more appealing, while she'd grown prickly and defensive in its wake.

Still, it was far better to be angry than pathetic . . . wasn't it?

Hal hitched his pant legs, then sat down close beside her. "He's staying with my sister for a while. His cousins are there for him to play with, and he seems much happier. I miss him so much, but . . . when he's at home, he has these nightmares. He cries out for his mother, and I can't think what to say."

Though her first inclination had been to slide to the extreme end of the sofa, Susan couldn't help feeling sorry for the guy. What would she have told a kid if she had one? It wasn't as if she could say, *Shhh, honey. Mommy's imagining roasting Daddy on a spit now.* Because, no matter what, Brian would still *be* his daddy, and only a true bitch would run him down to his child.

Peavy squirmed until she finally released him. Fortunately, he trotted off toward her mom's bedroom instead of sinking his sharp little teeth in Hal.

Hal glanced up at her, his blue eyes begging for understanding. "Sometimes when I come home from the bank, I hear—or think I hear them laughing. Robby and . . . and Alyssa."

Susan couldn't recall the last time she'd heard him mention his dead daughter's name. She swallowed hard and thought that, all in all, foreclosure would have been a safer topic.

Hal's smile looked both sad and distant. "I imagine Jessica's home, too," he said. "She's singing in the kitchen while she cooks, the way she always did before we lost Alyssa."

Tentatively, Susan reached out to pat his hand. No wonder the poor guy was getting maudlin. At least she had her mom here. How would she hold on to her sanity if she had to live with both the missing and the dead?

He grasped her hand and squeezed it, and she noticed that he'd finally removed his wedding ring. The day she'd heard that Brian had been seen with Jessica, Susan had hurled her ring as far as she could off the back deck. The memory remained raw, an abrasion on her heart. She could have sold that diamond-studded band to pay off some of her bills. She told herself that was the only reason she still cared.

"My friends and family and my pastor have all been wonderful," Hal told her, "but sometimes I think you're the only one who really understands. You've had— we've suffered some of the same losses."

His thumb caressed her knuckles, and he ventured a small smile. "I want to help you, Susan, with the payments on the house."

She jerked her hand free in an action more reflex than considered. Shaking her head, she said, "You can't do that."

"I can, and what's more, I want to." Anguish lurked behind the warmth in his blue eyes. "We're in the same boat, Susan, exactly the same. Don't you see? We *have* to stick together."

Something new flickered in his expression, something that made chill bumps erupt on Susan's arms. He wanted more than commiseration from her—or at least he thought he did. The idea struck her speechless. She'd been so certain he was still in love with Jessica.

Nausea stirred as Susan realized that his offer came with strings attached. A man like Hal wouldn't pressure her for sex or demand that she become a replacement mother for his child, but still, she felt dead certain that those strings would slowly, inexorably weave themselves into a noose. All she'd have to do was tell him yes. . . .

"Say yes, Susan. Let me do this for you." He gestured toward some boxes she'd stacked in a corner. "You and your mother shouldn't have to move, not after all you've been through."

The headache she'd felt coming rode in on a wave

of irritation. What was it about men that made them look past a crowd of interested females to find the one who wanted to be left alone?

Shaking her head more vigorously, she said, "It wouldn't matter if you helped me. If the bank doesn't get the house, the IRS will, sooner or later. For one thing, it's all in Brian's name. He bought the place before we married."

"We'll worry about that when the time comes," Hal argued. "Just pay what you can. I know a teacher's salary will never be enough, but I can—"

"You don't understand," she said, reaching for a lifeline. "I won't have a teacher's salary to rely on either, at least not if the school board has its way. I might even have to leave town."

"What?" He looked genuinely surprised.

Susan knew a moment's reassurance that not everyone in Clementine knew of her dismissal. Or at least not yet.

"They mean to fire me," she explained. "Some parents have complained about the rumors."

"Damn it, that's not fair. How could they be so stupid?"

She flinched, momentarily taken aback by the heat of his outburst. Cautiously she ventured, "Life's not always fair. You should know that."

His shoulders sagged, and he brought his hands up to his face in an apparent attempt to hide the gleam of tears. Was he thinking of the daughter who had died or the son who still suffered from his mother's absence? Despite the discomfort he had caused her, pity welled up in response.

"I'm going to bring them back," she promised, for her own sake as much as for his. "I'm going to find Jessica and Brian, Hal. I swear it."

He looked up sharply. "In eight months, no one has found a trace. No one."

"I have," she admitted. "Two, as of this evening."

"What?" At her hesitation, he pressed harder. "What did you find?"

She thought of how pathetic it would sound, how hopeless. A storage room, which might prove empty, and a broken hard drive, one she didn't, at the present, have any way to access. If she meant to give him some possibility to sustain him, it wouldn't do to give him details.

"I'd rather not say," she finally answered, "in case they turn out to be nothing. But something tells me that won't happen. Something tells me this is *it*."

"Have you turned this information over to the sheriff?"

She captured his gaze, held it. "He doesn't care, not really. What difference does it make to any of those guys? Sheriff Abbott isn't going to lose *his* job. Deputy Ramirez's mother won't end up in some California nursing home."

"You're right," Hal said. "Every time I press him for an update, the sheriff tells me it's past time to go on with my life. It's so damned frustrating."

"Tell me about it. They've had eight months to solve this. I'm finished waiting, Hal."

His face lit up, and he said, "Maybe you and I should look into this together."

Susan rose and started toward the door. Hesitating near the entry, she turned to see him standing just behind her. It surprised her to realize she was an inch or so taller; she had never noticed it before, perhaps because he was broader through the chest than most men. Brian had once told her Hal had wrestled back when he'd attended Rice University in Houston. Maybe that accounted for the build, or it might be the rock climbing he had taken up after his daughter's death. *To help him handle his loss*, Brian had added, leaving Susan to wonder who was helping Jessica with hers.

She knew now, of course, exactly who had slipped into that role. The bastard.

"If it's anything important, or if I need any help, you'll be the first to know," she promised.

Hal frowned at her. "Show me what you've found." An unexpected harshness had edged into his voice, but it collapsed into desperation. "Don't you think I've earned it? My God, do you have any idea what I've been going through—what your husband's done to me?"

His face looked so much like a wounded boy's, Susan had to remind herself he was a grown man, seven years her senior. Behind her, the doorbell rang. Her head turned toward the sound.

"I'm sorry," Hal told her, his voice a plea for understanding. "I had no right to say that, to blame you for what he did."

"It's okay," she said, more uncomfortable than ever. "Excuse me, I have to get the door."

"Susan," he called after her, reaching for her arm at the same time.

She decided on the spot that Hal could save his touching for the sympathetic ladies showing up on his doorstep. Turning away, she took several long strides and flung open the front door.

Only afterward did she stop to ask herself why she hadn't bothered to check the peephole first.

Chapter Four

Luke couldn't have been more surprised if Susan had greeted him stark naked. As the door swung inward, Hal Beecher stepped up from behind and draped his arm around her—an unmistakable claim of ownership.

The sight struck Luke like a gut punch. When he'd refused to help her, had she gone to Brian's lover's husband—the same man who was about to foreclose on her house?

"Maddox," Hal said simply, extending his right hand.

Luke ignored it. "I didn't realize you'd already moved in."

Susan shrugged off Hal's arm and shot the guy a look that could wither plastic flowers.

"Mr. Beecher has *not* moved in," she said emphatically. "In fact, he was just leaving."

Luke fought back a smile. That was more like it.

"I'm already running late." As Beecher frowned down at his Rolex, its diamond bezel flashed beneath the entry light. "I promised I'd stop by my sister's in time to tuck in Robby."

For a moment, Luke felt small, gloating over the poor bastard's botched attempt to stake a claim on Susan's affections. Until Susan leaned forward and brushed her lips across the banker's cheek.

"Thank you, Hal," she told him. "I very much appreciate your offer."

Her head turned slightly, and her gaze flicked toward Luke. Was she checking, seeing how he would react? He gritted his teeth before recovering with a shrug. Why the hell should he care whom she kissed?

"Let me know if you change your mind," Hal answered. "You can call me day or night."

Turning away, he glared at Luke on his way to the front walk. Lit by lights recessed into the brick path, it wound past a small stone fountain and between a pair of yuccas that stood like sentries guarding the approach. Above their sword-sharp foliage, long stalks ended in twin masses of creamy, bell-like blooms that unfurled after dark.

Their sweet scent stirred a memory of an even sweeter night. Luke felt his breath catch and his blood race at the thought.

Fortunately, he was distracted when a chirping disarmed Beecher's car alarm, and the banker climbed into a chromed-out black Hummer that Luke had figured belonged to a guest of Susan's neighbors.

"Expensive taste," he said of Hal, hoping to elicit some comment, or better yet, an explanation of why the man had come.

When Susan didn't bite—or ask him inside either—he ventured, "Maybe this is none of my business—"

"There's no maybe about that," she said. "And, for the record, it disgusts me to see two grown men posturing like that."

"What makes you think I give a damn what Beecher does?"

" 'I didn't realize you'd already moved in,' " she mimicked, making him sound as if he had a terminal case of testosterone poisoning. "Please, Luke. I teach high school. My sarcasm-detection skills are well honed."

He shrugged. "Maybe I didn't like the thought of that guy taking advantage of my sister-in-law. A woman . . . a woman in your situation can be vulnerable."

She rolled her eyes. "Not to a *man*, I can assure you. Believe me, right now I wouldn't give you two bucks for the entire gender, unless I need a jar lid loosened or a—"

"Broken hard drive fixed?"

She had the grace to smile sheepishly. "Touché, D'Artagnan, and . . . I'm sorry. I guess it is a pretty broad indictment, lumping all men in with your brother. Of course, I *could* include the sheriff and his loudmouth deputy, Ramirez, too. And let's not forget Dr. Winthrop and the male portion of the school board."

"After that run of bad luck, the law of averages guarantees you'll come across a decent man any day now. Maybe he can change your mind."

"Yeah, well, I can promise you, Hal Beecher won't be the one to do it. I can't even look at him without thinking about . . . about stuff I'd rather endure a root canal than relive."

And what about me? Luke wondered. *Can you look at me without thinking about Brian . . . without seeing him as well?* Though his brother was the fairer, all-American version, Luke knew there was a family resemblance, whether or not his mother claimed to see it.

"I figure you probably had some greater purpose for driving over than protecting me from Hal," she said.

He brushed his hair out of his eyes. "I need to talk to you. Would it be all right if I come in?"

Susan glanced over her shoulder before shaking her head. "Are you kidding? My mom's been dying to light into any handy Maddox, and frankly, I don't think she's up to the excitement. Why don't you wait out here a minute while I check on her and grab my purse? I promised I'd pick up shakes at Swenson's. You can ride along."

"You're not afraid we'll be seen together?" he asked above the growl of thunder. "You were worried enough to drag me an hour away this afternoon."

She shrugged. "This time of night, who's going to see us? You know Clementine. We pretty much roll up the sidewalks after seven."

He smiled at the memory, and at the thought that he didn't much miss Austin's nightlife. Maybe it was Ocotillo County's vast expanse of darkness, barely permeated by a smattering of man-made lights. Or perhaps it was the songs the insects cast up to the veiled moon. Or maybe thirty-three was simply the right age for nostalgia.

"Bring along that hard drive, will you?" he suggested.

Her eyes lit up, and she threw her arms around his neck. "And here I thought I was going to have to wear you down—or at least ply you with chocolate malts until you screamed for mercy."

It's only gratitude, Luke told himself, but that didn't stop his hands from stroking her back, or his body from responding to that lean, sweet length of female. Images flickered through his consciousness like lightning: mouths mating while he cupped a breast, two forms merging, melding beneath the canopy of stars.

Deeply embarrassed, he extricated himself before

insanity took hold. Praying she hadn't felt his arousal, he plucked up the threads of their conversation.

"Don't . . . don't get your hopes up too high," he warned. "I don't know if there's anything to find, even if I can get the drive to spin again."

She stood there for a moment, looking at him oddly, before she turned and went inside and closed the door behind her.

Oh, shit, he thought. She'd felt him, poking into her with all the freaking subtlety of a bayonet. For a moment, he hoped she wouldn't come back, for that rejection would be less painful than if she tried to talk about it.

What would he say then? *It's not you, Susan. It's just that I haven't held a woman in so long.*

He grimaced, hating how pathetic that would make him sound. Jeri, his last girlfriend, had hinted she'd turn down her job offer in Seattle if he'd give her some reason to stay. But something held him back, the way something always did with girlfriends, and she'd moved away—had it already been a year ago? Since then, he'd been so swamped with work, and then this mess with Brian, that he'd barely found time to do his laundry, much less start dating someone new. Still, it didn't excuse—

Susan came back, carrying her shoulder bag and holding her keys in her hand. "Sorry I took so long. I needed something from the kitchen."

"Why don't I drive?" he invited, praying she would be merciful and pretend away his lapse. God knows, that was *his* plan. "I'm blocking your Jeep anyway. I pulled into the driveway, right behind the garage."

As she closed the door behind her, she shook her head. "You know, I've never mastered the art of balancing milkshakes while sitting on the back of a moving motorcycle."

Luke roughly shoved aside the thought of her body—the same body he'd just held—pressed behind his on the Kawasaki's seat. What the hell was wrong with him tonight?

"I drove the truck here," he said quickly. "Come and see it."

As he led her to his pickup, he couldn't help wondering, what if he had been a little more patient back in high school, or a little more persistent? Would things have clicked between them the way he'd sensed they might?

He scowled, irritated at the way his body had commandeered his mind. He should make some excuse and leave now—take the hard drive and get back to the ranch to work on it.

He was about to say so when a motion detector switched on the lights in front of the garage. Even in the dim illumination, the old pickup gleamed.

"This is great." Susan hurried forward, then ran her hand appreciatively over the rear fender. "What year is it?"

"It's a 'fifty-three Chevy. You can't tell in this light, but it's turquoise with a white roof."

"Gorgeous. Did you fix it up yourself?"

"Top to bottom, and every bit of it original," he said, unable to keep the stupid grin off his face. Maybe it wouldn't hurt to take her for a quick spin.

"Very cool," she said. "Looks like a real labor of love."

Her admiration blew away the last of his resolve, as did her understanding. She wouldn't laugh, as Brian had, to learn he'd spent more on parts than the whole pickup was worth.

"You should have seen the thing when I first bought it," Luke said. "Some old farmer in the Hill Country had it stuck way back in a barn all crammed with junk. Mice had gnawed the interior to pieces. I found whole tribes living under the hood, too."

He thought of how Jeri had come to hate his "rat-infested" truck, or at least the hours he'd sunk into it. But then, Jeri hated everything that didn't revolve around her needs.

High maintenance, that was it. That was why he hadn't asked her to turn down Seattle.

"You always did like old cars," Susan said.

Her words reminded him all too clearly of the '66 El Dorado convertible he'd rebuilt in high school—and the use the two of them had made of it. Not trusting himself to speak, he sucked in a sharp breath instead.

Susan rubbed her hands together like a greedy little kid. "So, are you going to let me drive?"

"Uh, no. The gears are sort of fussy, and she's a little particular about the—"

Susan laughed and climbed into the passenger side. As he took the driver's seat, she told him, "You haven't changed a bit."

"What's that supposed to mean?"

She cranked down her window as she spoke. "You were never into sharing—unless you wanted to borrow my chemistry homework."

"Which you never lent me, I might add."

"You didn't need my homework," she said lightly. "You only needed to show up in class once in a while."

Since it was true, he let it pass, and for a while they rolled through the darkness in companionable silence. The headlights reflected off a sign that read "Welcome to Clementine, Pop. 7300," before catching the glowing eyes of several animals on the shoulder of the road. Slowing, Luke passed a family group of javelinas, a small, hairy, and cantankerous brand of wild hog.

Through the open windows, he heard their piglike calls and caught a whiff of smelly musk.

"Funky place for a school-board meeting," Susan commented. "I suppose it's more of the same pork-barrel politics."

He made a face. "Your students would've booed you out of class for that joke."

"Only after somebody explained it," she said, but the fondness in her voice belied her words.

During the awkward pause that followed, he wondered if she was thinking of the classroom and whether she would miss the teaching life. In spite of the long days he'd put in at the dealership, Brian had sometimes griped about all the extra hours Susan spent planning labs and grading papers. She'd sponsored some sort of club, too, that went on desert hikes and even camped out a few times each year, and she'd taken lots of photos for the yearbook.

"As if any of it brings in an extra dime," Brian had scoffed. *"Who'd do all that outside work for nothing?"*

Luke thought about her words to him, and the way they summed it up. *"Looks like a real labor of love."*

"We'll find a way to save your job," he told her, surprised at the determination in his voice. "If not in this hard drive, somewhere else."

Raindrops plinked against the windshield, not enough to bother flipping on the wipers but enough to keep Luke's gaze glued to the road. Even so, he felt her looking at him, staring. He would swear to it.

Finally she asked, "What changed your mind? Don't

get me wrong. I'm glad, but this afternoon, you were pretty insistent about staying out of this."

"I made a call," he explained, "to an old roommate from college. He married a woman who works for the Department of Public Safety."

"In the crime lab?"

They passed new businesses tucked between familiar landmarks. Some of the old places, like Pop Norton's Drugstore, appeared to have gone belly-up.

He shook his head in answer to Susan's question. "No, but Jane was there for a few years. She still has friends there, so I asked her to check into your computer's status."

"And you found out . . . ?" Susan prompted as it began to rain in earnest. She leaned over to crank up her window.

"Just a sec." Luke fiddled with the knob that ran the wipers. When nothing happened, he thumped the dash with the heel of his hand and was rewarded by the rhythmic music of the blades.

The headlights skimmed a construction site for a new gas station. From the size, he figured this one would have a mini-mart and flavored coffees, along with clerks working for some faceless corporation instead of for themselves.

"Place is growing, changing," he commented, surprised that something in him wanted his hometown to stay familiar, a time warp he could visit when he felt the need.

"You're stalling, Luke. Just tell me," Susan complained as he turned left into Swenson's.

But there was no line at the drive-through window, so he ordered three malts from a curly-haired teenager.

After Luke ignored Susan's offered twenty and paid for them himself, the girl mixed their shakes in old-fashioned silver cups. He was glad to see that in Clementine at least some memories remained sacred.

As soon as the mixer's whirring gave them privacy, Susan said, "Now spill it. What did this woman tell you?"

"Your computer never made it to the crime lab. Or at least it's not logged in."

"I *knew* it. I knew there was something—"

"That's not all," Luke broke in. "They don't have a record of any items taken from your house."

"Son of a bitch," Susan exploded. "Why would Sheriff Abbo—"

She stopped, apparently aware of the teen, who kept sneaking peeks over her shoulder.

"It's possible," Luke said, "my friend's wife might be wrong. Maybe the material's there but isn't recorded in the right spot. Or who knows? Could be they sent it somewhere else."

This time, Susan whispered, "Or maybe somebody here took it. Someone who doesn't want Brian found."

Luke had had the same thought, though he wasn't ready to say the words aloud. If Susan charged over to the ranch and started shouting accusations, his mother would clam up so tight they'd never learn the truth.

The girl handed him their milkshakes, then leaned out the window so far that Luke could count the piercings in her ear. Heedless of the rain, she called out, "Hey, Miz Maddox. I *thought* that was you. How's it goin'?"

"Just fine, Caitlyn. I didn't recognize you with the new hair." Susan wrapped one of her straight locks around a finger in demonstration. "Those curls are gorgeous."

The girl beamed, the way Luke thought he probably had when Susan had tossed a few kind words his truck's way.

"I think it's awesome that you're back out dating," the teen told her. "If the ball and chain's a player, why shouldn't you be, too?"

"I am *not* a player," Susan argued, "and this isn't a date."

"Sure, whatever." Caitlyn grinned as she winked at Luke and slid the drive-through window shut.

As Luke pulled away, Susan smacked her forehead and slumped in her seat. "Well, that was brilliant, coming here together. Now Caitlyn will tell everyone she knows."

Luke shrugged. "It's been eight months since Brian took off with another woman. If you did start dating, who could blame you?"

"Let's see," Susan said, clearly annoyed. "There's the school board, all the gossips who've laid wagers I did in the happy couple . . . and, lest you think you're off the hook, your mother. How's she going to take it if she hears you're 'dating' me?"

"I can handle my own mother," he insisted, though not without a few misgivings. "Besides, that girl didn't recognize me."

Susan gave a little bark of laughter. "You're underestimating Caitlyn. I'll bet you this twenty that by tomorrow, she and her friends will have it figured out."

"How're they going to—"

"The truck," she shot back. "It's not exactly inconspicuous."

"I've never driven it to town before. Besides, don't you think you're being a little paranoid?"

Even as it came out of his mouth, Luke realized it was the wrong thing to say. Of course she was feeling persecuted, between the gossip and the school board.

Before he could apologize, she said, "You know, it's a good thing you're driving—and I'm safety-minded."

"Why's that?"

"Because I really need your help with this hard drive," she said, pulling it out of her bag and laying it on the seat between them, "and you might not be inclined to give it if I dumped this milkshake in your lap."

He took a sip of his drink. The cold exploded in his mouth, rich and sweet and creamy all at once. "That would be a waste of a damned fine chocolate malt."

There was a pause, a slurp, and then a moan of pleasure that made the hairs behind his neck rise.

"Mmmm," Susan murmured. "This is so, *so* good. Ohmygod . . . it's been *way* too long."

Luke began to wish she'd dumped her milkshake on him after all—because right now he could use some cooling off.

Intent on reining in his wildly inappropriate thoughts, he concentrated on software codes, antivirus files, and the methods he would try to restart Brian's hard drive . . . on anything except the sounds she'd made. He was so fixed on his goal that, several minutes later, her gasp took him by surprise.

He shot her a look meant to say, *I'm going to choke you if you're back to the orgasmic noises.*

"Oh, God," she cried, her horrified gaze fixed on something in the distance. *"Mom."*

Following the direction of her stare, he saw the flashing red lights . . . and the patrol car parked haphazardly, door open, in front of Susan's house.

"Try not to panic," he warned as he slowed the pickup. "I'll come in wi—"

Turning his head, he saw that it was already too late. Susan had leapt out of the truck and was running blindly through her front yard.

And toward what Luke prayed would not prove to be the worst nightmare of her life.

Chapter Five

As Susan raced toward the partly open front door, the sharp spines of a yucca snagged her sleeve. Tearing it free, she called out, "Mom?" as she burst into the entryway.

The room lay empty, with no sign of her mother or a deputy, no sound at all to tell her where they'd gone. A premonition dropped her stomach to her sandals, or was it just a sense of déjà vu?

Finding nothing in the kitchen, she raced toward her mom's bedroom, her mind riffling through strobe-lit flashes of that awful night last winter when she'd come home to an empty house. The night she'd gone rushing through these same rooms while little stabs of panic sharpened into the bone-deep knowledge that her life would never be the same.

She froze as a sound reached her, a man's voice speaking softly, the way one did with a frightened child . . . or a dying woman. But the words were obliterated by pounding footsteps behind her.

She felt a hand on her shoulder, felt as much as heard the reassurance in Luke's words. "I'm here."

Together they stepped inside the guestroom, where a man in a deputy's tan shirt and dark brown dress jeans squatted across from Maggie Dalton, who was seated on the bed. The muted television flashed unsettling images: a bullet spinning in slow motion through the air.

Some crime show, Susan realized as she began to breathe again.

Her mother stared at her, her eyes wide, her now-loose hair a storm cloud around her pallid face. "There. There's . . . Susan. You see, I t-told you she'd . . . come back."

"Mom." Susan's legs shook like a newborn foal's. Luke's palm, squeezing her shoulder, lent her strength enough to keep her feet.

"Blood," said Susan's mother, her brown eyes cloudy. "There's blood on you."

"Blood?" asked Susan. "I don't . . . what's happening here?"

Deputy Ramirez stood and turned toward her, bearing a grim look on a face little like the one he'd worn when they'd attended high school. Thanks to an accident and the plastic surgery that followed, his features looked sandblasted, the skin too tight to disguise the shapes of the bone and muscle that it covered. He wore his black hair short, too, so it did little to disguise the scar that snaked along the scalp line.

It was Luke who answered first, touching Susan's upper arm and saying, "You must have scraped against the yuccas."

Tiny beads of crimson stood out against bare flesh, but Susan paid them no heed. Instead, she focused on Manuel Ramirez's dark eyes.

His wide mouth pulled into a frown. "While you were *out*, your sister Carol called the house. According to what she told the dispatcher, Mrs. Dalton sounded confused, couldn't say where you had gone or how long you had left her."

The censure in his voice was clear, as was the dislike when his gaze leapt to Luke. Susan could almost hear Ramirez wondering where they'd been together, and if they'd maybe held a little class reunion inside Luke's truck. She could almost hear suspicion snapping into place, filling up a hole he would call "motive."

Hell.

Taking a deep breath, she knelt before her mother and took the age-splotched hands in hers. "Mom, did you forget what I said? I ran to Swenson's to get milkshakes. Chocolate malts. Remember?"

"Looks to me like you forgot 'em," said Ramirez.

Maggie's gaze drifted up to Luke. "What in God's name is that boy doing here?"

But Luke hadn't taken his eyes off Ramirez. "They're out in the truck. Didn't seem important once we saw your lights."

Susan glanced from Luke to Manuel as they watched each other. If they'd been coyotes, their teeth would have been bared, their tails and hackles up.

More male posturing, she thought. But why? Hadn't the two of them been friends once, long ago?

"Did you hear me?" asked her mother. "What's a . . . a Maddox doing in this house?"

"Luke dropped by just as I was leaving, to see how we were doing," Susan explained. "He drove me into town to get the shakes."

"If you're all right," Luke said, turning a friendly smile on the older woman, "I'll bring yours in from the

73

pickup. Be a shame to let it go to waste. And I can walk Deputy Ramirez out as well. Now that he knows there's no trouble after all."

As Ramirez shot Susan a hard look, she could see a muscle working in his jaw. An exhalation hissed out of his nostrils, like steam out of a kettle's spout. "Better call your sister," he said. "Let her know you're with your mom—at least for now."

"I'll do that, Deputy." Susan rose to her feet, a move that forced her to look down to hold his gaze. "Thanks for checking on my mother. I appreciate the—"

The thread of the thought unraveled as she recalled the open front door. Glancing around the room, she said, "Wait. Where's Peavy? Have any of you seen my dog?"

Ramirez glanced down at his ostrich boots and shrugged. "Something brushed past my legs when your mother let me in. Was that thing really a dog?"

"Not much of one, but—"

Her mother interrupted. "He must have zipped right past me. I don't . . . I don't remember. But he never . . . goes far."

"I'll help you find him," Luke said to Susan. "Just let me get your mom that shake."

He turned and started back down the hall leading toward the family room. Something stopped him, and he looked back over his shoulder. "You coming, Deputy?"

Even as Ramirez nodded to Luke, his gaze rested on Susan. She stared back, feeling the skin prickling behind her neck, the fine hairs rising on her arms. Her apprehension mounted as she waited for some question, or perhaps an accusation.

Instead, Deputy Ramirez was the one to break eye contact, the first to walk away.

Susan turned, then sank back to the bed and threw her arms around her mother. On the muted screen behind her, a woman's body arched as she fell face first to a stark white driveway. Before the hug was over, rivulets of blood ran downward, forever staining the concrete.

It was almost midnight when Susan told Luke she'd given up on finding Peavy.

From the back deck, she swung her light's beam one last time across the gray-green needles of a clutch of juniper. Still wet from the earlier shower, they sparkled as if strung with fireflies.

"If he were here," she said, "we would have found him, or heard him anyway. Mom's right. He's never gone far."

Luke switched off his own flashlight, which had faded into yellow with the passing hours. "He's probably holed up underneath a neighbor's deck or in a corner of a tool shed. I'm betting he'll turn up come morning."

Still staring toward the foothills, Susan sighed. "I know what's out there, Luke. A dozen things that would be glad to eat him. There's a reason the neighbors keep their cats indoors. The few who don't, find tails and tufts of fur, or maybe paws. More often they find nothing."

Luke thought of the sign he'd seen when he'd driven by her neighborhood's bank of mailboxes earlier. Beneath the words "Missing" and "Reward," a yellow tabby had stared out with big green eyes.

"I hope you're wrong," he said, though if he were a gambling man, he would have laid good money on coyotes.

"Stupid dog's always been more trouble than he's worth." She flipped off her flashlight, too, leaving them only the illumination from the kitchen window and the partly shrouded moon. Still, she turned her face away, hoping, he supposed, to hide her tears.

Whether or not she would admit it, he knew damned well she loved the fuzz ball. The thought made him want to reach for her and pull her into his arms.

Bad idea, something warned him.

"It's been one hell of a long day," Susan said, fatigue or grief putting a quaver in her voice.

He moved nearer, close enough to hear her breathing in the stillness of the night. Close enough to catch the light scent of her skin. Close enough to want to taste it, too . . .

Again, something whispered in his head. Something that had never gotten past that one night, had never forgotten how she'd sounded when he had made her come, how she had felt and smelled and tasted . . . and how he'd been too young and stupid to realize he couldn't go back to relive those moments with anybody else.

Closing his eyes, he turned and kissed her head, above her ear. Her hair felt like warm silk as his lips brushed against it, just the way it had before.

It was nothing but a chaste kiss, a kiss any relative, even an in-law, might bestow upon a woman who had lost so much. But coiled within the simple gesture was the secret they had kept for far too long.

He wanted to ask her in that moment, *"Did you really keep it? Or did you tell my brother?"*

Yet as she moved away from him, he kept up his end of their unspoken pact. Never to mention it again, not even to each other.

She ran her palm over her hair as if to smooth it, then said, "Thanks anyway . . . for staying out so late to help me look. And thanks for saying you would fix that hard drive."

"I'll see what I can do," he said quickly. "But let's not get our hopes too high."

"You'll do it."

Her words were so soft, he could barely make them out. Yet the faith he heard in them echoed in his ears throughout the short drive home.

The watcher's heart was racing still, with the thought of how close *she* had come to where he waited.

Her feet crunching on the cooling earth, she'd walked within yards of him, so near that all he would have had to do was reach out of the juniper to caress those long, bare legs, to slide up underneath her skirt and—

The mere thought had his cock standing at attention, the burning shaft of heat contrasting with the icy film that overlaid his vision.

And then the man caught up to her, a man whose presence made the watcher's hands shake, made him so fucking mad he wanted to grab the nearest stick and snap it right in half.

But he thought, after a moment, that a bone would do as well. Or maybe he would wring—or was it ring?— a neck instead. *Yes.* That would remind the woman that a sacred vow, once given, could not be cast aside the second some other guy came sniffing around.

And there was no mistaking that the bastard was encroaching on his territory. The watcher saw that, saw them silhouetted against the kitchen window when the man ducked his head to press his face against her hair.

He waited for her to cry out as she should have, to jerk away and slap the interloper's face. When she did neither, the ice across his vision thickened, and he felt a fragile shell of cold constrict his beating heart.

So once the pickup vanished and the lights inside the house blanked out, the watcher emerged from the damp juniper and strode back toward the cage where he had left the tiny dog . . . the same one she'd held pressed between her breasts.

Chapter Six

Tired as she was, it took time for the sound to permeate her consciousness. Time for her to realize there was someone in her house.

Susan's eyes snapped open, and her pulse boomed loud and fast in her ears. Faster still when her vision focused on the shape that loomed above her in the darkness.

"God, how I've missed you."

The tall form was silhouetted, yet she would know Brian's voice anywhere, no matter how long he had been gone. Yet she couldn't speak or make her limbs work, couldn't break through the paralysis of fear.

And couldn't do a damned thing to stop him as he crawled into bed with her.

She felt his nakedness, felt his big hand move along her side and touch her breast. As if he'd never left her or made her life a living hell. As if, even before that, they had been on the same page when it came to sex.

"I can't tonight. I just can't," she had told him, turning away with the sheet clutched in both her hands.

"Jesus, Susan. It's not as if you're the first woman in the world to have a couple of miscarriages. How're we supposed to try again if you won't even let me—"

The memory unlocked her frozen muscles, made her fling her arms at him and cry out, "No."

Yet still, he pressed his nakedness against her, his mouth finding her neck while his fingertips trailed both guilt and pleasure from her nipples to the shameful pool of heat between her legs.

It was not until he rose up over her that she saw he wasn't Brian, not until he drove into her that she finally cried out, *"Luke,"* and saw the stars glowing in the summer sky above his head.

She woke inside the sweat-drenched tangle of her own sheets. With a groan, she sat up, then pushed her damp hair off her face.

The dream had meant nothing, nothing at all, she told herself . . . just as she realized that some part of it was real. She swallowed at an unfamiliar noise.

What?

Chill bumps erupted on her arms as something thumped the wall to her right, the one that separated her bedroom from the office. The same something she'd been hearing in her sleep.

Whatever the noise was, it was here, inside the house. As her gaze flicked to the glowing numbers of her clock, she tried to tell herself it was her mother. But why would she be rummaging around the office at 3:58 A.M.?

At the sound of scraping, Susan frowned, remembering how Mom's confusion had prompted Carol to call the sheriff's office earlier. Rising from her bed, Susan thought, too, of Roberta's warning about the gas stove. Could her mother be suffering some sort of relapse?

80

Wide awake now, Susan pulled on a pair of shorts to accompany the oversized T-shirt she had slept in. After feeling her way to the door, she turned the knob carefully so it would make no telltale sound.

She scanned the hallway. Other than the night-light she'd plugged in to help her mom find the second bathroom, not a glimmer breached the darkness of the house.

She had just stepped from the carpeted bedroom onto the cool tile of the hallway when she heard a muffled thud. As she glanced toward the closed door of the office to her right, the thought of Peavy blazed like a meteor across her mind. Could someone have accidentally shut him in the office earlier? Or purposely, she amended, recalling how often her mom lost patience with the Chihuahua's misbehavior. She could easily imagine the scenario: her mother scolding him for digging up a potted plant or shredding a throw pillow, then banishing him to the office just before Carol's call. It was just as easy to imagine that her mother had forgotten, especially when she could not even explain to Carol where Susan had gone.

The idea was so plausible that warm relief spilled into Susan's limbs. It was weird that Peavy hadn't barked when he'd heard them calling, but it would be just like the little idiot to scare the hell out of her while he was sleeping somewhere cozy.

As she walked toward the office, she couldn't help laughing at what a fool she'd been to worry.

"Peavy-boy," she called softly, picturing him fanning his fringed tail behind the door. "Come on out, you little terror—"

Something clicked from farther down the hall. The sound was harsh, metallic, one that brought to mind the crime drama she'd glimpsed in her mother's bedroom earlier.

Gun, her mind shrieked as she spun toward the sound. Just in time to see a human shape rush toward her.

Before she could scream, the office door banged open. A second intruder's hand clamped, hard and painful, on her neck.

She felt herself yanked forward an instant before she slammed headfirst into the door frame. Wood cracked—or maybe something in her forehead. When her attacker let go of her, she tumbled to the floor.

It might have been a minute or an hour later when more noises roused her. A sense of wrongness rushed in with the sounds.

Somewhere nearby, voices murmured, and she put meaning to the noises: drawers pulled open, boxes emptied, then running footsteps and a hungry crackling. The last triggered bone-deep instinct, a certainty she had to move away from here.

But when she tried to lift her head, pain—God, how it hurt—arced around her forehead and made her want to vomit. Lying back, she whimpered under the combined assault not only of her head, but of a twinge in her elbow, a stiff ache in her hip. The floor felt hard underneath her and sticky below her cheek.

Confusion spiraled into panic.

An orange flickering worked its way into her awareness, even though her eyes were still closed. Forcing them open, Susan recognized the hallway in the lurid yellow light. The way it swam and shifted made her groan with nausea.

But she couldn't stay here, for she understood now:

There was fire in the office to her right, fire chewing its way hungrily through papers strewn across the floor.

She flinched at the sound of a door opening and the shuffling of feet. Was someone coming back to hurt her again?

"Susan?" Her mother sounded tremulous and old against the crackling. "Susan!"

Susan's eyes snapped open, and in the hazy yellow light she saw her mother leaning over her walker just beside her.

Her mom was saying something, but the sounds refused to resolve themselves into any sort of sense. Susan shifted slightly, thinking to move closer, but at the change in her position, a black wave rolled over her.

"*Up*," her mother ordered, and this time, there was pure grit in the older woman's voice, a firmness not unlike the days when Susan had tried pulling her covers over her head instead of waking up for school. Her mother bumped her with a toe.

A burst of siren just outside joined forces with another nudge to convince Susan there would be no going back to sleep.

Moments later, a man shouted from the entryway. "Miz Maddox, are you in there? Maggie, you hear me?"

"Hector—" Her mother coughed before continuing. "Hector, I need . . . I need your help. Susan won't get up."

Hector Abbott? What did Mom mean, calling in the law to get her out of bed?

Susan threw an arm over her eyes as an overhead light flipped on, and the sheriff's footsteps pounded down the hall.

"Maggie, get outside." Hector, too, began to cough.

"I'm gonna try to knock this back, and then I'll bring her out."

Frightened at his tone, Susan looked past the bend of her arm to see him edging by her, a fire extinguisher in his hands. The air was thick with what she finally recognized as smoke.

When her mother made no move to obey the sheriff's order, Susan found the strength to roll over, then push herself onto her hands and knees.

Pain bloomed in her forehead, but she managed to focus on the whooshes of the extinguisher and the stench of ash. Groaning, she struggled to her feet, her mother coughing and pulling at her elbow.

No sooner had she stood than her lungs began rebelling, and both her eyes and nose ran at the insult. The air was worse here than it had been near the floor, she realized. But since her mother couldn't crawl, Susan merely bent forward at the waist instead of resorting to her hands and knees.

With her first step, her legs buckled, but Hector Abbott's firm hand wrapped around her waist and held her steady.

"Just move, both of you," he growled, then firmly shut the office door. "I think I got it, but there's still a lot of smoke."

With sudden shocking clarity, Susan recalled the clicking of the gun she'd heard earlier.

"The men," she said, filled with terror at the thought that the intruders were still here, that they might shoot her or her mom or Sheriff Abbott.

"He left," the sheriff answered as he towed her forward. "I saw him running when I pulled up. I radioed for backup, but I 'spect he'll be long gone."

"Two," Susan gasped after a round of coughing. "There were two of them."

As they made their way toward fresh air, Susan wondered if she was still dreaming. It was the only way she could make sense of a night in which white-haired Sheriff Abbott played the hero, saving not only her house but quite possibly their lives.

For something told her that the two men had been scared away before their work was finished. And that once they found whatever they had come for, they had meant to leave her and her mother dead.

Though Sheriff Hector Abbott had radioed to assure them the blaze was extinguished, the Clementine Volunteer Fire and Rescue couldn't be talked out of running through the subdivision with their sirens blaring— the neighbors' sleep be damned—before stampeding through the house. Once a call woke those boys, they had to have their fun.

As it was, the volunteers were mad as hell to find out he'd intruded on what they saw as their domain, no matter that Hector had been county sheriff for close to thirty years.

"What were you doing, running into a fire?" demanded Captain Arturo Rivera. "Don't you know that's what we train for? You didn't even have gear on."

Arturo was a small man, small enough that he could have ended up a jockey instead of selling insurance down on Prickly Pear Avenue. But on the scene at any incident, he always stood a little taller, especially in the eyes of the volunteers he led. To Hector, this was all well and good, except when Arturo felt the need to tell him how to do his business.

Distracted by the sound of swearing, Hector glanced over to where Susan was trying to prevent the rescue crew from strapping her to a backboard so they could transport her to the ambulance that was en route. She was sitting in the driveway next to his patrol car with a towel pressed to her head to stanch the bleeding.

"I'm fine," she argued, and she seemed it, in spite of the champion goose egg Hector had seen. "Didn't you hear me? I'm refusing treatment. I'll sign anything you want."

The youngest Miller boy, an acne-scarred fellow barely out of high school, was valiantly attempting to explain to her the risks of untreated concussions. Hector could have told him not to waste his breath; Susan Maddox wasn't the kind of woman who needed a man to make her mind up for her.

He noticed how often her gaze flicked to her mother, who was sitting in the back of Hector's car. Maggie looked lost there, her pale face glowing in the emergency lights. Enough so that Hector imagined Susan was more worried about the older woman than herself.

He thought of volunteering to look after Maggie for the time being, but Arturo was lecturing him again.

"All three of you could have died in there," the insurance man was saying.

"But we didn't," Hector all but barked. "I got a call. Neighbor got up to snitch some of his wife's pie, thought he saw someone slip around the side of this house. I came to check it out and spotted a man running. He'd left the front door standing open, and I spotted what looked like fire inside the window there. Ran to the door with my extinguisher. I could hear Mrs.

Dalton yelling for Susan to get up. What the hell would you have done, man? Left them both in there—maybe hurt—with some pissant fire that would only grow?"

Arturo ignored the question. "I saw a lot of damage, but it's mostly unrelated to the fire. Drawers pulled out and strewn around, boxes dumped out everywhere. Looks like robbery to me, or maybe vandals."

"So now that I've done your job, you think you oughta take a stab at mine?" Hector asked, still irritated that Rivera hadn't allowed him back inside. Arturo had cited his crew's need to check for fire in the walls, since Hector's extinguisher had blown bits of burning paper all over the office, and "cross-ventilate," as they insisted on calling their window-opening operation. "Smoke ought to be clear enough by now. I'm goin' in to have a look. Deputy Forrester gets here, you send him right in."

"I'm not sure it's safe yet," Arturo started, but Hector was already walking toward the house.

Inside, the scene was pretty much as Rivera had described it: boxes of kitchen stuff and books dumped at random, music CDs pulled out of the entertainment center, photographs scattered across the family room as if some joker had been playing fifty-two pickup— and everywhere the reek of smoke and the chemical odor of his extinguisher.

As Hector's booted foot crunched an errant light-bulb, he heard someone come in behind him.

"Oh, God . . . look at this."

His head jerked to take in Susan, who stood inside the doorway, a white square of gauze taped above her left eye.

"How'd you get in here?" he asked, surprised she had escaped the volunteers—and Deputy Forrester, who should have kept her outside.

"It's still my house," she told him, her eyes gleaming with moisture. "I had to see what . . . what they'd done to it."

He frowned, anticipating tears and maybe even hysterics. But, stubborn as she was, he knew he'd have the devil's own time getting her to leave before she'd seen the whole place. So Hector decided to walk her through it and glean whatever he could from her reactions to the scene.

Instead of breaking down as he'd expected, she cursed as they paused at the office doorway. Though the reek of smoke hung heavy and papery ash lay against a charred spot on the Sheetrock, her attention was riveted on several red-brown splotches on the tile outside the door.

Her blood, Hector figured, but nonetheless he chalked a line around it. "We'll have this typed and cross-matched against yours, in case any of it belonged to one of the intruders. You never know. You might've scratched one in that scuffle."

While he drew, she turned away, as if the sight disturbed her. Before he could think of what to say, she brushed past him and walked into what must have been her bedroom.

Tangled skeins of clothing littered the carpet, and the mattress had been dragged off the bed frame. Susan stepped around the mess and knelt beside her purse, which had been dumped beside her nightstand. Picking up the wallet, she pulled out two twenties and a ten, along with a few ones. "They didn't bother with the money. Look, the credit cards are here too. And I saw my camera stuff out in the family room."

After slinging the purse's long strap over her shoulder, she dug around inside her jewelry box, which stood open on her dresser. "Weird," she said. "There's nothing missing."

From what Hector could see, her jewelry consisted mainly of silver and some turquoise, but she pointed out a pair of good-sized diamond studs.

"Anniversary gift," she said. "I would have thought they'd take these and the cash, if anything."

"So they didn't come to steal," he said, liking the way she'd wrestled her shock into submission and started thinking logically. "Or could be they got scared off— maybe they heard my patrol car driving up, or one of 'em saw me coming through the window."

But that didn't really wash. Thieves should have had a vehicle parked close to carry off TVs, VCRs, and other bulky items, yet the man he'd seen had fled on foot. His gut told him she was right, that robbery had never been the motive.

"What about kids? You know, some of the ones you've taught?" he asked. "Anybody come to mind, some troublemaker you had to flunk or discipline? You heard about how your school's assistant principal had all that vandalism at the new house he was build-ing a couple of months back. I'm pretty sure it made the paper."

She shook her head. "My students—my kids would never hurt me."

He shrugged. "Maybe you surprised them. Could be they thought you'd already moved out and they were busting up an empty house. If kids get scared enough, they're capable of things their own mamas wouldn't credit. I've seen plenty of it."

But as he and Susan checked the other rooms, he couldn't make that idea fly either. More than likely, kids would've panicked and run off after hurting Susan instead of sticking around to paw through her belongings as she'd described. And even if they'd stuck around, vandals would have kicked in the big screen in the family room, smashed the contents of the fridge, maybe busted all the china and run out with the cameras. This destruction had another pattern, one that troubled him.

He and Susan drifted back to the office, where most of the damage had occurred. The charred contents of desk drawers and file cabinets littered the tiled floor. The office closet, too, had been thoroughly tossed, leaving small boxes and shiny disks scattered alongside those little plastic ones folks stuck in their computers.

"What were they looking for in here?" Hector mused.

Susan hesitated for a beat, then shook her head. "What a disaster area. Catch the bastards, will you, so I can thank them personally?"

Was it only his imagination, or was she trying to change the subject? Did she know—or guess—something she wasn't telling him?

He thought of calling Manuel Ramirez, comparing notes to see if he'd noticed anything strange during the welfare check on Susan's mother earlier that evening. He decided against it, not because he was worried about waking his off-duty deputy, but because he was afraid he'd catch Ramirez in the sack with Grace Morton, a twenty-two-year-old certified jailer who was married to a bar owner known to be a poor sport about such things. Better not to know than to dive headfirst into that cesspool. Especially since his first inclination—to fire Grace, whose superior had complained she had a mean streak—would likely trigger a complaint with the Equal Employment Opportunity Commission. If anyone could be counted on to cry sex discrimination, it was Gracie.

Dismissing Ramirez and Morton from his mind, he said to Susan, "If you have any ideas . . ."

She nudged the burnt edge of a file folder with her foot. "If I could just sift through this mess, maybe I could figure out what's missing. What if they took old tax returns or passwords for accounts, even receipts with credit-card numbers? Couldn't they use stuff like that to run up all kinds of charges?"

Hector scratched his mustache as he thought about what she said. "It's not a half-bad suggestion, but I can't see professionals bypassing free-and-easy cash, credit cards, and diamonds to go after some homeowner's file cabinet, especially when they can get stuff just as good by rifling mailboxes. No, what you've got here feels a lot less random, more like somebody came looking for something in particular."

Susan had grown pale, and he thought he detected a tremor in the hand she used to brace herself against the door frame. "It's this smell," she said, apparently aware that he was staring. "It's making me sick."

He walked her back outside and had her sit down on the fender of the fire truck. "You catch your breath," he said. "But don't go anywhere. We need to run through what happened once or twice more for the record."

"But I've already told—"

He smiled. "Folks always complain, and I tell 'em all the same thing. We ask you to go over it a few times because you'll remember more with every pass."

She groaned, and he turned away to go and talk to Forrester about taking prints and running a blood type on those splotches. His senior deputy didn't move too fast, but Forrester was sharp enough that he might catch something Hector hadn't.

Maybe even something to explain why someone would come back to search the same office Hector and his deputies had gone through last December. As if the intruder suspected that the potential evidence they'd deemed immaterial held some clue. Or was desperate to get his hands on the missing man. Desperate enough to risk a nighttime break-in in an occupied residence. And to try to kill when he was caught.

Besides Susan, who would want so badly to track down Brian? Not his mother, certainly. As she'd let Hector know on numerous occasions, Virginia Maddox preferred that her son stay missing rather than return to face charges for his financial shenanigans. His brother Luke, on the other hand, appeared to want him found, but Hector thought Luke was too smart to get his hands so dirty as to ransack the office, especially since Hector couldn't imagine Susan being anything but eager to cooperate in whatever amateur detecting Luke might suggest.

Hector dismissed the idea of those automaker fellows as well. For one, the Detroit corporation could well afford to write off whatever it lost on one dishonest dealer. Besides, whoever had made this mess had a more personal grudge.

Hal Beecher crossed his mind, too. Although the banker wasn't half the thorn in his side that Susan had been, he'd made it abundantly clear that he wanted his wife back. To add insult to injury, Brian Maddox had taken out some bad loans, but Hector couldn't make that idea fit, either. Like Luke Maddox, Hal Beecher could have simply asked to look for anything that might help. Besides, if he was going to do something so stupid and reckless, he would have done so in those first tense days, when he had been so torn up about the whole thing.

That left one other possibility, one that Hector, try as he might, could not discount: the idea that Brian Maddox had come back himself . . .

Because the man had realized he'd left something in that office, something he'd risk anything—even the murder of his own wife—to recover.

Chapter Seven

By the time the blood-smeared dawn yielded to a pale blue morning, Susan had had enough of questions. How many ways could she explain that it had been too dark to make out her attackers' features and that she hadn't recognized their voices? How many times could she say she had no idea what they might have wanted?

Even though each time she repeated it, doubt flickered like heat lightning just beyond her mind's horizon. Had one of the voices seemed familiar, or had the sheriff's and the deputy's relentless questions planted the suspicion?

When Deputy Forrester asked her to recount "the events" for him one more time, she turned to Sheriff Abbott and played her trump card. "I need to take my mom to her apartment. She needs to rest somewhere she'll feel safe."

Hector's expression softened as he glanced at her mother, who sat in the cruiser's backseat in her bathrobe, her eyes closed and her head tipped forward. Though her gray-streaked hair had fallen untidily around her shoulders, sleep and the morning sunlight had conspired to smooth her face's creases, offering a glimpse of the younger woman she had been.

Hector nodded at the deputy, a round-faced fifty-something whose belly strained at his tan uniform shirt. "We've got enough."

As soon as Forrester lumbered back to his patrol car, Hector added, "You'll be staying at your mother's apartment, too, right?"

"There's no way I'm sleeping in this house again," Susan answered. "Not with those men still on the loose. I'll grab a few things for now, if it's okay for me to go back."

"It's all right. We're done inside, and the volunteers shoveled out the burnt papers from the office. Still, watch your step in there. Your visitors left quite a mess."

Thinking about the work depressed her. "I'll come back and clean up later."

"Better rest first," he said, sounding more like a grandfather than a lawman, "and see your doctor like you promised. Otherwise, I'm gonna have to call Big Sister, get her out here to ride herd on both of you."

"Don't you dare call Carol," Susan snapped, noticing too late the smile beneath his full white mustache.

He stopped to scratch it, a habit so homely and familiar that it made her feel at ease—until she remembered with a sick jolt that this was the same man who might have destroyed or hidden evidence taken from her house.

"You shouldn't be driving," he advised. "Anyone you do want me to call?"

She thought of Luke immediately, thought of how

good it had felt last night when he'd embraced her, how wonderful it would be to feel his arms around her now.

And how very dangerous. For if Luke came, she knew her carefully built composure would collapse, and right now she needed it more than ever. Besides, she couldn't chance having the sheriff guess that the two of them were not only looking into evidence, but scrutinizing his investigation.

"My head's much better, just a little sore," she answered carefully. "I don't need anyone."

Sheriff Abbott looked right at her, his blue eyes so intent, she worried that he knew about the hard drive she had found. *Had* her mother let it slip, or Agnes or Roberta? And even if one of them hadn't, should she come clean about it now? Especially since she could not stop worrying that the hard drive and its secrets had been her attackers' goal.

"It's not a crime, you know," he said.

Confusion short-circuited her guilt. "What?"

"Needing someone."

She puffed out an exhalation, a sound too soft and cynical to qualify as laughter. "I used to think that, too. Or at least I did eight months ago."

Turning on her heel, Susan walked inside, eager to collect both her essentials and her wits. Instead, when she peeked into the office on her way to her room, she started trembling at the sight of the dark charring on the office wall—and the realization of how close the house had come to going up in flames.

Backing away from the doorway, she glanced down at the bloodstained tile with its chalk lines. A sick chill gripped her at the thought of how helpless she had been while she had lain there—and how powerless she would have been had her attackers rushed into her mother's room.

Her world tipped on its axis at the thought.

Fighting off her dizziness, she demanded of the silence, "What was it you wanted, you sons of bitches? Why in God's name did you come—and why last night?"

The house she'd lived in for six years yielded her no answers.

It was her red Jeep, when she climbed into it fifteen minutes later, that offered up the first heartrending clue.

At the moment of truth, Luke's bedroom door swung open.

"For heaven's sake," his mother said in lieu of good morning. "I've asked you a hundred times not to let that smelly dog up on the furniture."

At the message on the computer's screen, he swore.

"*Luke.*" His mother's voice was sharp with disapproval. "Did you hear me? I was saying, about the dog . . ."

"What?" His gaze jerked from the screen and landed on Duke, who was sprawled happily across Luke's still-made bed. "Oh, sorry. Get down, boy. I hadn't even realized he was in here."

Or that it was morning, he added mentally. Yet it clearly was, judging by the light streaming through the eastern-facing window and the steaming mug of coffee in his mother's hand. When the aroma reached him, it was all he could do not to grab the mug and down its contents.

The fat black dog stood and stretched, turned once,

and lay back down in the same spot on the denim comforter.

Already dressed and ready for the day, Virginia blew across the coffee's surface before sipping delicately and remarking, "You've been playing on that fool thing all night. *Off,* Duke."

The old Lab mix jumped down before stalking to the corner, where he moaned dramatically while finding a comfortable position.

"Somebody had to break this thing in." He touched the side of the flat-screen monitor, then smiled up at her, softening the gibe about her lack of interest in the state-of-the-art PC he'd given her last Christmas. Though he'd spent hours setting it up and showing her how to use the Net to plan travel, shop for mystery novels by her favorite authors, and explore her family tree, he'd returned a few months later to find the whole system moved to his room, where it was covered with a layer of fine dust. "Besides, it's not *playing,* it's business I'm doing. I told you I'd need to do some telecommuting as long as I stay here, and I needed your computer to do the job."

Not that the project that had kept him up most of the night had a thing to do with P.O.M.—Peace of Mind, Inc.—but Luke didn't want his mother to guess that he was working on anything to do with Brian. He needn't have worried, because, as he'd expected, her eyes glazed over at the reference to his work.

He wondered if things would change if she had any inkling of how much money his "messing around" had earned him. But he'd never been able to bring himself to try to buy her approval that way, and this morning, when he was tired and frustrated with his lack of progress, proved no exception.

She was predictably quick to change the subject. "Would you care for breakfast? I haven't broken out the waffle iron in an age."

A peace offering, he suspected. One that he would do well to accept. Maybe a full stomach and half a pot of coffee would bring some fresh ideas.

"Thanks, that would be great. Let me jump in the shower to clear the cobwebs first, and I'll be right out."

While he washed and shaved, he mentally ran through the steps he'd taken to get the damaged hard drive spinning. As he'd told Susan, his expertise was in data security, not recovery, but he'd picked up a few ideas that had served him well in the past. Suspecting that the drive's heads were sticking to the platter, he'd tried time-honored Jedi geek tricks such as rapping it with a rubber mallet, dropping it onto the desk from a few inches, even sticking the damned thing in a static bag and popping it in the freezer for a couple hours while he dozed in a chair. Yet each time he'd rein-stalled it into the free bay on his mom's PC, the old drive had stubbornly refused to function.

Afterward, he'd cruised the Net in search of an iden-tical, working hard drive so he could swap out the on-board controller and, if absolutely necessary, the motors themselves. Locating the drive had proved a challenge, since the model had been out of produc-tion for at least three years. Finally, on an all-night tech chat, he'd run across some guy who'd claimed to have a good one. In return for Luke's promise to air-express some barbecue from a world-famous Austin joint to him in Boise, the homesick Texan had promised to overnight the drive to Luke.

Even though Luke had already made good on his part of the bargain, he'd been unable to resist one more shot at the freezer fix. One more shot that had failed. No surprise. He had a feeling that every effort to recover the data from this drive would be doomed.

He had always hated giving up on any broken thing, yet this particular failure ate at him in a way no other had. Maybe it was because he kept seeing Susan's face, hope shining sunlike in her long-lashed blue eyes.

How could he stand to crush it out again?

After toweling off, he pulled on fresh jeans and a plain black T-shirt. He ignored the ringing phone, which was undoubtedly for his mother, and instead took a few moments to drag a comb through his dark hair. Needed cutting, he thought before a whiff of something burning drew him to the kitchen.

His mother was standing at the sink with the phone pressed to her ear as dark curls rose from the unattended waffle iron. Luke pulled the plug and threw open a window before the odor set off the smoke alarm.

"Is it still standing?" his mother asked the caller.

He hadn't meant to eavesdrop, but the anxiety in her voice froze him in his tracks.

After a brief pause, she answered, "I wouldn't be surprised if she set the thing herself since she can't have it."

His heart thumped with the conviction that his mother was talking about Susan. Whom else would she speak of with such ill-concealed hostility?

Before he could catch her attention to mouth a question, his mother added, "Hmmm. Well, how *badly* could she have been hurt, if she refused the hospital? I don't know about—"

"What is it?" Luke burst out. "What's happened?"

She clapped one hand over the phone's mouthpiece. "Your manners, Luke, have gotten completely out of—"

He wasn't about to put up with a scolding. It must have shown in his expression, for she abruptly nodded, then excused herself to the caller.

After hanging up, she frowned at the smoldering waffle iron. "That was Jessie Miller. Her youngest, Ray, lends a hand at the fire department when he's not off at college. He's so caught up in it, she says she's half afraid he'll quit school and—"

Luke hurried her with a gesture of impatience.

"I was getting to it," his mother said. "There was a fire at Brian's home last night. Nothing serious, Ray said. Hector Abbott put it out with an extinguisher before it got much of a foothold."

"What about Susan? Was she the one hurt, or did you mean her mother?"

Virginia wrapped her fingers around her half-full mug of coffee. "They're fine. That Dalton girl bumped her head somehow. She claims someone hit her, and the place *was* fairly torn up. But I can't imagine anyone here in Clementine—"

"Someone broke into their house?" he demanded, all fatigue forgotten. "An intruder trashed the place and set the fire?"

"That's what she says, but don't you see? This could be a bid for sympathy, a story she thinks could save her house and job. What are you doing?"

"I'm going to see her," he said as he filled a silver travel mug with coffee. "I want to find out if there's anything she and her mom need. If her place is messed up, I can help—"

"They're not even at the house now. They went to

stay at that little apartment where her mother was living. You remember the place. It's in that old white house over on Mirage."

He nodded. "Good. Then I'll know where to find them."

She spared the smoking waffle iron a rueful glance. "But what about your breakfast?"

He snapped the lid on top of the mug. "I'll skip it, but thanks anyway."

Before leaving, he trotted to the bedroom to pull the hard drive from his mother's desktop. It was possible, he thought, that whoever had torn up Susan's place had been looking for something. As unlikely as it was that anyone would know or care about the defunct component, he didn't want to leave it too far out of his sight.

He was almost out the door when his mother came up behind him.

"Luke?" she said, her voice uncharacteristically hesitant.

He turned in her direction.

"Don't you . . ." She straightened her spine and raised her chin proudly. "Don't you have any loyalty?"

He bowed his head to kiss her cheek.

"Yes," he said in answer. "I'm finding that I do."

Turning from her, he was careful not to let the door bang in his wake.

Chapter Eight

Just the empty collar, hanging from the turn signal lever. That was all Susan found when she climbed inside her Jeep.

Though her eyes were bleary with fatigue, she stared until the tiny blue loop wavered with her unshed tears. Dear God, what kind of heartless bastard would want to—

"Susan?" asked her mother. "Is everything all right?"

Glancing at her mother's pale face, Susan couldn't bear to tell her that the predator that took Peavy might well have been human. Not until she had to, or at least until her mom had had a chance to rest in her own bed. There would be time enough later to tell both her mother and the sheriff about what she had found.

"Everything will be fine," Susan promised, speaking past the painful lump in her throat.

With a single deft movement, she slipped the collar off the turn signal lever and stuffed it beneath the seat. The dog's tags jingled as she did so, but her mother didn't seem to notice.

Susan was in no hurry to get the collar out again, to think about who might have put it there and what it meant for Peavy. Like each of the calamities bearing down on her, this one seemed surreal—something from the nightmare her whole life had become.

On the gearshift and the wheel, her hands began to tremble. With a will, she put herself in this moment, in this place—driving toward town with her mother beside her in the Jeep, and brilliant sunshine streaming from a cloudless summer sky. All she had to do was get her mom settled in and maybe take a warm bath, wash off the smell of smoke and the dried blood.

She could do that much, she told herself. By the time she reached Mirage Street, the trembling had stopped.

Roberta was waiting for them, her face more flushed than usual, when Susan pulled into an open spot beside the big Victorian Old Man Littleton and his two sons had converted to apartments fifteen years earlier.

Roberta, who had been widowed four years earlier, lived two doors down, in a blue Queen Anne that had seen better days. Like the Victorian and the few other survivors, Roberta's house was a holdover from the days when ranchers made enough to retire to town once they'd turned over their operations' reins to one of their sons. It was a sad thing, Maggie Dalton often remarked, that hardly a soul was left in Clementine who remembered cattle bringing anyone that kind of prosperity. Nowadays, the remaining ranchers were barely hanging on, and many had resorted to raising exotic game, selling hunting leases, or even allowing well-heeled city "dudes" to pay for the privilege of working a real roundup.

"Are you all right?" Roberta asked as she helped Maggie from the Jeep. "Helen Rivera, Chief Rivera's wife, called to tell me about the fire."

Roberta hugged Susan's mom, who seemed to have perked up at seeing her friend. Either that or, judging from the way her gaze lit on the door to her apartment, she felt glad to be finally going home.

"We'll be . . . all . . . all right," Maggie told Roberta, sounding mulish as ever despite the quaver in her voice. "We're both Daltons, after all."

Roberta must have phoned Agnes, because the larger woman piled out of her Buick minutes later, her double Ds bouncing with her hurry.

As she stared at Susan's face, Agnes said, "Good Lord, you're a sight, with Mount Vesuvius rising on that forehead."

"You always have known how to make a girl feel special," Susan told her.

"What did you do, forget to lock the doors last night? Don't you watch the news? There's crazies out there everywhere."

Susan turned on her, in no mood to put up with any insinuations. Before she could define a crazy as someone who habitually stirred up squabbles, Roberta took her arm.

"You poor thing," she crooned. "We'll get some ice on that, and then you can tell us all about what happened."

After Susan waved off her attentions, the two women reassured themselves by fussing over Maggie, who was too tired to make more than a token protest. By the time Susan emerged from a long soak and changed into fresh shorts and a Grand Canyon T-shirt, Agnes and Roberta had already made her mother tea, helped her into her nightgown, and tucked her into her freshly remade bed. They were still inside her room, dissecting the events of last night in low voices, when Susan thought of calling Carol—before one of her sister's friends could beat her to it.

She stalled, sipping the tea left for her while she held a bag of ice wrapped in a dish towel to her forehead for several minutes. She wished she could numb her emotions as easily . . . maybe with an icepack to the heart.

Sitting at the honey oak dinette with the phone in hand, she thought how fortunate her mother was to have Roberta, who had been using her key to periodically clean up the place in her mom's absence. Thanks to Roberta's efforts, there wasn't a speck of dust in evidence.

Wishing her own friends had been as loyal, Susan took a deep breath, then punched in her older sister's cell-phone number and gave Carol an abbreviated version of what had happened at the house.

At her sister's shriek of horror, Susan's headache came roaring back.

"Someone tried to kill you," Carol practically screamed into the phone. "He could have hurt Mom, too!"

Her tone left no doubt that she considered the latter possibility far more serious. So much, thought Susan, for the idea that sibling rivalry could be outgrown.

As Susan could have predicted, Carol's blubbering reaction was closely followed by insinuations that Susan's "sordid" troubles were at least in part to blame.

"Ever since Brian *left* you"—as usual, Carol said this as if she had no doubt that Susan had done something to drive off a man Carol had always considered a prime catch, one who had been utterly wasted on her younger sister—"these *problems* of yours have gotten worse and worse. And now they're wearing on Mom's health. I could tell when I spoke with her last night, when I—"

"Turned me in to the sheriff's office for picking up some milkshakes?" Susan shot back.

"How was I to know? Mom sounded so distracted. She couldn't tell me anything—"

"She was watching TV, that's all," Susan interrupted. "I've told you how attached she's gotten to her shows. She's not so bad I can't leave her to run a twenty-minute errand."

"You mean you'd do that *now*, after someone's broken into your house and—"

"I won't leave her again. Roberta's only two doors down, and Agnes and her husband are close by, too. I'll call one of them if I have to step out."

"Bring her here," begged Carol. "James and I would be glad to get her the therapy she needs—and we have the means to hire a home-care aide if necessary."

Susan made a face at Carol's reference to her pompous husband, an engineer who pulled down big bucks and made sure everyone knew about it. Yet neither Susan's sister nor the man she'd chased to California had felt "comfortable"—whatever the hell that meant—helping to pay for Maggie's rehabilitation after Medicare claimed she was no longer eligible. Brian, on the other hand, had manfully volunteered to take on the responsibility—before skipping town with his pockets stuffed with every cent he could take.

Mentally Susan held a lit match to her voodoo husband's groin.

"I can take care of Mom myself—" Susan began, but her older sister wasn't listening.

"Or I can come and get her." There was no mistaking

the genuine distress in Carol's voice. "I need to have her here so I can sleep at night. Please."

Susan bit back her first impulse—to argue—and chewed her lower lip instead. *Could* she keep her mom safe from the kind of person who would creep into her house at night, the kind of sick son of a bitch who would take—and maybe kill—her little dog? She didn't even have a job now, unless something dramatic happened in the next two weeks.

Was it fair to risk her mom's life—and her sister's peace of mine—out of pride and stubbornness and petty grudges?

"I'm really beat," Susan said after a pause. "I need a little time to rest and clear my head. But I'll consider it, I promise."

"You will?" Clearly, Carol had not expected the concession.

"If you really meant what you said. If you weren't just asking me to bring Mom for the sake of argument."

"Of course not, Susan. I just . . . are you sure you're going to be all right? Maybe you should go and get those X-rays after all."

After reassuring her, Susan ended the conversation. And wondered what kind of sister she had been up to this point, if by agreeing to consider Carol's suggestion, she had raised the suspicion that her egg must be cracked.

As Luke parked the truck along Mirage Street, he saw Susan just ahead of him, pulling something from inside her red Jeep. A duffel bag and a small suitcase stood beside her on the pavement.

Pocketing his keys, he hurried to her.

"You should have called me." The words sprang out

before he could contain them. "Someone from the family should have been there."

As she turned her head toward him, the bottom dropped out of his stomach at the sight of the livid bump above her left eye.

"From the family," she echoed, but it didn't register at first. Not while he was staring at the purple bruise with its small cut. Behind the wound, her face was deathly pale.

With a sickening jolt, it sank in that whoever had hurt her might have done worse, might have even killed her.

At the realization, his world slanted off-kilter and his hand reached toward her face, seemingly of its own volition. "Susan . . ."

She jerked back as if she feared he'd touch the sore spot. He noticed then that she was clutching some small item in her right hand.

"What can I do to help?" He swore to himself he would do anything she asked, right down to murdering the bastard who had dared to touch her. He was shaking with fury, as close to exploding as he had felt in years.

"You can . . . you can . . . oh, God," she stammered, then dropped what she was holding into his outstretched palm. Something metallic jingled as it fell. "Take this. Take it, please."

He stared down at the blue loop, at first not comprehending. Then he realized it was Peavy's collar.

In an attempt to clear his head, he took in a deep breath. Right now she needed gentleness, not anger. "You found him?"

"*Look* at it," she demanded. "At first I missed it, too. I thought it was the tags I heard, and then . . ."

She swayed then, and he thought she would have

fallen had he not thrown a supporting arm around her waist.

"Susan," he said. "Come on. Let's get you inside where you can sit."

She leaned into him and draped her arms over his shoulders. Helpless against the impulse, he embraced her tightly.

"The ring," she whispered in his ear. "Look at it—the ring."

He didn't want to loosen his grip, didn't want to ease up even for a moment. But her voice had made the hairs at the back of his neck rise.

That was when he saw the thick gold band that hung between the rabies and ID tags. Still holding her, he turned it to stare at the three diamonds—diamonds he remembered winking on his brother's hand.

Reflexively his fist clenched around it. "Brian's?"

She stepped away from him, seemingly recovered from the initial panic that had gripped her. Nodding, she said, "Yes."

"But where? How?"

"Inside," she said and reached down for the bags.

He beat her to them. "Let me get those."

She didn't protest when he picked them up, or when he stopped at his truck to grab the damaged hard drive. If he'd thought for a moment she would allow it, he would have carried her inside as well.

She let him into Maggie's first-floor apartment, a small but neat place, homey despite the infestation of doilies on every available surface. There was even one underneath the monitor of an old 486 computer that sat atop a delicate-looking writing table in a corner of the living room. In a window, an air conditioner thrummed steadily against the day's heat.

He glanced at a door along the hallway as Susan closed it.

"Mom's room," she explained. "She's just drifted off to sleep. Her friends have gone, thank God, or I'd never hear the end of it."

Puzzled, he looked at her for further explanation.

She must have read his look, for she supplied it. "Between your mom and your brother, Maddoxes are none too popular right now. I, uh, I imagine you're sick of being blamed for stuff your family's stirred up."

"After a while you get used to it," he said. He never had, but he supposed one might, in time.

Moving past a blue recliner, Susan sat on an overstuffed sofa with an old-fashioned floral print. When he followed suit, their knees touched. He felt gratified when she pretended not to notice. Maybe she needed the contact. Or perhaps, like him, she felt the current passing from one to another, as dangerous as it was irresistible.

He unbuckled the small collar, then slipped the ring off, into his sweating palm. He had never thought he'd see his brother's wedding band again. "Where did you find this?"

"The collar was hanging in my Jeep this morning. Someone must have left it, but I don't know when. There were plenty of people running around last night, at the fire."

When he tried to pass the ring to her, she shook her head. "No, I don't want to . . . I can't . . . touch it."

He understood the feeling. He set down both the collar and the ring on the coffee table. "I heard you had a break-in."

She nodded, her blue eyes looking huge and glassy. "There were two of them, at least. I heard a noise, and when I came out of my bedroom—oh, God, Luke.

113

Could it have been Brian? Could he have left his ring—and what about poor Peavy?"

Trying to put the Chihuahua's fate out of his mind, Luke took her hands into his. They felt icy despite the warmth of the apartment, and he sensed her fault lines spreading, threatening what remained of her composure.

"Let's take one thing at a time," he told her, his thumb stroking her hand. Maybe if he asked the easy questions first, he could get her back on track. "You didn't find the dog, only the collar?"

Once more, she nodded. "Do you think someone's ki—"

"Let's work with what we're sure of. Someone got close enough to take off his collar. That's all we can really say until we know more."

He heard her sigh. "All right."

"And whoever it was had access to Brian's wedding band, or one that looks enough like it to pass."

"It's his. Look inside."

Turning it so the inner band caught the light, Luke read what was inscribed there: the date of Brian and Susan's wedding. He sucked in a sharp breath at the reminder that the two of them were married still.

"You're right," he admitted. "Brian could have lost the ring before he left here, or he might have pawned it somewhere. I don't think he's come back."

In spite of everything his brother had done, Luke couldn't imagine Brian physically harming anyone, not even the little scrap of fluff he'd once rescued from the death chamber of Animal Control. But even if Luke was wrong, even if his brother intended to kill Susan for some reason, could he be insane enough to bother torturing her with the dog collar and the ring left in her

Jeep? No, thought Luke. Maybe, like his mother, he was deluding himself, but he had to believe there was someone else at work here.

"I would have known him." Susan nodded, as if she had just now come to the conclusion. "Even in the dark, I heard some voices. I would have recognized his."

Luke set both the collar and the ring down beside the hard-drive box on the coffee table. "Were any of the voices familiar?"

"I—I don't know. It seemed . . ." She shook her head. "I was so damned scared and stunned, and everything happened so fast. Before I could make sense of any of it, one of them grabbed my neck and slammed my head into the door frame."

As Luke stared at the wound on her forehead, his mind flooded with terrifying images: Susan lying on the floor with blood pooling beneath her, two men looming over her as she lay there in shock. Rage resurfaced at the bastards who had done this—rage and a new fear.

"Did they . . . did they do anything else, Susan?" he managed, his voice rough with emotion. "Did those sons of bitches—"

"No, Luke, no." She looked alarmed, perhaps at the intensity of his reaction. "They didn't try to rape me. After I went down, they went about whatever it was they were doing in the office. I'll be fine."

"How do you know? Did you get checked out by a doctor?"

Her lips pursed in clear annoyance. "I already have a mother. I said I'll be all right."

"And what about your mom?"

"She wasn't hurt, just a little shaken up. But I didn't show her those." Susan gestured toward the ring and collar. "You're the only one who's seen them."

"You haven't told the sheriff?"

Her mouth flattened in a grim line. "I meant to, once I'd gotten a chance to clean up and rest awhile. But now I wonder: Is this going to disappear like all the other stuff? And how's it going to look if I suddenly turn up with Brian's ring? Hector Abbott might not give a damn about this case, but you can't tell me Manuel Ramirez doesn't suspect that I've done *something*."

Recalling the way Manuel had acted toward her, Luke nodded. "You could be right, but how's it going to look if you get caught with it if you *don't* report it?"

Her eyes closed, and she leaned back, saying nothing while his thumb caressed her hand. He wanted to release it, but he didn't dare, so strong was the impulse to soothe her like a child who had just awakened from a nightmare.

She wouldn't welcome it, he told himself. And worse yet, he could all too easily imagine his caresses sparking other, far less innocent forms of comfort.

Her eyes slid open, and her gaze was so intent, he was certain she must have guessed what he'd been thinking. Pulling her hand free, she turned her knees from his.

"You're right. I'll call the sheriff later and tell him what was in my Jeep. I don't care what he does with it anyway. I just want that thing out of my sight."

Snatching a few tissues from a box on the coffee table, she wadded them around the ring before tucking it inside the pocket of her shorts.

Susan pointed to the hard drive in its box. "Have you found anything?"

He shook his head, "Not yet, but I'm—"

A knock at the front door interrupted him.

116

Susan rose, frowning, and said, "Maybe that's the sheriff now. I can't imagine who else—"

Luke grabbed the hard drive and slid it underneath the sofa just as Susan opened the door.

"Marcus?" she said to a tall boy who grinned at her from beneath the greasy fringe of hair draped over his eyes. The color was anybody's guess, a black-gold mix of several different dye jobs, but at least it distracted from the painful-looking zits that marked his face.

"Hey, Miz Maddox, look what we found," he said cheerfully.

"Peavy!" There was no mistaking the delight in Susan's voice as she moved past Marcus to where a second, shorter boy stood close behind him, his dark gaze seemingly cemented to ground level. In his arms he held the Chihuahua, who struggled wildly at the sight of his mistress.

"Or Jimmy found him, anyway," said Marcus. "But *I'm* the one who recognized him from that picture on your desk. And I'm the one who figured out where you were after we found that 'no admittance' sign on your door. What happened, anyhow? You look like you've been in an accident or something."

He tapped his own forehead as he looked at hers.

Ignoring the question, she took the squirming dog out of Jimmy's hands. Though he'd at first appeared smaller than his friend, Luke realized from his vantage behind Susan that Jimmy had been slumping. And no wonder. Someone appeared to have recently shorn the kid's head, nicking the scalp in several places and leaving only about a quarter-inch of dark brown fuzz. His clothing, too, fit poorly, far tighter than the oversized jean shorts and T-shirts that Luke saw other teens the boy's age wearing.

He watched Jimmy's gaze flicking to Susan's face as the little fuzz ball licked it, then dart away as if he figured she would swallow him alive. Or as if the poor kid had it bad for her.

Luke could sympathize, especially when the thought occurred to him that he was just as bad, pining after his own brother's wife.

But she was mine first, something foolish in him whispered—something that forgot how it had ended, stillborn, long ago.

"Thank you so much," Susan told them. "Thank you both. I've been so afraid—but where'd you find him, Jimmy?"

"Out"—the boy had to clear his throat, but he didn't look up—"out wandering around near where I live. You know, on Rocky Rim."

"On Rocky Rim?" Luke echoed. If memory served him, the only things up that way were some abandoned housing units. If Jimmy lived in that rat hole, it would explain his neglected look, along with the broken shoes Luke had just noticed. "But that's at least five miles from Su—from Mrs. Maddox's house. There's no way Peavy could have gotten so far on his own."

Marcus looked up sharply. His lips curled back over his teeth. "What are you saying? That we took him? Because if you understood anything about us, man, you'd know—"

Luke held up a palm in an attempt to defuse the boy's anger. "I didn't mean that either of you took him. Only that *someone* must have." Looking to Susan, he said, "Probably the same person who broke into your house."

"Someone broke into your house?" Jimmy erupted, emboldened enough to risk eye contact. "You tell us who they are and we'll—"

"If I find out, you'll be the first to know," Susan said. "This is my brother-in-law, Luke Maddox. He's helping me out with a few things. Luke, meet Marcus Bingham and Jimmy Archer. They're ace biology students, when they remember to show up."

Marcus grinned sheepishly while Jimmy shrugged. Both looked surprised when Luke reached out to each one in turn and shook his hand.

"We always show up for the hikes," Marcus said to Susan.

"Ecology Club's not graded," she commented. "I hear you turn up for lunchtimes too."

"And auto shop," Marcus added. "Takes both of us to keep my old crate running."

"Come on in," said Susan. "I have something to show Jimmy."

As Luke took his earlier spot on the sofa, he noticed the way Marcus walked straight in and claimed the sole recliner. Jimmy, on the other hand, barely edged far enough inside to allow Susan to close the door behind him. Luke saw that the kid's right hand was bandaged.

Still in Susan's arms, Peavy stopped wagging his tail long enough to bare his teeth at Jimmy before barking fiercely at both the teens and Luke.

"Hush up, you little ingrate," Susan scolded, though she hadn't stopped stroking the tan fur. "Let me stick him in the back room with a pan of water and some biscuits before he wakes up Mom."

When she returned, she retrieved her purse from the kitchen counter and dug out an envelope. Smiling at Jimmy, she said, "Come on, sit with us."

His dark gaze flicked upward briefly. After several moments' hesitation, the boy veered around the living room, then pulled out a straight-backed chair from the dinette set. Resting one arm across its back, he stood there waiting until Susan brought him the envelope.

"Do you recognize that address?" she asked.

To judge from her rapt attention, the boy's answer was important to her. With as much as she had to worry about, Luke wondered what could be bothering her about a letter.

As if she'd read his mind, she looked at Luke. "It's a bill addressed to Brian, for a storage facility out on Rocky Rim. Place by the name of U-Store-All. Only I've never heard of it, and the phone book has nothing by that name."

"It's one of the units," Jimmy murmured, staring at the return address.

"What?" asked Susan.

"One of the units where I live. Weird old hippie by the name of Boone rents out the empties."

"I don't get it," Susan said. "Why on earth would Brian rent a place like that?"

"Sometimes," the kid said, more audibly this time, "somebody's got stuff he don't want to get caught with. You know, like barrels that's expensive to get rid of legally."

"Drugs?" Susan asked.

"Or maybe hazardous materials," Luke said. "Disposal's regulated now for everything from refrigerants to motor oil to old computer monitors. A lot of people don't want to put out the extra money."

"You mean they're storing toxic waste there?" Susan sounded horrified. "Where there are people living?"

Jimmy shrugged. "Nobody worries much about a few squatters. Who cares if we—"

"I do, man," said Marcus. "And it's not right, rich bas—I mean jerks—dumping off their garbage."

"I agree," Susan added, "but I still can't imagine Brian wanting to hide that sort of thing. For one thing, I know he was paying to have the waste material from the dealership recycled. So he must have been using the unit to hide something else."

"Could be he needed a place where stuff could be sent where no one would know about it," Jimmy suggested. "People do that sometimes. You'd be surprised. They can get mail there."

"But if Brian wanted to get mail, why not just rent a post office box?" asked Susan. "Who would question that? He could say he needed one for the dealership, same as half the businesses in town."

Luke's mood darkened at the mention of his father's legacy, now lost. But that didn't stop him from thinking of another explanation. "There are things you can't send to a P.O. box. You need a physical address for packages from other shippers like FedEx and UPS, big stuff—and certain official documents."

"For instance?" Susan asked.

Luke glanced from one teen to the other, and Susan nodded, understanding.

"I'm not sure," he said for the boys' benefit.

"Well, whatever he has over there, I'm going to find out." Susan reached for the envelope.

Instead of handing it to her, Jimmy said, "Boone's not going to let you. It'd wreck his business if anyone found out he let a renter's old lady get his stuff. Besides, you don't want to go there. It's not . . . somebody might hurt you."

"Someone already has," she said quietly.

Jimmy gave no sign that he had heard her. "Let me hang on to this for the time being. Then me and Marcus can get whatever's in there for you—"

"I don't want you doing anything illegal," Susan said.

Both teens lifted their right hands, thumbs folded to their palms, and said in unison, "Scout's honor."

The two of them laughed then, leaving Luke no doubt they'd falsely sworn the same oath more than a few times.

"Don't worry," Marcus said, rising from his chair. "With me and Jimmy on the case, what could possibly go wrong?"

Susan watched the two of them climb into an ancient Cadillac convertible, a rust bucket painted in the tans and browns of desert camouflage. A spider's web of fractures on the windshield made her wonder how Marcus could see to drive.

"If those two get arrested—" she began.

"Who's going to file a complaint against them?" Luke asked. "Surely not this Boone character. He can't afford to call attention to an illegal operation."

"I see your point."

"That car . . ." Luke nodded toward the receding Cadillac. "It looks almost like the one—"

Susan closed the door behind her, cutting off his view. She didn't want to talk about the convertible Luke had in mind, the sleek, blue El Dorado he had owned in high school. They couldn't risk that conversation, or the memories it would jar free.

As if he'd read her mind, Luke dropped the subject, and Peavy started whining from the back bedroom. After turning him loose, she came back to the living room.

"What were you thinking earlier?" she asked Luke. "Something about what can't be sent to P.O. boxes?"

"Copies of birth certificates, social security cards—those kinds of documents usually require a physical address. The kind of papers someone would need if—"

"If he meant to manufacture a new identity," Susan finished for him.

"Exactly."

She lowered herself onto the sofa and sighed at the thought. "I don't have the energy to think about that bastard and his honey living somewhere under different names. Baking on a beach somewhere, living it up on other people's money."

Uncomfortable, she turned and stretched along the sofa's length, bending her legs so she wouldn't crowd Luke. She felt him pick up her bare feet, then place them across his lap. It didn't strike her as a good idea, but she was too tired to argue.

"You must be wiped out," he told her, his big hands resting on her lower legs.

It made her wish she'd painted her toenails lately and had her sister's dainty-looking feet. But even when her life wasn't in shambles, she couldn't muster more than fleeting interest in such girly things.

"You don't look so perky yourself," she managed, though her eyes remained closed.

When his fingertips trailed along her ankles, she worried that he might be perkier than she could handle. And yet that simple touch became an oasis of peace within her maelstrom, bringing her such comfort that, before she realized what was happening, she had drifted off in a deep sleep.

* * *

"Get your . . . your damned hands off my daughter."

Time was, Luke had often wakened to similar statements, or often enough to sharpen his reflexes so that he could hit the ground running at a moment's notice. Now, he only opened his eyes to see Maggie Dalton hunched over her walker, glaring at him as if she'd like to have him gelded with the yearling colts.

He tried to push himself into a sitting position, but Susan's weight and warmth surprised him. Somehow she had turned around while he'd slept and spooned herself against his body. His arm was draped casually over her waist, and her silky hair was tickling his nose.

Despite her mother's anger, Susan remained asleep, or at least he thought so from the spacing of her breathing and the soft snores that, under other circumstances, would have made him smile. Not wanting to wake her, he extricated himself as carefully as he could, disturbing the Chihuahua, who'd been curled against her leg.

Peavy bared his teeth as Luke climbed over to stand in front of Susan's mother.

Luke tried on a contrite expression. "I know how this must look, but we were both exhausted, that's all. We were sitting on your couch and talking, and I don't know what happened."

He nearly laughed aloud when she rolled her eyes, exactly as her daughter would have.

"She's had . . . had a hard time of it lately," Maggie told him. "Last thing she needs is . . . you, taking . . . taking . . ."

Her face contorted as she struggled for the word. Instead of helping her, he waited her out in silence.

A light came into Maggie's eyes, and she continued, "Taking *advantage*."

"I would never," he began, then stopped himself. Because in that moment he realized that he would. That he hadn't reformed *that* much since his wild years, and that he still wanted Susan. Badly—no matter if the law, the town, or God Himself still considered her his brother's wife.

"Don't bother lying," she said. "You . . . you Maddoxes are all . . . are all alike. But I don't . . . I don't have to let it go on in my home. So get out of here now. Shoo."

With one hand still clutching her walker, she pointed to the front door with the other.

"Hey, Miss Manners." Susan's sleep-soaked voice rose from the sofa as she stretched and sat upright. Her gaze, leveled at her mother, was equal parts fondness and reproach. "You charming my guests again?"

She covered a yawn with one hand, but her blue eyes glinted with amusement.

"He's damned . . . damned lucky I don't still have your . . . your father's shotgun," Maggie said. "And you, you should be ashamed, young lady. A married wo—"

"Interesting that you would pick now to acknowledge that fact," Susan quipped. "Look, Luke's not the Antichrist, and he's not out to seduce me. He's just helping me look into a few things I'll need to make my case against the school board."

"Helping *himself* is more like it." With that, Maggie turned and clumped into the kitchen.

Luke glanced at his watch and saw that it was mid-afternoon already. "I'd better get home anyway. Yesterday I promised Mom I'd be there when the farrier comes to shoe the horses."

125

"She's keeping them?" asked Susan. "She told me months ago that she'd arranged to sell them."

"Of course she's keeping them," Luke told her, and despite his best effort, he couldn't keep bitterness from seeping into his voice. "They were Brian's, weren't they? She'd have them both bronzed if she could."

"Penny's mine," Susan corrected, "or at least I thought of her that way. But it's a damned good thing your mother didn't."

"Why's that?"

"Because then, instead of having her bronzed, your mom would have already sold her to the cannery for dog food."

Her smile let Luke know she didn't really believe his mother capable of such an act. She might dislike, even hate, Brian's choice of wife, but Virginia Hale Maddox, daughter, granddaughter, and great-granddaughter of ranchers, had firm ideas on the sanctity of horseflesh.

"You can come and ride her anytime," Luke offered. "Both horses need the exercise. I might even take Jet out with you."

Her gaze softened, and he wondered if she was re-membering riding along the edges of pastureland now leased to other cattlemen, or into the rugged little draws that marked the border of what had once been a great ranch. Or was she recalling picnics there with Brian, days the two of them had packed a blanket so they could make love beneath the open sky?

It was a painful thought, one he could not easily shake off.

As if she'd read it in his eyes, Susan frowned at him. "I'm not a Maddox anymore, even if I'm still a few weeks from making it official. It's time to stop pretend-ing that I'm family to you."

He stared hard at her, wanting desperately to ask what he was to her, why she'd come to him for help. Wanting even more to take her in his arms and show her the kind of relationship he'd begun to have in mind.

But, mindful of her mother's presence—and unwilling to risk giving her another stroke—Luke only nodded and murmured, "See you around, then."

He walked out without another word, not realizing until later that along with his pretenses, he'd left behind something almost as important: his brother's broken hard drive, which still must lie beneath the couch.

Chapter Nine

As Susan navigated her way through the seven-layer bean dip her homeowner's insurance company had made of its automated phone system, she began to suspect the powers that be were trying to minimize claims by defeating their customers' efforts to report them. What they succeeded at, in her case, was making certain she was pre-pissed when she finally managed to speak with a live person.

Fortunately, the customer-service representative placated her by offering to send a claims adjuster to look at her house that afternoon.

After she made a brief call to Roberta, the phone rang. Thinking her mom's friend was calling back to clarify some point on the plans they'd just discussed, Susan snatched up the receiver. "Yes?"

When no one answered, a queasy lump of dread slid around her stomach.

"Hello?" she repeated, then listened intently.

And heard nothing but a heavy silence . . . or was that faint sound the susurration of a breath?

Independent of her conscious mind, her fingers touched the bump formed by the wedding band inside her pocket. *Brian?*

Before she could speak his name aloud, there was a click, followed by a dial tone that sounded loud as sirens to her ear.

"Who was . . . who was on the phone?" her mother called from the kitchen.

Susan left the bedroom to join her. "Just a hang-up."

They were a fact of life, she told herself, inconsiderate jerks who heard an unfamiliar voice, then didn't bother explaining they had dialed a wrong number. Nothing to freak out about, no matter what had happened last night or what she'd found inside her Jeep this morning.

Liar, warned some instinct. *You know damned well there wasn't anything random about that call.*

Her mind conjured the soft hiss of breathing, and the fine hairs rose along her arms. But her mother was asking her something about the insurance agency.

"They kept me on hold forever, but I'm meeting the adjuster at five-thirty at the house," Susan explained. "I talked to Roberta, too. She said she'll pick you up around five-ten for dinner and a video at her place."

Her mom deftly stirred a bowl of some sweet-smelling, pale mixture. In her kitchen, surrounded by her own things, she seemed far more at home, and more competent, than she ever had at Susan's.

"I don't need any ba . . . babysitter." There was defiance in her voice and a stubborn set to her jaw that Susan recognized.

"She says she's fixing her famous tuna casserole for dinner, so what you might need is an antacid—or maybe an emetic."

Maggie scowled, clearly not amused.

"What are you making?" Susan ventured. There wasn't much left in her mom's pantry, and Susan had cleaned out the refrigerator months ago, except for a few condiments and an open box of baking soda.

"Sni . . . you know, those cinnamon cookies you're so . . . so fond of," her mother answered.

"Snickerdoodles?" Susan's gaze snapped to the oven, which her mother had set to five hundred degrees. "Little hot for them, don't you think?"

As she turned the oven to the proper setting, she thanked God that unlike the one at her house, this kitchen was electric. Maggie might burn them up, but at least she wasn't likely to blow them to high heavens. But Susan had also meant to remind her mother that July was no time for baking, particularly not within the close confines of this kitchen.

"And what are you using for ingredients?" Susan added.

"Agnes and Herb dropped . . . dropped by while you were on the phone. They'd been to the store and picked us up some . . . those round things . . . white . . . oh, *eggs,* and milk and such. Thought I'd put some of them to good use. I'll take so-some cookies to Roberta, too."

Susan glanced across the counter at the open containers of cinnamon and shortening, the empty wrapper from a butter stick and a couple of eggshells in the sink. At least it didn't look as if her mom had put anything indigestible in the dough.

"All these . . . all these years," her mother said as she mixed up a small bowl of cinnamon and sugar. "I've made them pr-pretty . . . tempting, haven't I?"

Susan smiled. "You know I love those cookies."

Colleen Thompson

Maggie looked up sharply, skewering Susan with her brown-eyed gaze. "Ma . . . the *Maddox* boys, I mean. You knew . . . how I felt . . . how I feel about . . . about them buying our ranch in that . . . in that tax auction, and so you re . . . re . . ."

"Rebelled," Susan supplied. "And yes. I suppose that was part of the attraction when I first met Brian."

But she wasn't thinking about Brian. Instead, her memory had carried her back to the night she'd sneaked out for that ride with Luke in their senior year. The act had been forbidden in itself, but at the time, she had brought to it a teenager's sense of drama, imagining the two of them as a West Texas version of Romeo and Juliet instead of a pair of teenagers struggling against the typical flash flood of hormones.

Maggie was pinching off bits of dough, which she rolled between her palms into walnut-sized balls. She dipped each one in the mix of cinnamon and sugar, then lined them up on an ungreased baking sheet.

"It's why," began her mother, "why you . . . married that—that son of a—"

Susan shook her head. "I didn't marry out of spite, Mom. If anyone did, it was Brian—or at least that's the way I see it now."

After Susan had met him at the dealership, where she'd hand-held a friend through buying her first car, she and Brian had dated on and off for a couple of years. They'd had fun together, riding the Maddox horses and camping in the rough country during her vacations but drifting in different directions during the school year—until his mother had started giving him a lot of static about "the class of woman you're seeing."

Soon after, he had redoubled his attentions before surprising Susan with a proposal. She had been so swept up in the excitement, so badly afflicted with Bridal Fever, that she hadn't seen what he'd done for the act of defiance it had been. In hindsight, it seemed so perfectly transparent that she thought her younger self a fool for having missed it.

"I'm not sure Brian even knew it," she told her mother. "Maybe he imagined it was love. For a while anyway."

So did I, she thought, but she couldn't bring herself to admit it.

Maggie popped the sheet of cookies in the oven before turning back to look at her. Susan braced herself, certain her mother had plenty more to say about the Maddox brothers.

Susan wasn't sure how much she could take, not now, while the wounds of the present had left her so vulnerable to those of the past.

Instead, Maggie surprised her by coming around the counter to hug her fiercely. Which proved conclusively, thought Susan, that whatever her mom's deficits, the mothering center of her brain hadn't suffered any damage from the stroke.

As Jimmy and Marcus walked Susan to her Jeep later, she had to laugh at how gingerly each one held his plastic sandwich bag of cookies in his fingers, as if the snickerdoodles were likely to explode.

Under her mother's smiling supervision, each boy had eaten one inside, despite the fact that the bite Susan had taken had been as salty as the Dead Sea.

"Delicious, aren't they?" her mother had prompted, and, bless their hearts, neither boy contradicted her by word or deed.

Susan had tried sneaking the remnants of her

cookie to Peavy, but she would have to say this for the little bugger: He had standards.

"I'll take those off your hands," Susan offered.

"I don't know," said Marcus. "My butt-head little brother's always busting into my stash of candy bars. Could be he deserves to find these."

"I-uh-I think I'll contribute mine to the cause." Jimmy handed him his bag. "It'll do Simon some good to eat them. Put some hair on the kid's chest."

Fortunately, Susan had just remanded her mom to Roberta's custody, so there would be no more unsupervised cooking this evening.

As Marcus dug out his keys, Susan said, "Thanks, guys. I owe you both—for Peavy and for this."

She shrugged a shoulder to indicate the beat-up manila folder she held pinned under her arm. When Marcus had handed it to her earlier, she'd glanced at the handful of envelopes inside.

"That's all we had the chance to grab before we heard Boone hollering and had to take off," Jimmy explained. "Maybe we can go back later for the rest."

"Don't even think about it," she insisted. "I won't have you getting hurt. What's here is going to have to be enough."

She had wanted to go through the mail when they first gave it to her inside, but she had no intention of doing it while the boys were present. By the time they finally left, Susan had to meet the insurance adjuster. She took the folder with her, afraid to leave the thing behind where her mom, Roberta, or even Agnes might show up and start pawing through it.

Ten minutes after she left Mirage Street, Susan turned onto the small road that had so long been her address. Slowing the Jeep to a crawl, she scanned the adobe exterior and the desert plantings in search of some sign of the violence that had taken place inside.

The house looked as it always had, welcoming and peaceful, a beautiful oasis against the summer heat. Yet she nearly allowed the Jeep to move past it, to take her far from the memories of the clicking of a gun and the hard hand on her neck, the whispers in the darkness and the voracious voice of flame.

"They're gone," she reassured herself, but her forehead throbbed a warning, and she decided that instead of going inside, she would wait for the claims adjuster in the driveway. Still uncomfortable alone here, she left the engine running and both doors locked.

A glance at her watch informed her she was at least five minutes early. Time enough, she thought, to go through some of Brian's letters. Or at least it would be if she could bring herself to look. Anxious as she was to find a clue to her husband's whereabouts, she was equally afraid of the answers she might unearth. For more than eight months, doubt had simmered behind the anger she wore like armor. Doubt that whispered damning answers to the single question: *Why?*

Could one of the letters explain Brian's actions? Could some message offer her a hint as to how she had lived so long, oblivious, with someone who had hated her so much?

A sickening suspicion bubbled to the surface, and she wondered once again if his discovery that she'd gone back on the pill after her second miscarriage could have been the catalyst. Had she been responsible for Brian's actions, as his mother had implied? Or had it been something else she'd done or failed to do that had driven him away? The way she'd graded papers late, or spent untold hours photographing wild creatures, or bitched about his habit of leaving damp towels on the bathroom floor or—

"I really *do* need to see a freaking doctor," she growled under her breath. She must have rattled something loose, if she was starting to think that any of the issues that cropped up in a marriage could begin to excuse what Brian had done.

Grabbing the unopened envelopes from the folder, she flipped through them. And realized immediately that Jimmy and Marcus must have stolen someone else's mail instead of Brian's.

Great, she thought, *now I'm an accessory to a federal crime, too.* As if she didn't have enough problems.

The envelopes were addressed to several men. The first, Sean Wells, had two letters. The second, Roger Ewing, had three, and the last two were addressed to David Spencer. She had never heard of any of them, which struck her as strange in a town the size of Clementine.

Until she recalled what she and Luke had discussed earlier today. Something about Brian needing a physical address so he could receive official documents, the type he would need to reinvent himself. If he'd been doing something of the kind, he wouldn't want to use his real name, would he?

Ripping into one of Spencer's letters, she found a credit application, the same sort banks sent unsolicited every day of the year. She then chose a handwritten envelope with a Colorado return address which had been sent to Wells. Inside, she found physical data in the same neat print: *Ht.: 5'9", Wt.: 158. Eyes: brown, and Hair: dark reddish brown—what's left of it, anyway.*

She frowned and scanned both sides of the paper, looking for some further explanation. But the only other writing consisted of what appeared to be a pair of scribbled initials: *R.E.*. Could that be Roger Ewing, or was it only a coincidence?

Next, she tore open one of the letters addressed to Ewing. She noticed first the bright red "Final Notice" stamped on the corner. The bill for $75.80 was for something called a "pre-employment criminal check" on Sean Wells from some firm called SafeWorks, out of San Francisco.

"What the hell *is* this?" she muttered. Had Brian been attempting to establish credit in a false name, hire someone, or—she couldn't begin to come up with a reason why he'd want to know some guy's physical data.

A sharp rap at her window made her bite back a cry of alarm. Jerking her head toward the sound, she stared at a balding man in a short-sleeved button-down shirt and what was obviously a clip-on tie. Grinning at her, he held up a clipboard with a sheaf of papers and a pen attached.

Smiling at the familiar face, she stuffed the ill-gotten mail into its folder and shut off the Jeep before stepping out into the blazing afternoon. "Mr. Foley, you're working for Serenity Plus now?"

He nodded rapidly. "Pays a lot better than substitute teaching, I can tell you. And nobody's locked me in a supply closet lately either."

"Good for you," she said, and meant it. Hall-of-fame nerds like Millard Foley had no business setting foot in a high-school classroom. Not if they wanted to live to reach retirement age.

While Mr. Foley made small talk, Susan locked the

Jeep. And saw, behind the adjuster's brown sedan, a deputy's patrol car inching by.

Manuel Ramirez stared at her from behind a pair of mirrored lenses, his scarred face set in an expression that might have denoted either indifference or contempt. Surely by now the deputy had heard about last night's events, but when Susan nodded in his direction, he glided past without acknowledging her in any manner.

"Must be on his way to find a donut shop."

Mr. Foley's laughter at the lame joke grated, but at least it took Susan's mind off Ramirez for the moment.

She didn't think of him again until almost an hour later, when she returned to the locked Jeep to find that both the manila folder and the letters it held had disappeared into thin air.

Chapter Ten

The blood thrummed hot and fast through Luke's veins as he scanned the lines of code that tumbled down the screen. With adrenaline pumping through his system and a fierce grin pulling at his mouth, he could think of nothing better than electronic breaking and entering—except for being paid to do it in perfectly legal tender.

His keystrokes went from tentative to lightning swift as he struck at his competitor's defenses. Meanwhile, half a continent away, a brilliant young hacker he'd recruited—and hopefully reformed—launched her own attack on the investment institution's network, her keystrokes striking defenses from Z to A as Luke's attacks raced in the opposite direction.

Meeting in the middle, they created a hole, allowing Luke to dart inside. In the split second before the security noose tightened—and, well designed as it was, it took no more than that—Luke snatched personal data from thousands of customer accounts: everything from trade history to Social Security numbers to mother's maiden names. Enough, in short, to wreak havoc on these individuals had he been of a larcenous persuasion.

Since he still was not entirely certain whether Sibyl, as she preferred to be called, had curbed her appetite for living large at the expense of others, Luke deftly funneled the data away from her and sent it in an encrypted file to the institution's vice president, an arrogant twit who'd been fool enough to boast that his company's new system was completely hack-proof. Following that, Luke outlined a proposal for his team at P.O.M., Inc., to correct the vulnerability, and drew up an invoice for his services to date before he heard someone at the door.

"Computer parts," he explained as he met his mother in the front hall.

She unlocked the deadbolt, then backed out of his way, the banana-walnut scent of baking muffins that wafted around her contrasting with her frown. "How many could one person need?"

"That's easy," Luke told her as he opened the door. "The answer's always 'at least one more than you have on hand.'"

But instead of the delivery-truck driver he'd expected, Sheriff Hector Abbott stood there, his hat held in his hands.

"If I could have a few moments of your time . . ." The gravity of his expression convinced Luke he hadn't come to discuss the upcoming election with his mother, as he had often done in past years.

Judging from the nervous flutter of the dish towel in her hand, Luke's mother understood, too, that this visit was more serious in nature.

140

"Is it," she began, "is there some news about Brian?"

"I was hoping you could tell me," Abbott answered.

In the kitchen, a buzzer sounded.

"I was baking," Luke's mother said faintly, but she didn't move. Remembering yesterday's smoking waffles, Luke excused himself to turn off the oven and pull out a muffin tin.

Duke stretched his nose toward the pan, which Luke had set on top of the stove, and snuffled noisily.

"Don't even think about it, buddy," Luke warned on his way to find his mother and the sheriff.

The two of them were sitting in the formal living room, on the fussy chintz sofa that his mother had long ago reserved for visitors. Luke drifted in behind them but couldn't bring himself to sit.

Abbott's glance touched him before settling on his mother. "First of all, I want to make it clear that I consider you a friend, Virginia, both personally and professionally. Without your support, and your ladies' help, I know I wouldn't have spent the better part of these past thirty years behind this badge."

In the pause that followed, Luke waited for the other shoe to drop.

"But since I do stand behind it," Abbott continued, "part of the job is bringing up things that have to be said, whether or not they're pleasant or someone might take offense—"

"Oh, for heaven's sake, Hector," Virginia interrupted. "I won't have all this pussyfooting about. If you know something about my son, just tell us."

When she pinned the sheriff with her most formidable stare, the man scratched his mustache. "All right, then. I need to make it clear that if Brian shows up, or

141

you've had any contact with him to this point, it would be a big mistake to hide it. The consequences could be extremely serious, for everyone involved."

"Well, of course." His mother managed to sound both perplexed and insulted.

"Trust me," Luke said. "If my brother shows up, I'll personally hand you his ass on a silver platter. But why tell us this now?"

The sheriff drew Brian's ring from his shirt pocket. "I saw Mrs. Maddox—Susan Dalton, that is—first thing this morning. She reported that this had been left in her vehicle, along with the collar from her lost dog."

When Luke's mother reached for the ring, Hector let her take it. Perched on the edge of her seat, she held the band carefully and stared at it intently, as if she expected it to take wing at any moment.

"And then there was the break-in the night before last," Abbott continued. "I'm guessing the damage and the assault on Susan were both beside the point. Someone was looking for something in that house. Maybe something he forgot."

"And you think it might be Brian," Luke said.

Virginia Maddox looked up sharply. "If my son had come back, he certainly wouldn't skulk around like some common criminal."

But he is *a criminal*, Luke wanted to remind her.

"How do any of us know that Dalton girl didn't have the ring this whole time?" his mother burst out. "She could have easily put it in her own car. And the damage to that house could have been intended—"

Abbott shook his head. "I've told you before, Virginia, you're barking up the wrong tree. Your daughter-in-law didn't bash her own skull or set that fire, not with her own mama in the house. And if I'm any judge of character, she had nothing to do with this ring turning up either."

"I helped her look for her dog the evening he went missing," Luke said, since he figured Ramirez had mentioned the incident to the sheriff. "She was pretty upset about it at the time. And plenty surprised when one of her students found him running loose without his collar."

His mother speared him with a look that all but shouted, *Traitor.*

Hector nodded at her. "Susan's not a suspect."

"But *we* are?" Virginia rose from her seat. "That's what you meant by coming here to warn us. You think we're harboring my son. Well, I can tell you right now, I haven't heard a single word from Brian. But if he turns up on my doorstep, I won't send him away. And he'll have the best—the very best attorney that can be provided."

As Hector stood, he looked resigned. "Yes, ma'am, I understand that. But understand me. Any decent lawyer's going to tell your boy he'll be better off if he comes in of his own free will. And, Mrs. Maddox—Virginia?"

"Yes?"

"I'll need to hold that ring for now. It's evidence."

With obvious reluctance, she dropped it into his palm. "Have it your way, Sheriff."

"There's one more thing we need to talk about, a rumor that's been buzzing around town these past few weeks. I haven't been able to verify it, at least not yet, but I was wondering if you'd . . . Could be, folks wouldn't mention it to you, but—"

"Straight talk, Sheriff," Luke said. "What are people saying?"

"That Jessica Beecher was in a family way. And that she ran off because your brother was the father."

Luke braced himself for his mother's horrified outburst.

Instead, she stared down Sheriff Abbott, her bearing regal, her words quiet and controlled. "When I wish to hear gossip repeated, I'll go and have my hair done. All I expect from you are unvarnished facts."

Her reaction left Luke to suspect she'd been prepared for Hector's news. As if the gossips had already gotten to her—or she knew the rumor to be true.

As Abbott's patrol car left, he had to move over for the delivery truck bouncing up the narrow drive. To Luke's relief, it brought the used hard drive he had been expecting.

Instead of rushing off to Susan's to retrieve the broken drive, as he would have liked to do, Luke sat down with his mother and ate some of the muffins she had baked, along with a spoonful of last year's muscadine preserves and some stout, black coffee.

Her own breakfast untouched, his mother stared at him, her expression unfathomable.

"This is good stuff," he said, hoping to make conversation. When she didn't respond, he ventured, "Mom?"

"Your brother can't have come back. If he had, he surely would have called. He must know how very worried we all are."

"You're probably right about that," Luke agreed. For one thing, his brother could have counted on a happy—and utterly blameless—reception from their mother. And Luke wouldn't put it past the asshole to hit her up for more money.

"Besides," she said, "he might have been angry with Susan, but I can hardly imagine him trying to frighten her or hurt her after all these months. It makes no sense at all."

"No, it doesn't." Luke thought, too, that Susan had probably been right. She *would* have recognized her husband somehow, even in the dark. "But what do you mean about him being mad at Susan?"

"I've appreciated all your help," she said as if she hadn't heard him. Her words sounded cautious, giving him the impression she was weighing every possible shade of meaning. "I honestly don't know what I would have done if you hadn't come to take care of the . . . the dealership. And all the . . . all the details you've tended, the way you've fixed the well pump and seen to my car, and your .... your assistance with getting my finances in order. It's been so much . . . so much more than I . . . ah . . . than I would have expected."

He tried another sip of coffee, but the taste turned bile-bitter in his mouth. He wanted to ask, *What exactly was it you* expected *from me?*

Instead, he prompted, "But . . ." for he was suddenly convinced that gratitude was not her point.

She stood up and began to clear the table. "But I believe it's time for you to get on with your life. In Austin."

"You want me to go *home* now?" Luke asked. A few days ago, she'd suggested that he extend his stay indefinitely, noting how much she preferred cooking for two, having his help with the maintenance the big old place always seemed to need, and simply knowing there was someone else living on the ranch.

But up until yesterday, he hadn't had more than the most perfunctory contact with his brother's wife.

"Is it Susan?" he asked bluntly.

His mother brought a sponge to wipe the table clean. "I don't want you mixed up in her troubles."

145

"She is—or was, maybe I should say—Brian's wife. He betrayed her in the worst way a man can, and if she hears this latest rumor, that's going to hurt her even more." He hoped to God no one would be cruel enough to mention it to her. "I think she deserves our support, don't you?"

"I won't have it, Luke. I won't have you running down your brother when you don't know what *she* did."

"What she did?" he echoed. "Hector told you, she had nothing to do with—"

His mother picked a stray crumb from her vacant chair. "I told her to be careful, especially after she had that first miscarriage. But she wouldn't listen."

Luke felt his forehead crinkle in confusion. "What are you talking about?"

"She was careless, reckless, even though she knew how much your brother wanted children. She kept saying her doctor told her that exercise was good for a woman who'd always been so active."

"I'm no expert," Luke said, "but it doesn't sound unreasonable. And her fall was an accident. It might have happened on a trail, but Brian was with her, and he told me himself it wasn't any rougher than what you'd find in their backyard. Besides, didn't the doctor tell her the miscarriage had nothing to do with a couple of bumps and bruises? And I know she was plenty broken up about it—especially the second time."

Luke didn't mention that he had sent her flowers afterward, just to let her know that she'd been on his mind. The night she'd called to thank him, she'd wept on the phone, hard enough that she had had to hand it back to Brian. Luke had felt like shit, knowing there wasn't a damned thing he could do to fix the problem, especially after his brother blew off her tears with some flip remark about her hormones being out of whack.

As a string of short-term girlfriends would line up to testify, Luke wasn't exactly a sensitive new-age guy, but Brian's comment had seemed obnoxious. Maybe, Luke thought, he should have realized then that there was trouble between Brian and Susan, or that there soon would be.

His mother shook her head. "That Dalton girl never wanted children. That's all there was to it. She told Brian she didn't plan to quit her job, even if the baby had to go to day care. Imagine, *day care,* for a tiny infant, when he made more than enough to support a family."

Luke winced. "You're blaming Susan because she has different ideas about raising kids than you? And because she listened to her doctor instead of taking your advice?"

"Did Brian tell you that, afterward, she went back on the pill? When he found them in her handbag, he was so furious that—"

"That what? That he thought he'd work out their problems by getting another man's wife pregnant, embezzling from the business, taking out huge loans, and disappearing? I'm sorry. It doesn't wash, Mom." Disgusted with her, he picked up his keys and the box containing the used hard drive from the counter. "We can talk about this later. I have some things to do in town now."

"With *her*?" his mother accused.

"I'm not one of your CLC friends," Luke said, "and I'm not planning on running for election, either. So yes, I'm going to see Susan, because helping her is the decent thing to do."

147

She crossed her arms in front of her. "In that case, I'm giving you 'til week's end to clear your things out of this house."

This time, as he left her, the door slammed hard behind him.

It was so much more difficult to watch her now that she had moved to the apartment. There was no vacant lot nearby, conveniently overgrown with foliage that could hide him. There was no way, either, to cruise past too often, not without raising the suspicions of the neighbors or of the old ladies who seemed to come and go around the clock.

He hated the old bitches, the way the lot of them pecked away at her attention and prevented her from dealing with the promise she had made. Someday, he meant to put a stop to those distractions, forbid her to spend time with anyone but him. The day was coming soon, he thought, when he could show his love directly, in ways more straightforward and sacred than any fucking useless words.

With any other female, such a thing would be impossible. The others were no more than embryonic versions of themselves, half-formed mock-ups with blind eyes and empty souls. Their grasp of the symbolic went no farther than the streamers on corsages or the crowns set upon fair heads at homecoming.

Not like *her* at all.

Reverently, the watcher withdrew a woman's wedding band from his left pocket, then kissed each of the three diamonds that starred the gleaming gold. Three for *third*, he understood, because third period had been their special time together. Three, too, for the number of nights he had watched her through her window before she'd left the ring hidden in the junipers, where he had waited until her bedroom light came on.

Considering what she had done for him, he was not surprised at how she cloaked her feelings whenever there was someone near. He understood her need for secrecy; he was certainly no fool.

But *she* was a fool if she thought he would put up with any more of her attempts to make him jealous. She needed to understand that what they shared was too sacred for any foolish female games.

With her, he played for keeps, and if she hadn't gotten that message from his earlier warning, she would—even if he had to write the words in blood.

"Yes," Susan hissed when her mother's out-of-date computer sputtered its way onto the Internet. Thankful for the free trial membership disks that clogged mailboxes nationwide, she'd plugged her mom's modem to the phone line and hobbled into cyberspace.

Though she was by no means an expert, in the wake of Brian's disappearance she had spent a lot of hours on a library computer after the sheriff's department hauled off hers. With the help of a friendly genealogist she'd met in the library, she'd learned to search publicly accessible databases in an attempt to find something—anything—that would lead her to Brian.

The whole enterprise had proved an enormous waste of time. Of the dozens of Brian Maddoxes she'd tracked down and contacted, none, of course, had been her missing husband. To make matters worse, the public venue had exposed her to the suspicious glares of those convinced that she had done her husband harm. One tart-mouthed old biddy had even gone so far as to ask if she was checking on her offshore bank accounts.

But now Susan had a private venue, along with a different quarry. Three of them, in fact.

After coming home last evening, she'd racked her brain for hours trying to come up with the men's names from the mail that had been taken from her Jeep. For some reason, the name Sean Wells had stuck in her mind, and several hours later she'd remembered David Spencer, too. But it hadn't been until earlier this morning, over a cold cereal breakfast, that she'd suddenly burst out, "Robert Ewing—no, *Roger,* that was it."

Her mother had glanced up from a half-eaten slice of peanut butter toast. "Are you sure . . . sure your head's all right? I can't go tr-traip . . . *running* off to see your sister if you're hurt."

Susan had offered up a grin. "It'll be such a relief when this bruising fades. Maybe then people will stop implying I'm a head case. I'm all right, Mom, I promise. I was just trying to remember the name of a contractor the adjuster recommended to take care of the damage to the house."

Susan had hated lying again, but she'd just convinced her mother that a brief trip to California would provide a much-needed break for both of them, as well as getting Carol off their backs. Susan would breathe easier, too, to know her mom would be out of reach of whoever had broken into the house two nights before.

Now that the two of them had made plans and Carol—bless her—had bought Susan and their mother tickets for a flight to Oakland tomorrow morning, Maggie seemed as excited as a child about the trip. While Susan searched the Internet, her mom was waiting impatiently for Agnes to pick her up for an appointment at the beauty parlor to get some "California style," whatever the hell that was supposed to be.

"I'll . . . I'll be late if she doesn't . . . doesn't hurry," Susan's mother fretted. "Do you think I should try some color, too?"

Susan turned away from her search screen of U.S. telephone listings, which had just assured her there were no fewer than three hundred David Spencers in the country. Probably a lot more, if one considered those going by initials, or those who had unlisted numbers.

If she could only remember the return addresses from the envelopes, or at least the city, maybe that would help her narrow down—

"Susan?" her mother prompted.

"Oh, sorry. I think a cut will be enough for one day. You don't want to tire yourself before our trip tomorrow. Remember, we're going to have to drive out to El Paso to catch our flight."

There were other considerations as well, including the fact that she had seen her mom's beautician's color work around town. Susan was convinced that most of it would glow under black light.

"That Agnes ne-never was on time," fumed Maggie. "Even back in school, her a-assign . . . her *homework* . . . always came in two days late."

"Don't gripe at her, please. Agnes is doing us a favor, taking you. And it was really nice of her and Herb to stop by with those groceries. I don't know what I'd do without her and Roberta."

Her mother smiled. "Me neither—and don't you forget to visit them when you get back to town. I don't want them getting lonesome."

Susan wasn't fooled. She'd overheard her mother on the telephone asking both of her best friends to keep a close eye on her younger daughter. Doubtless, Susan could expect to be the happy recipient of a couple of homemade meals a week. She breathed a silent prayer that Roberta's tuna casserole wouldn't be among them.

Agnes showed up a few minutes later, and soon afterward, Susan had the apartment to herself.

Drawn by the tapping of her keys as she turned back to her search, Peavy hopped onto her lap and watched the changing screen with interest. When Susan swore at the results, he licked her face until she set him on the floor.

How was she supposed to know which of the dozens of Sean Wellses or Roger Ewings had written to her husband?

"That's the problem with this country," she told the Chihuahua, who was staring meaningfully at her in an attempt to worm his way back onto her lap. "Too many people with the same damned names."

If she only had the rest of the mail, maybe she could piece together . . .

But what exactly would she do then, call a stranger out of the blue and ask what business he'd had with her husband? Still, even that awkward plan was moot, thanks to Deputy Ramirez, or whoever it had been who'd gotten into her Jeep.

Frustrated, she disconnected from the Internet. While she was thinking of what to do, she could call the cleaning service Mr. Foley had recommended to take care of the house. At least she'd learned that the insurance would cover the expense; with everything she had on her plate, that disheartening job was the last thing she wanted to tackle.

Just as she found the number, the phone rang. Reminded of yesterday's mystery caller, Susan let it ring four times before she convinced herself she was being ridiculous. It was probably a telemarketer, or maybe her mother calling to ask if Susan didn't think she would look much more "California" as a blonde.

"Hello?"

No response, only the same hollow silence she had heard before. This time, she couldn't even make out the suggestion of a human breath.

"Who *is* this?" she demanded, her mind rushing through a host of possibilities. Since Ramirez had stooped—if it really had been he—to stealing evidence, did he imagine that harassing her would prompt a spontaneous confession? Or was it some former student, too tongue-tied to respond? Try as she might to suppress the thought, she could not help imagining Brian, calling from wherever the hell he was.

Maybe somewhere far closer than she had imagined.

Nausea roiled in her stomach, and she shouted into the receiver, "Don't call here anymore if you don't have anything to say."

Without waiting for a response, she slammed the phone down hard enough to make Peavy tuck his tail between his legs and run into the guestroom.

She could hardly blame him. She'd like to hide under the bed, too.

Instead, however, she picked up the receiver. With her heart thumping, she dialed the code the telephone company's advertisements promised would phone back the last incoming caller.

She held her breath as someone on the other end picked up.

"First Bank of Ocotillo County, where great customer service is not only our tradition, it's our pleasure," rattled off a female voice. She sounded both young and breathless, probably from reciting that stupid spiel all day. "How may I demonstrate our excellence today?"

Susan blinked in surprise. Her bank?

"You can start by telling me who just called me," she managed after a brief pause. "This is Susan Dalton Maddox; I have an account with you. I've been getting hang-ups, and the last one came from this number."

"If you could hold for a few moments, I'll be happy to check into it," the Stepford receptionist answered brightly.

Susan made a face at the bank's flaccid choice of hold music, but at least she didn't have to listen long.

"I'm sorry, Mrs. Maddox. No one here remembers making such a call." The girl sounded genuinely disappointed.

On a whim, Susan asked, "Is Mr. Beecher in? If he is, I'd like to speak to him, please."

"I'll see—I'll find out if he can take your call."

"If he could, I'd consider it a demonstration of your excellence," Susan told her.

She was forced to revise her opinion of the receptionist when the young woman laughed. "Yeah," she said, "isn't that some script? They paid some consultant beaucoup bucks to come up with that stuff. Let me transfer you."

After another brief delay, Hal Beecher picked up on the second ring. "Susan," he said, "I've been trying to get hold of you, but this new phone system is a nightmare. This management consultant said we needed to—"

"What you need to do is stop making that poor girl out front recite propaganda. Trust me."

"Duly noted," Hal said.

"Were you calling about the house?"

"I called about *you*," he said. "I was very disturbed when I heard what happened at your home. I can't imagine—it must have been a terrifying episode."

"Yes, it was. And I appreciate your concern." She did, though his sincerity sounded warning bells inside her mind. She'd hoped that she'd discouraged his personal interest in her during their last conversation.

"Are you all right? I was told you'd been hurt. I would have come right over yesterday morning when I heard, but this management consultant, he couldn't be put off. And the bank's board of trustees has been breathing down my—"

"I'm fine, and it's just as well you didn't come back yesterday. I would have probably been asleep by the time you got here."

Asleep beside Luke on the sofa, she thought, overwhelmed by a memory of how incredibly well they'd fit together. His arm resting so comfortably along the curve between her hip and waist, her back pressed so close to his broad chest.

"Are you still there, Suz?" Hal was saying. "I was asking if you'd lost much personal property."

"I don't think so," she said, making a face at the hated abbreviation of her name. "Nothing I can't live without."

"About those things you said might help you, help us find . . ." He struggled for the words, reminding her acutely of her mother.

"Listen, Hal. I'm sorry I ever mentioned those to you."

"Do you still have them?"

"I do, but I really hate to get your hopes up. They'll probably turn out to be nothing."

He said nothing for so long, she began to fear his phone had gone dead.

"Hal?"

"I'm very sorry, Susan," he said, regret dampening his words. "I've held off for as long as possible, but there's a lot of pressure on me now, and I can't—"

"I told you, it's all right. Foreclose. I can't—I won't go back there anyway."

As if he hadn't heard her, he said, "There still might be a way. I need to meet with you in person . . . as soon as possible."

Instinct warned her that she wouldn't want to hear whatever plan he had concocted—not unless she wanted to end up as his replacement wife. Shuddering at the thought, she said, "I don't think that's necessary—oh, someone's at the door. Sorry, but I'm going to have to let you go."

Luke wasn't actually at the door yet, but she saw his truck pulling into the empty spot behind her Jeep. As he climbed out of it, she felt relieved at the thought that he was the one person she could confide in about the disappearing mail.

She ignored the whispers that warned she would be better off trusting the grieving banker with his kind heart and his motherless child than the man who had taken her virginity, then never deigned to mention it again.

Chapter Eleven

With her hair sleeked back in a neat twist and her impossibly long legs highlighted by a pair of hiking shorts, Susan was proving to be one hell of a distraction as Luke worked on the hard drive.

And that was only taking into consideration the sight of her. The story she had told him about the strange mail Brian had received, along with its subsequent disappearance, made him put down the on-board controller he had just removed.

"Ramirez?" He watched her pace the room. "But why in hell would he do that? It's not as if he can use anything he's illegally taken as grounds to arrest you, if that's his goal."

Susan stopped pacing and frowned. "Maybe it isn't. Maybe he's involved in some other way that we don't understand. After all, *somebody* from the sheriff's office got rid of the evidence taken from my house. Who's to say it wasn't him?"

"He might be a better bet than Abbott. Hector stopped

by this morning, and he told my mom straight out that you're not a suspect—"

"I'm sure she'll be calling any second to apologize." Turning toward the telephone, Susan cupped her ear with one hand and pretended to listen for the ring.

"I wouldn't count on it. When I said I was coming over, she gave me 'til the end of the week to get out of her house. Preferably to leave for Austin, where I won't be tempted to aid the enemy."

"Nice." She'd resumed her stalking, reminding Luke of a captive cougar circling its cage. "So what are you going to do?"

He wished she would stand still, because the way her legs moved filled his head with far too many inappropriate responses to her question.

She's your brother's wife, for God's sake. He repeated the thought like a mantra in the hope that it would finally sink in.

Fortunately, she perched on one of the two barstools up against the counter. Even so, those legs remained at eye level.

"I'm here," he said, "for as long as you need me. I can always rent a room somewhere. Is the Sportsman's Inn still doing business?"

She nodded. "Yes, and they always have plenty of space when it's not hunting season. But maybe your mom's right. Maybe you should go back to your business."

She met his gaze and held it, but unlike his mother's stare, hers said that she really wanted him to remain. He hoped his interpretation was more than wishful thinking.

"I'm taking Mom to Oakland in the morning anyway," she added. "I'll be gone a couple of days to get her settled in. You don't want to wait around for . . ."

Getting up from the sofa, he crossed the room to stand before her, so near that she turned her head away. As if she were terrified of whatever his gaze might unlock.

"That's too close," she whispered. "*We're* too close, working together like this."

He cupped her chin and turned it toward him. "What are you afraid of?"

She jerked her head back from his touch and blinked away the moisture that had pooled in her blue eyes. With a sneer that didn't quite ring true, she shot back, "Do you want that answer in list or novel form?"

He didn't push her, didn't dare, for he was far too close to crossing the line the two of them had drawn so many years ago. And he was afraid that if he did, she'd surely send him packing, just as his mother had.

Luke drew a deep breath, then glanced at the desktop computer across the room. No time like the present for a change of subject. "Mind if I pop that open? I just switched out your hard drive's onboard controller, and I want to see if it did the trick. I'd use my laptop, but the drive's too big to fit."

He could swear he heard her sigh of relief.

Nodding her permission, she followed him to the computer. "Do you really think this might work? Do you think we'll be able to get to Brian's files?"

"I wouldn't get my hopes up," Luke said as he unscrewed the old PC's case, "especially if it doesn't boot on the first try."

It didn't. Nor did it spin up on the second or the third. Luke shook his head. "I'm sorry, Susan. I really thought that would do it."

For a long while, she said nothing, so he removed the broken drive.

"Maybe if I swap the motor too . . ."

"Don't bother." She was looking out the window, probably to hide her tears. "I should have known it wouldn't work. I should have known it all along."

That was when Luke noticed the kinked cable he'd used to link up the two hard drives. He dug inside a pocket of his laptop bag, then replaced the cable with a new one. Without another word to Susan, he tried to access the bad drive one last time.

"It's spinning!" he burst out as her mother's old workhorse computer listed the drive's contents.

Standing at the desk, he began dragging folders, copying them to the other hard drive. Tax folders, e-mails, documents, and then—

"Shit." A box appeared on screen to announce another failure. "I've lost the damned thing."

He turned to look at Susan, who was now standing behind his chair. Her hands were balled into tight fists, and she seemed to have stopped breathing.

He checked the files he'd just copied and grinned triumphantly. "Doesn't matter, Susan. We got 'em anyway. We've copied Brian's files, and most of them look to be intact."

Her frozen expression melted into joy, and she threw her arms around him. Before he could react, her mouth had covered his in a kiss so vibrant, so compelling, that neither of them stood a chance against its power.

Not that Luke was bothering to fight it. As his body shouted *Hallelujah*, he pulled her even closer, reveling in the way her curves molded to his hardness, the way her mouth opened, hot and wet, to take his tongue.

A jolt of pure pleasure leapt from mouth to groin, and despite all vows to the contrary, Luke couldn't help himself. Before his mind registered what he was doing, his hands were sliding up beneath her T-shirt, palming the soft roundness of her breasts. At her throaty murmur, he reached around to unhook her bra, then hurried to expose the small, tight nipples.

He was wild to taste them. The problem was, he had to break off his kiss to do it. And in that single moment, he heard the startled intake of her breath.

Crossing her arms over her breasts, she shook her head and told him, "No. No, Luke. Oh, God, I'm so sorry. I don't know why I did that."

Luke swore, disappointed beyond words—and furious with himself. He'd crossed some lines in his day, but he'd never made love to a married woman. What kind of brother was he, to start with Brian's wife? And what kind of man, to expose her to more heartbreak and scandal?

Yet inside him, something whispered, *Brian never did deserve her. Never understood or appreciated for a moment what he had. Never loved her the way I—*

He couldn't afford to let the thought play out, so he clamped down on it ruthlessly.

"Yes, I do know why," Susan continued. "I was so relieved to finally have some chance of finding Brian."

"This has nothing to do with Brian." Luke tried to stop himself, but he heard the words gushing like an unstoppable torrent. "This is about something we started and never finished back in high school."

He willed her to demand that he never mention it again, or, better yet, pretend she hadn't heard him. Instead, she said, "You're wrong there." Quietly, emphatically, as if she understood this would change everything between them. "We *finished* it all right, in case you've forgotten."

"I remember just fine." It was easier, simpler, to withdraw behind the smart-ass facade that had served him so well before. "And believe me, honey, I was only getting started."

She paused to hook her bra. "You always were a cocky bastard. Too bad I was too love-struck to see it at the time."

"If you were so damned 'love-struck,' you had a funny way of showing it. You wouldn't speak to me for weeks." It felt strange, bringing up the past after so many years, but it seemed their kiss had put a match to the covenant of silence. Something in him muttered sullenly, *Let the damned thing burn.*

"I was in huge trouble, you idiot," Susan answered. "I was grounded for weeks just for being seen with you at school. And with Carol spying on me night and day, there was no way I could risk letting her find out I'd . . . letting her guess what we'd done."

While he absorbed what she said, a new silence coiled like a snake between them.

This time, she was the first to break it. "I was so young, and it was all so new to me. I was scared, too, that I'd handed my heart over to a troublemaker . . . along with my virginity. And by the time I finally got a chance to talk to you in private, there you were, pinning Linda Finch against her locker."

"When you didn't talk to me the next day, I figured you were embarrassed about what we'd done, that you didn't want to be reminded. But I couldn't just leave things, not after . . . You never said a word, but I knew I was your first." He winced, remembering how she'd cried out and how he'd wished he could take it back.

And the way she'd smiled up at him so sweetly and whispered, "*Show me more.*"

He drew in a deep breath before he was able to continue. "By the time I got up the nerve to call the house, your mother told me you didn't want to speak to me, that she'd bitch to my parents if I didn't leave you be. I'd already been in trouble—cutting classes catches up with you—and my dad had said he'd take away my car if I didn't straighten up. So, yeah, I did move on."

He didn't say how many times he'd thought back on that decision and cursed his younger self. And now that he knew that if he'd only acted differently, there might have been some chance—

"You called?" she asked, then shook her head. "What does it matter? It couldn't have made any difference. We were only seventeen."

"And what about now?" he couldn't stop himself from asking.

She only shook her head. "Too late. For one thing, my lawyer tells me that in thirty days I'll be a Dalton again, and I intend to keep it that way."

"You haven't changed much," he said.

"In what way do you mean?"

"In so many ways you're still that same scared girl."

"Yeah, well, you're still a cocky bastard, so we're even. Now let's see what you got off that hard drive. Let me judge for myself if it warranted a kiss."

He brushed the wispy bangs from her eyes. "And if you find it's worth more," he murmured, "can I collect the balance due?"

"Don't get too far ahead of yourself, geek boy. I might come looking for my change."

She turned away, but not quickly enough to keep

him from seeing that the look in her eyes belied the acid in her words.

While Luke transferred the data from Brian's hard drive onto his much faster laptop, Susan kept her distance, her mind struggling for purchase on memory's well-greased slopes. Fragments blazed like meteors across her consciousness, flashes of the kiss they had just shared igniting older memories of that night beneath the stars. Her breathing quickened, and her breasts tingled where he'd touched her, where she knew he'd meant to put his mouth.

To hide her own rough jumble of emotions, she moved into the kitchen, where she threw together a couple of slapdash sandwiches. Her hands moved on autopilot as her thoughts circled back relentlessly to Luke.

If she hadn't protested, she realized, there would have been no stopping either of them. She was appalled at how regret tinged—perhaps even overshadowed—her relief.

Pinching her lower lip between her teeth, she attempted to regain her focus. Even if she weren't still married in the law's eyes, a relationship with Luke would bring her nothing but more suspicion and more grief. *Unthinkable,* she told herself over and over until the word melted into meaninglessness, like an ice cube in the rain.

Though she remained wary, even more distrustful of herself than of Luke, she edged closer as he began to open files. After setting the plate with his peanut-butter-and-jelly sandwich at his elbow, she stood behind him and looked over his shoulder to focus on the screen. She prayed he couldn't feel how hard her heart was still beating.

Luke clicked a file, and his monitor went bright blue. Against this backdrop, a message in white letters read: *Fatal Error: Operating system will shut down in 1 minute. All unsaved data will be lost.*

"Damned blue screen of death," Luke muttered as he depressed the keys to reboot his laptop.

Susan put down the half sandwich she'd been nibbling. "That started happening not long before the hard drive went kaput. We figured it must have been a warning the drive was at death's door."

"This has nothing to do with the hard drive failure and everything to do with overeducated, underemployed assholes who are pissed at the whole world."

"What?"

"It's a worm—like a virus, or close enough."

Susan wanted to cry or curse, she wasn't sure which. "After all you went through to get them, does this mean we won't be able to look at Brian's files?"

"I can't be sure yet. Let's knock out this worm first and see what we have. I fixed this on one of my company's computers a while back; I think I still have the application on my hard drive that will . . . There it is."

As he ran the program that removed the worm, his matter-of-factness grated on Susan as much as it relieved her. She should be thankful that their near miss hadn't rattled him too much, thankful she could devote all her attention to keeping herself under control. Waiting while the program ran, she forced herself to eat.

Once the system restarted for a second time, Luke announced their success.

"But the bad news is, it looks as if some of these files

are corrupted," he added. "They'll look like garbage—random symbols—if we open them. But let's see what else we have."

She helped him scan file after file. Gradually, the intense concentration loosened the knot of anxiety in her stomach. Or replaced it, at least, with another worry.

Her apprehension mounted as one file after another yielded nothing except routine financial records, business correspondence, and e-mails—sometimes from Brian to Luke or to one of her husband's college buddies, more often an electronic newsletter or a receipt for one of the classic rock CDs her husband had often bought online. By the time they neared the list's end more than an hour later, she was certain they would not find anything of use. Clearly, Brian must have used some means other than his computer to lay the groundwork for his disappearance. Or failing that, he'd been careful to erase incriminating files as he went along. The idea didn't mesh with her memory of his panic the day the hard drive crashed, but since when had any of what he'd done made sense?

She was so caught up in her fears, she almost missed it. "Wait—back up one. No, one more. Right there."

Her finger shook as she pointed out the header of an e-mail sent to Brian. It read: *Receipt for payment to D. Spencer.*

"David Spencer," she said. "Some of the envelopes in Brian's storage unit were addressed to him. Do you think this could be the same guy?"

Susan scanned the message and found it to be from an electronic money transfer service. She blinked at the amount, thinking her vision was blurring from scanning so many e-mails. The decimal point, however, remained stubbornly in place. Brian had transferred $9,999 from their joint bank account to D. Spencer.

"That doesn't make sense," she blurted. Brian sure as hell hadn't bought CDs with that amount.

Luke swallowed his last bite of sandwich. "Banks report transactions larger than ten thousand to the feds. This must have been something he wanted to keep under the radar."

"But *what?*"

"Look," Luke said. "Here's another one, from a month later."

On this occasion, Brian had sent D. Spencer five thousand dollars even.

"Why?" asked Susan. "I need to find out what this guy was selling."

When Luke searched the other files for the name Spencer, he came up empty.

"Let's see what we can find out about him." Luke plugged a wire into the phone jack and tapped a few keys. Moments later, his laptop connected to the Internet.

She watched, fascinated, as he accessed databases she'd never dreamed of, then typed in D. Spencer's e-mail address, which had appeared in the body of Brian's receipt. Luke grumbled as he hit one roadblock after another.

"This e-mail address is no longer active," he said, "but if you give me a few minutes, I may be able to find who used to have . . . Bingo."

Normally, Susan would have found it frightening, how much personal information was floating around in cyberspace, but at the moment, she thanked her lucky stars when the name David Spencer popped up on the screen. By clicking another link, Luke found not only a telephone number, but a San Francisco address—with directions to the man's home.

"That's unbelievable," she said as she jotted down the information on a scrap of printer paper. "Any stalker could use this to—"

"Unfortunately, they do all the time," Luke said. "But don't worry. I blocked your public info and your mother's a long time ago, while I was protecting mine and my mom's."

"Uh, thanks. So now what? Do we call this—"

In her peripheral vision, she caught sight of a patrol car creeping along Mirage Street. Moving to a spot alongside the window, where she hoped she wouldn't be seen, Susan saw the car stop beside Luke's pickup.

"Ramirez," she said quietly, as if the deputy might hear her. "Or at least I think it's him."

She heard Luke tap a few more keys before he disconnected his computer and then joined her beside the window.

"Let him look," Luke said. "My insurance, registration, and all that are in order."

She frowned, thinking of the folder taken from her Jeep. "Hope you didn't leave anything important on the inside."

He shook his head. "He won't bother with it. He could be seen too easily on this street. Could be he's just trying to intimidate us. Fits pretty well with the Ramirez I remember."

"He's treated me like some sort of black widow ever since Brian disappeared," said Susan as she watched the patrol car turn onto Oasis Drive. "But what does he have against you? I thought you guys were friends."

"We were," Luke said, "until our senior year, when he finished fixing up that old Mustang he bought. Once he did that, he was always after me to race him. Got real pissed off when I told him no."

"Good thinking on your part. Isn't that what happened to his face? Some crash, after a drag race?"

Luke took a deep breath and let out a sigh. "I didn't tell him no forever. I wish to God I had."

"You don't mean—"

"I'd had enough of the son of a bitch and his new friends shoving me around, calling me a pussy. Stupid, I know, but . . ." He shook his head hard, as if to dislodge the painful memory. "He lost control and rolled his car around a curve, that sharp one over by the old municipal dump."

"I remember hearing about it when it happened. It was awful. They didn't think he'd live."

"The other guys took off—even Lupe, his half brother. But I couldn't—there was no way I could leave him. The car was on its back, and flames were shooting out the windows. The smell of gas was everywhere. I did what I could, dragged him out at least, and then I went for help."

"That was really brave, Luke. But your name wasn't mentioned in the papers. In fact, wasn't the whole incident sort of glossed over at the time?"

He shrugged. "My mom's doing, I guess, and Sheriff Abbott had a hand in it as well. Manuel was in the hospital, and my dad had just died. And then there's this: It was just about election time."

"And so it went in Ocotillo County, the way it always has." She tried and failed to keep bitterness out of her voice.

"Don't forget, 'it went' for Manuel, too. If Abbott had

charged us, he might never have been able to become a deputy. He could've ended up an ex-con working part-time as a mechanic, just like Lupe."

"Somehow, I'm not grateful."

"Neither is he," Luke said. "He's hated my guts ever since the wreck."

"Even though you saved his life."

Luke shrugged. "Sometimes in this life, a man needs nothing more than someone else to blame."

He held her gaze for a long moment, until she thought of saying, *I guess that goes for women, too.*

But before she did, the phone rang. Susan made a face, thinking of Hal Beecher's phone problems. Still, if he meant to set up some sort of heart-to-heart between them, she hoped his telephone was still on the blink.

When she picked it up, however, she was greeted by her mother's familiar stammer. "Su-Susan? Larinda just got back from a sty-style show in . . . in—"

Over the hum of a blow dryer, someone in the background shouted, "It was Lubbock, honey. And very cutting edge."

Susan raised an eyebrow at the notion of Lubbock, Texas, as the cutting edge of the hair world. But she kept her comments to herself, since her predilection for ponytails didn't put her on the high ground in terms of hairstyle snobbery.

"Well, Lar-Larinda says that red is the new . . . the new blond. And Noreen can make over Ag-Agnes at the same time. So what . . . what do you think? Should I . . . should we do it?"

A vision of her mom shuffling behind her walker and sporting fuchsia hair made Susan wince. But before she could say anything, she thought of how much closer she and Luke might come to finding Brian in the time it would take Larinda to deface her mother.

"Go for it," Susan told her. "And you and Agnes have fun."

After hanging up the phone, she turned to Luke. "I just sold my mother's soul to the devil to buy us a couple more hours, if you're game."

She didn't miss the mischief in his wry grin. Maybe he wasn't as unaffected by what had happened earlier between them as she had imagined.

"Oh, I'm game all right," he told her. "The question is, are you?"

Time to play it cool. She rolled her eyes. "Just hand me that phone number. Let's find out what this David Spencer knows about your brother."

"You might not reach him at that number," Luke said as he passed it to her. "Before I got off-line, I cross-checked that street address with another database. Someone else is living in that apartment now. A couple by the name of Van Doren."

"Doesn't ring a bell, but Spencer could have kept the same phone number. People do sometimes, you know."

He picked up the receiver and handed it to her. "Guess there's only one way to find out."

Chapter Twelve

Though Susan didn't hesitate to take the phone, Luke could tell she was nervous. He saw it in her eyes and in the tension of her shoulders, in the way she fumbled in the midst of dialing twice.

Yet when he touched her arm to convey strength, she shrugged him off in the irritable way a horse dislodges a fly. He would have offered to make the call for her, but he couldn't be certain that she wouldn't kick. It was for damn sure she'd rather do that than admit she needed help.

"It's ringing," she whispered urgently. Her hand trembled where it gripped the receiver. A moment later she clamped it over the mouthpiece. "A machine's answering. It's not—"

But someone must have picked up, for she broke off to say, "Hello. May I please speak to David Spencer?"

To Luke's surprise, her voice belied none of the edginess he'd witnessed. Instead, she sounded professional and focused. His opinion of her rose another notch.

"It's a business matter," she was saying. "It's really important that I speak with Mr. Spencer personally."

Her brows rose at what was said next. "I see," she said. "I'm terribly sorry. Could you—it might be helpful to know when this happened. Would it be possible to . . . Hello?"

After another vain attempt to solicit a response, she set the receiver in its cradle, then looked up at Luke. "Dead," she told him.

He thought she was referring to the line until she added, "David Spencer's dead."

"And Brian's missing," Luke commented, "after originally being thought dead, too."

"Such a coincidence." Her tone said that she didn't buy it for a minute.

"So who'd you get on the phone?"

"I have no idea. He sounded nervous, and he was none too talkative. Hung up when I asked about the timing."

"You think it might have been Spencer himself, trying to dodge some kind of bad news? Maybe he has bill collectors on his case."

"And here I thought the guy was living large on my fifteen thousand," Susan said, referring to the bank transfers. "Well, whoever he is, he's a California transplant. He has some kind of a Southern accent, but definitely not Texan."

Luke picked up the phone and jabbed redial. "Let's see if my luck's any better." *And hope the guy doesn't have Caller ID,* he added mentally.

On the third ring, someone picked up.

"Hello?" The man's voice was tentative, suspicious. As if he suspected the call had come from creditors— or worse.

"I'm trying to reach a Mr. David Spencer." Luke infused his own words with all the goodwill he could muster.

"You all need to understand the man's passed—"

"It's regarding a refund of four hundred twenty-three dollars and fifty-eight cents owed as a result of the state's recent utility settlement," Luke interrupted. Occasionally, he'd helped one of his client corporations entrap a saboteur—usually a disgruntled former employee who'd launched malicious code on the company's mainframe on his way out the door. Even the savviest among them loved the idea of free money.

Susan smiled and gave him a thumbs-up, obviously amused.

"Uh, who did you say this was?" the man asked.

"This is J.D. Marshall of the California Utility Commission's Office of Settlement Distribution." Luke doubted any such department existed, but it sounded sufficiently official. "Can you tell me, is this Mr. Spencer?"

During the brief pause that followed, Luke leaned forward, willing the man to step into his trap.

"Mr. Spencer's indisposed at the moment, but you can mail a check here."

"Let me take down that information," Luke said, and Susan slid him the pen and paper she'd been using. As soon as he'd recorded the information—a different San Francisco address from the one he'd looked up earlier—he added, "Mr. Spencer should receive his check in four to six weeks, Mr. . . . ?"

"Oh, I'm no one. Just a friend." A click and then a dial tone concluded the proceedings.

After Luke recounted what the man had said, Susan asked, "Do you think it was him? Do you think he knows something about Brian?"

Luke shook his head. "Could be, on both counts. But we're still a long way from proving either."

She eyed the address Luke had written. "So what's next? Should I look him up in San Francisco? I'll be in Oakland anyway, and maybe one-on-one I can convince him to tell me something."

"*No* way you're going there alone." Luke didn't give a damn if she got bristly over his mandate or not. "We don't know anything about this guy, not even his name. If you show up on his doorstep, you could scare him into running, or—worse—he could hurt you."

Gingerly Luke used the pad of his thumb to stroke a spot beside the bruise on Susan's forehead. His stomach lurched as he thought of how the intruder could have cracked her skull with just a little extra effort, could have left her dying while her house burned.

"Hell, Susan," he breathed. "Wasn't this enough to convince you you're dealing with something very dangerous? No thief or vandal broke into your house; we both know that."

She jerked her head away, irritable once more. "I know that. I'm not a child. But you have to understand. I only have twelve days before my appeal goes to the school board. I *have* to have something—something concrete—to show them I haven't been mixed up in anything illegal."

"So you're guilty until proven innocent? Don't those jackasses have it backward?"

She snorted in disgust. "Mark Twain said it best, I think. Something to the effect that God made idiots for practice. Then he came up with school boards."

"Fight them in the courts," he urged. "They're firing you because of rumors."

176

She shook her head. "They'll still have won, because I'll have to go elsewhere in the meantime to find another job. And what school district's going to hire a teacher who's in litigation against her previous employer?"

Luke wanted to offer her money, whatever it would take to win the fight. But he knew that pride—or good sense—would prevent her from accepting. Even if she grew desperate enough to accept such an offer, their relationship would be forever changed, and he was having trouble enough maintaining his emotional equilibrium around her as it was.

"There are other things you can do," he said. "Don't you have a degree in environmental science? I have clients around Austin who do cleanup projects, reclaiming polluted areas, turning them into safe and useful places: airstrips, golf courses, that sort of thing. And the pay would be a whole lot better."

She shook her head. "I'm a teacher, Luke, and a damned good one. I know you're going to think this sounds like some bleeding-heart bullshit—God knows Brian gave me enough grief about it—but I love making a difference in kids' lives, especially the ones the system's given up on—and lots of times, their parents, too. I don't want my students to see me run off because of gossip, and I sure as hell don't want them to see me sell out to help make rich corporations richer, even if their goals are good."

Luke had heard such intensity before, in his own voice when he'd turned down a huge incentive package offered by a telecommunications giant who wanted him to write code that would help annihilate its already struggling competition. The recruiter had said flat out that Luke was nuts to go to work instead for a tiny start-up company in the brand-new field of electronic security. But that had been his love, and he had made it pay.

He had no illusions that Susan's high ideals would earn her the kind of money his job had, or even the respect that she deserved. But there was a payoff in the passion, in doing the job a person felt he had been born to do. And a man who'd sunk more money into restoring an old pickup than the entire truck was worth had no problem comprehending the concept.

"I'll tell you what," he said. "I'll go back to the ranch and see what else I can find out about this David Spencer. I'll cross-check this new address, too, see if I can attach any other name to it." He wanted, too, to dig into bank records, to see if the money trail from Brian to Spencer would yield any clues. Since what he was suggesting was illegal, he didn't want Susan to know anything about it. And since he might very well have done work for the banking entities involved, it would be unethical as well. Sibyl, on the other hand, would draw no such distinctions. Except that she would probably raise her rates.

"I'll be leaving around seven tomorrow morning," Susan said. "Can you call and let me know what you've found out?"

"It's a deal, as long as you'll promise not to do anything about this Spencer until we find out more."

Holding up her hand just as Marcus and Jimmy had done earlier, she smiled before repeating their words. "Scout's honor."

The pickup backfired so loudly that all along Mirage Street, heads appeared in windows or popped out of front doors. Feeling sheepish, Luke gave a little finger wave to let them know it was all right, then drove off quickly, before some busybody called 9-1-1 to report that a big-city drive-by shooter had come to terrorize their town.

When he got home, he'd have to look at the spark plugs and check to see if one of the valves was sticking. But that problem faded into insignificance beside the larger question: How long would Susan's shaky vow hold before need pushed her past its boundaries?

He remembered Brian complaining, *"She never listens when I tell her to be careful. Some of those losers in that club of hers are huge. But she goes traipsing off on desert hikes with them, sometimes even camping overnight. Doesn't think a thing about it."*

Luke had to admit that if Susan were his wife—a thought that jabbed needle-sharp into his consciousness—he would have worried, too, even though her "kids" had borne out her belief in them thus far. But in the case of David Spencer, would Susan's natural confidence lead her to bite off more than she could chew?

Just past a shot-up sign marked *Rocky Rim,* Luke pulled over, then backed up to the intersection of the highway and a rutted dirt road barely deserving of the name. Even the ocotillos and the shindaggers growing nearby looked scraggly. The only other sign of life came in the form of the flies that swarmed over a squashed and desiccated rabbit lying in a tire track.

Above him, thin slivers of metallic cloud speared the pallid sky. This time of year, they might be harbingers of a sudden shower that would turn this track into a torrent. But that threat was hours off yet; he could take the turn-off now. He could talk to the old hippie, too, maybe get the remaining mail that Susan had told him had been left there.

What had Jimmy said the guy's name was who rented out the empty units? Something that sounded like Moon—no. *Boone,* that was it.

Luke wasn't sure what he could expect to get out of the meeting, but one thing was certain. The old man would doubtless perceive both the law and any "client's" wife as natural enemies. A brother willing to pay Brian's storage bill would likely be another story, especially if said brother kicked in an extra fifty bucks.

Luke kept the pickup in low gear as it followed sagging power lines uphill. Whoever had planned Clementine's low-income housing project had taken pains to isolate it, so much so that instead of overlooking the town, the inhabitants were treated to a view of endless, empty desert, its starkness softened only by a purple smudge of mountains in the distance.

Luke hadn't come this way in years, but just as he remembered, the cinder-block cubicles still resembled nothing so much as a derelict warren of jail cells. As if to heighten the impression, some of the squatters had added what appeared to be scavenged iron bars to mostly glassless windows, reminding Luke that the criminal poor preyed upon each other first and foremost.

That didn't mean, however, that they left out others. The power company, for one, he thought as he noticed a tangle of obviously jerry-rigged wires tapping into the main lines. As Luke slid his laptop into a locking compartment he'd installed beneath the passenger seat, he understood that he, too, would be a target if he didn't watch himself.

What he couldn't fathom was the idea of his brother coming up here. Like Luke, Brian had the physical confidence of a big man, but unlike his younger brother, he'd never had to learn to fight—or fight dirty, anyway. He'd always been contemptuous, too, of the poor, and certain that all their problems came of their own shiftlessness, stupidity, and promiscuity. Luke had never shared his opinion, but he figured that maybe part of Brian's attitude resulted from his brother's business. Brian claimed he'd lost a lot of money over the years on deadbeats who disappeared with cars he couldn't find to repossess.

Luke spotted no new vehicles among those parked haphazardly around the property. Of the half-dozen junkers he did see, the majority looked as if they hadn't moved in years.

After climbing from his truck, he stood and listened to wind whistling through the mostly vacant units. He could almost feel the squatters straining their eyes and ears, trying to guess whether he was the law or immigration or maybe some knee-breaker for another loan gone bad.

But maybe that was only his imagination, for other sounds soon drifted to his ear: a radio tuned to a Spanish-language station, the fretful whimpers of a child born without a fighting chance. Luke smelled something cooking, too. He guessed it would be beans reheated once too often on a small hot plate. He wondered, would the crying kid have nothing better? No meat or chance of milk?

Because he had no way of knowing where this Boone might be, Luke followed both his nose and the child's cries to one of the units near the front. It looked much the same as all the others, except that the brown paint on the door had bubbled and begun to peel in strips that reminded him of sunburn. Behind the bars, someone had replaced most of the broken glass with cardboard.

But there must have been a peephole, for a dark-haired white female in a stained pink bathrobe emerged before he could come close enough to knock. She couldn't have been more than twenty, and a filthy, scrawny toddler, naked but for a sagging—and reeking—diaper, clung to her leg like a leech. From inside, another child continued whimpering.

She brandished a crusty spatula as if it were a weapon. "If you're huntin' for my man, I ain't seen him lately, so you can take them papers you come to serve and shove 'em up your goddamn—"

Who would have guessed they'd hidden hell right here, on a road outside of Clementine? "I'm looking for a guy named Boone. I've got some business with him."

Her expression changed her in an eye-blink from vicious harpy to seductress. Or at least that was the look Luke *thought* she was going for.

"I'll take you to him, but first, maybe me and you can do some business of our own."

In the right light, she might be almost pretty, but as she edged nearer, Luke smelled a rank accumulation of greasy food, old cigarettes, and what he thought was menstrual blood. He couldn't help stepping back, before he lost his lunch.

"Uh, sorry," he told her. "I don't have time right now, but I'd be happy to pay you for your trouble if you'd point me in the right direction."

She smiled knowingly. "Sure, honey. Let me take you there myself."

As she proceeded to scrape off the clinging toddler

and shove the child toward the door, Luke realized she meant to go with him and leave her kids alone.

"You should stay," he advised, shoving a twenty toward her. "Just tell me where he is—and get the little ones some milk or something when you get to the store."

Her thin eyebrows shot up, and she gave a dismissive little snort, almost a laugh. "Sure thing, mister. You'll find old Boone four units down and then one more to the inside. If he don't hear you the first time, pound hard on the door. That bastard's stoned half out of his mind most of the time."

But Luke didn't find the aging hippie stoned, as he expected. Instead, he found the man stone dead.

As Luke squatted down to check for signs of life, what came up behind him was something altogether different. And altogether deadlier than any corpse.

Chapter Thirteen

Virginia Maddox had gotten out of the habit of worry-ing over Luke. Heaven only knew, he'd given her enough cause in his youth, when there had always been some teacher to mollify or some trashy girl trying to improve herself by snatching up a Maddox. But she'd given up the effort after discovering that, like an old tomcat who might disappear for days before show-ing up with blood on his whiskers and a gleam in his eye, her younger son was a survivor.

Or at least he had been before Susan Dalton set her sights on him. Now here it was, long after midnight, and she'd seen neither hide nor hair of Luke.

He could only be there for the sex, Virginia thought, her mouth shrinking into a puckered moue of disapproval. Susan was doubtless the sort of woman who went in for all that rolling around and sweating, or at least thought it was in her best inter-ests to pretend she did.

What else could that female giraffe have that would ensnare both of her boys? Certainly not connections, and no money either. And if it was looks her sons were after, Virginia couldn't imagine why either one would choose a woman with so little interest in displaying her features to their best advantage.

Barely registering the sound of the wind rustling in the mesquite trees, Virginia lifted the receiver for the second time that evening. She was furious enough to call that Jezebel and demand she send Luke home immediately. If the Dalton girl had forgotten she was still a married woman, who better to remind her than her husband's mother? Who better to give Susan the dressing-down she so richly deserved?

Yet the thought of Brian being cuckolded by Luke festered, like a splinter buried in Virginia's heart. When it came to Brian, Luke had always been distant, sometimes even resentful. Her late husband had claimed that her obvious favoritism had driven a wedge between the two boys, but that was nonsense. She was certain Luke was only jealous of Brian's many accomplishments, from his stellar athletic career, to his successes with the family business, to what had appeared, at least to the casual observer, to be a successful marriage.

Hampered by a drifter's sensibilities, Luke had achieved none of these things. She'd told herself again and again that her younger son's deficiencies explained his anger after Brian's disappearance, just as it explained Luke's refusal to understand that his older brother never would have betrayed them—betrayed *her*—unless he had been forced to it.

She realized now, however, that Luke's hatred must run far deeper than she had imagined, if he had taken the appalling step of sleeping with his brother's wife.

Either that, or her younger son had the morals of an alley cat as well as the survival instincts.

But as she had before, Virginia found herself staring at the phone instead of dialing. Raindrops popped against her bedroom window, and she thought she heard one of the horses whinny. A night like this left them as unsettled as she felt.

What if Luke had only stayed away out of anger over this morning's argument? After the way he'd stormed out of the house, Virginia could easily picture him renting a motel room out of spite. And she could all too readily imagine the reactions of both Susan and her mother if she were to call them in the dead of night and make false accusations. Besides, even if Luke *was* there, it wasn't as if he would come home just because she asked him to.

As she peered into the empty blackness outside her window, Virginia hesitated. Her index finger hovering over the telephone's number pad, she considered the frightening possibilities that visited all mothers after midnight, weighing them against the much more likely—and much more terrifying—specter of her own humiliation.

After a moment's hesitation, she laid down the receiver and slapped shut the open phonebook. Returning to her bed, she called up Duke and let him snuggle in beside her. Before Brian's disappearance, she had never allowed the smelly old dog on any of the furniture, but sometimes, on her worst nights, the warm presence of another living creature was the only thing that had the power to take her through to dawn.

*   *   *

The cold and damp seeped into Luke's awareness first. Pain came next, hard on their heels. Yet for a time, these feelings remained nebulous, impossible to pin down.

His first conscious thought was that something round and hard lay underneath his shoulder, a presence he could no longer tolerate. He would have to move, to do something about it.

This proved more difficult than he had imagined, for the moment he shifted his position, the abstract pain became concrete—concrete enough for him to wonder if someone had smashed a cinder block against his skull.

Groaning, he fought waves of nausea to force open his eyelids. He raised an arm, trying to shield himself from what looked like a great dark wing silhouetted against a pewter sky.

The sudden movement made his vision disintegrate into fat black dots edged with venomous yellow. Buzzing like a plague of wasps, they blotted out his world.

But only for a while, for when he recovered, he could focus once more on the dark shape. Gradually he recognized the thing for what it was: his truck's door, flung open just above him. He seemed to be lying flat on his back beside the passenger side of his own abandoned pickup. On a damned softball-sized rock, if he was any judge.

Turned out he was lying on a host of smallish rocks, he learned as he wormed his way off the sharpest. That distraction gone, he was able to concentrate more on his surroundings.

He thought he was in a depression, which reinforced the notion that this was a creek bed. Though dry now, it must have run a little water earlier, for the backs of both his jeans and T-shirt remained clammy. Judging from the round shapes of prickly pears and the skeletal cholla cactus he made out along the nearest bank, he was somewhere in the desert, without a building or a house in sight.

That narrowed his location down—to about a thousand square miles of empty wasteland.

He had no better luck determining *when* he was than where. The weak light could mean either dusk or predawn—he had no idea which. When he went to check his watch, he found it missing.

The watch's loss jolted his attention from his bodily discomfort. It probably hadn't been worth much, but his dad had given him that timepiece for his sixteenth birthday. The memory played inside his head like a jittery scene from an old-fashioned movie camera: the father smiling warmly, laying his hand on his boy's shoulder, and saying, "*Now maybe you can make it home in time for curfew, son.*"

In the echo of his words, Luke fully came back to himself. Enough to risk the painstaking movement needed to sit up.

Once the swarming black dots cleared, he carefully hauled himself into the passenger seat of the pickup. For one thing, it was a hell of a lot more comfortable—and warmer—than the chill stones of the creek bottom. For another, the higher vantage point offered him a better view.

The light was perceptibly better now, too, which answered his earlier question about time. Judging by the greasy smear of light at what must be the eastern horizon, daybreak was fast approaching. Even so, he saw nothing but the empty desert stretching out in all directions. He strained for signs of human life, but he couldn't make out even a tire track to lead him back in the direction he had come.

"Oh, *shit*," he swore, his voice so dry and rough he barely recognized it as his own.

He'd been in tight spots before, but it was dawning on him that this one might be his undoing. God alone knew how long he'd lain there while his body heat seeped into the creek bottom, or how long he had gone without anything to drink. Or how he had come to be here in the first place. Not willingly, he was certain, but when he tried to look back for more detail, he remembered nothing, nothing except . . .

Had he kissed Susan, or had that been a dream? Images licked around the edges of his mind like summer lightning: brilliant, devastating, and every bit as fleeting when he tried to grasp one.

He did remember for a certainty the repair of the hard drive, the location of the e-mail, and the phone call that had followed. After that, he had gone somewhere alone, somewhere . . . rough and squalid? He remembered blood—the smell of it—the sight of it— then nothing.

But if he was to have a future, he must put aside the puzzle of his past for now. He glanced, and because the light remained weak, felt around the truck's interior and his pockets, praying to find something that would get him out of this mess.

To his surprise, both his credit cards and his driver's license remained inside his pocket, but like the silver watch, his cash was missing. He'd forgotten his cell phone at the house, primarily because in this part of West Texas, he could only rarely get a signal. He counted it a worse disaster that whoever had dumped him out here had taken the truck's keys, too.

Luke groaned, thinking how those keys would have allowed him to drive along the creek's bank when the light was better and to find the tire tracks that would lead him home from hell.

He thought of leaving the truck here to attempt the search on foot, but even if his injuries didn't make him collapse, the sun would, once it rose to smite the open desert with the heat of late July.

And the sun, unlike whoever had attacked him, would surely finish him for good.

The eastern sky was already blushing in anticipation of the dawn's kiss; Susan couldn't afford to wait for Luke's call any longer. Pushing aside a frisson of unease, she told herself that more than likely he'd worked late into the night and was asleep now. Probably, he'd call her sister's place this evening to let her know if he'd learned any more about David Spencer.

Susan slung her mom's suitcases and her duffel bag onto the Jeep's rear seat. She dreaded the thought of the four-hour drive to the El Paso airport, especially with her mother's weak bladder and the dearth of rest rooms to consider.

"Don't worry about your fellow," Roberta said as Peavy snuggled in her arms against the morning chill. "He and I will get along just fine."

Still half asleep, the Chihuahua looked angelic, or at least he would to someone who didn't know him better. Though Susan certainly did, she gave him an affectionate scratch behind the ears, where the hair was silkiest. Closing his brown eyes, he gave a little moan of canine satisfaction.

"Bet-better keep a w-watch on your good linens," Maggie Dalton warned her friend. "L-last night, the little . . . little poop chewed up my . . . my favorite ecru doilies."

Roberta looked properly horrified. "Not those darling pineapple ones Matilda Walker made you?"

Maggie nodded gravely, while Susan bit back an unkind comment commending Peavy's decorative tastes, if not his manner of expressing his opinions. She was in enough trouble already for her comments on the new hair color.

"Thanks again for watching him. You're a brave woman." She leaned to kiss Roberta's cheek. "We'd better hit the road, Mom. I still have to get gas."

They stopped at an old station near the intersection of the vacant end of Mirage Street and the ranch road leading toward the interstate. As Susan walked around the corner of the station to pay the attendant, she caught sight of a black Hummer making a fast turn toward town. Remembering Hal's insistence that he needed to see her, she wondered if he was trying to catch her early at her mom's apartment.

She thought of waving to attract his attention and explaining that she was leaving town, but a strange reluctance stayed her hand. She didn't have the energy to deal with any more of his sticky sincerity, or the offers of assistance that had more to do with his needs than her own.

But as she looked after him, a sheriff's department patrol car swung into view, driving up behind Hal with its lights flashing, though its siren remained mute. When the Hummer stopped along the shoulder, Deputy Ramirez stepped out of his vehicle with the swagger of a man who enjoyed lording his authority over county residents.

She wondered what minor infraction he'd detected.

Had Hal failed to signal his turn, or had he been driving a few miles per hour over the oft-ignored speed limit? He put down his window and passed something to Ramirez. A driver's license, possibly, or his insurance card.

She wondered if Hal felt singled out for bad luck, as she sometimes had these past eight months. Only his misfortune had started even earlier and struck deeper, with his daughter's death.

And like Susan, the guy kept treading water, thrusting his head above the current tide of trouble.

But that doesn't mean I owe it to him to let him use me for a ladder, she thought as she paid for her fuel. *It doesn't mean I have to let his grief and loneliness drown us both.*

The crystal made a satisfying crackle when he smashed it with the hammer, but with a few more blows, the watch went all to pieces. Swearing violently, the watcher swept them from the table. He had wanted to smash the interloper's face, not just his timepiece, for he'd seen the bastard's truck again, parked outside the place the faithless bitch was staying.

But just when fate handed him his chance, when he had the interloper helpless, the witness had shown up—the same asshole who always seemed to be there—and the watcher had been forced to drop back into his false self. He'd had to settle for a petty theft and a petty warning, one he feared the interloper would survive.

So go back and finish him, sang the icy floes that drifted through his bloodstream. *Take the bastard out, and she'll remember you.*

The watcher kicked the table and roared with fury,

for he knew things would never be the same. After all he'd been through, all they'd had together, she had proved too fickle to deserve his love.

She would damn well have his hate, then, he thought as he pulled her ring out of his pocket. Let the bitch see how much screwing around she'd get to do once he spilled her secrets . . .

And once she figured out she couldn't get away with murder after all.

Chapter Fourteen

Since his wife's death sixteen years earlier, Sheriff Hector Abbott had spent more and more time on the job. With his daughter and grandkids living in Colorado, he'd found filling the empty hours with work far more satisfying than watching TV or shooting the shit over a cup of coffee with his retired friends. One by one, he'd watched them drift into irrelevance, and he'd sworn to himself he wasn't leaving office without one hell of a fight. He especially wasn't going to hand over his department to some smart-ass outsider who thought it was time to bring big-city policing to Ocotillo County.

He'd worked late last night, after the old hippie's body had been found in that concrete shit-hole out on Rocky Rim. But that didn't stop Hector from coming in around five-thirty this morning in hopes of clearing some of the paperwork from his disastrously disheveled desk. He started by running through the file on the Boone murder to see if Deputy Ortiz had found anything else to add.

Frowning, Hector absently scratched at his mustache. As he'd expected, there was nothing helpful, only the photographs of a small hole in the victim's chest, a larger exit wound in his back. They'd dug the bullet from a wall and sent it off for testing, but they still had no idea of the man's full name or next of kin.

With no relatives, at least there'd be no one breathing down Hector's neck to solve the murder. Of course, he meant to give it his best shot, but when crimes occurred on Rocky Rim, as they did far too often, there were never any witnesses, never any leads. After the last murder a few years back, Hector had gotten so fed up with the place that he and his deputies had cleaned out all the squatters and painstakingly boarded up each door and every window.

It hadn't lasted two months. The funding didn't come through to raze the complex, for one thing. Besides, the squatters pried their way back inside faster than he and his men could throw them out. The decent citizens of Clementine didn't want to see the homeless in the streets and parks, either, or camped out scaring schoolkids by the public library. And they sure as hell didn't appreciate the increase in petty thefts from sheds and garages as the displaced helped themselves to both essentials and any items they figured they could sell. So Hector and the complex had fallen into an uneasy truce. Every so often, he'd show up and rattle cages, but otherwise he left the heathens to themselves.

An hour later, he was signing off on a DWI arrest report when the night-shift dispatcher slid her wheeled office chair into his doorway.

"Weirdo for you on line two." Gladys's round cheeks dimpled with a smug smile. She was famous for her ability to screen and sort incoming calls. It was a skill that came in handy, since the county commissioners kept voting down Hector's requests for an upgrade in communications. Hell, his office didn't even have the ability to pinpoint the location of incoming calls.

The fortyish brunette scooted back to her desk, an act that offered Hector a glimpse of her posterior, which lapped over her chair on both sides. He shuddered. He'd always enjoyed her company, but there wasn't enough coffee in the world to prepare him for that sight this early in the morning.

After reaching for the phone, he punched the flashing button. "Sheriff Abbott. What can I do for you?"

The person on the other end murmured something indistinguishable. The voice sounded male, but Hector could pick up nothing else.

"Can you put the receiver closer to your mouth, sir?" He raised his own voice, in case the problem was a bad connection. "I can't make out a word you're saying."

The caller tried again, but only intermittent words broke through. "Su . . . Maddox . . . saw her near the park . . . back on December . . . she . . . dumping something . . . shot . . . canyon . . ."

Hector frowned. This fellow sounded as if he were talking through a stack of thick sweat socks. "I still can't hear you. Who *is* this?"

He wasn't a bit surprised when the caller refused to identify himself. He did speak up a little, repeating himself patiently until Hector wrote out the directions the fellow was set on giving him.

Finally the caller added, "You'll find what you've been looking for ten feet to the left of the fifth pool of water. Just watch for the three rocks, like I said."

"If you could leave a number where I could reach you in case I have any questions . . ." Hector ventured.

There was nothing muffled about his informant's outrage. "You think I'm stupid, old man?" he demanded before banging down the phone.

"A few manners will get you a long way in this life," Hector advised the dial tone.

When he looked up, Gladys had slid her chair back into view and gestured at him with the half-eaten egg-and-cheese burrito that had dripped grease onto her eye-searing orange blouse. "Well, what did I tell you? A real nutcase, right?"

"More than likely," he said. Unidentified informants, especially those who attempted to disguise their voices, were more often pranksters than reliable witnesses. Still, the details in the man's description troubled Hector. People didn't usually go to that much trouble to flesh out their fabrications. "But I think we ought to check out his story, just in case."

He counted it a blessing that the location the caller had described was just outside the boundaries of the national park. Though Hector had the authority to investigate criminal matters anywhere within the county, he would rather be dragged buck naked through a patch of prickly pear than deal with the latest namby-pamby East Coast college boy the park service had promoted to keep out of harm's way. In the unlikely event there was something to be found, that fellow would be on the horn to the Effing BI, as his younger deputies called the bureau, without a moment to lose. And the last thing Hector wanted was a bunch of feds sticking their noses into his investigation.

"Who's on this morning?" he called to Gladys, who had drifted back to her own desk.

"Ramirez is supposed to come at seven all this

week. I wouldn't count on him, though. Francine said he went home sick yesterday morning."

The sheriff swore under his breath. After what he'd learned yesterday, Ramirez was one of the main reasons he didn't want outside agencies sticking their noses into county business. And sick or not, Hector wasn't letting the deputy get within ten miles of the Maddox case again.

The affair with Grace Morton was bad enough, but if this new wrinkle was discovered, Hector would lose a hell of a lot more than a couple of oversexed employees. He knew the day was coming when he would have to deal firmly with the matter, but he was hoping to string it out a few more months, until he could slide safely past this next election . . . and into the next four years of the career that had become his life.

"I'll take care of this myself," he told Gladys on his way out of the office. "Here's a copy of my notes, but do me a favor, will you? Keep 'em to yourself unless I don't check in in a few hours."

Susan ought to have been impressed by the costly view James and Carol's lakeside town house offered. The sky was clear and vibrant blue this morning, displaying the shimmering water, the thick-limbed evergreens, and the pricey real estate that lined the waterfront to spectacular advantage. Instead, her full attention was focused on keeping her rising frustration from her voice.

Wearing an ivory sweater she'd borrowed from her sister with a pair of jeans she'd packed, Susan stood on the condo's balcony, a cordless phone clutched in one hand. "Are you sure you gave him my last message?"

On the other end she heard Virginia Maddox's sharp intake of breath. "Are you insinuating I would stoop to lying? I told you he doesn't want to speak to you."

Nice try, Susan thought. Maybe that tactic would have proved successful if she had been as young as Luke was when her own mother had used it. Ignoring the older woman's claim, she answered, "Yes."

"Yes? Yes to *what?*" her mother-in-law demanded.

"I'm sorry to have to say it, but, yes, I do think you would lie to me if that's what it would take to keep me from speaking to Luke. Where is he?"

"He's . . . he's not here now, so stop calling."

A harsh click and a dial tone convinced Susan that the two of them had come to an impasse.

At least Virginia hadn't bothered to deny the accusation, but Susan wondered if her claim that he was out was just as false. It was possible, of course, that Luke was elsewhere at the moment, but that did nothing to explain why he hadn't called yet.

The more Susan thought about the lack of contact, the more she worried. What if she had scared him off by throwing herself at him in her mom's apartment? He hadn't *acted* scared—far from it—but maybe he'd thought better of helping her once he left her sight.

She could hardly blame him if he had, for more than once she'd come to the conclusion that she'd lit a fuse the day she'd asked Luke to help her—a fuse that was slowly, inexorably burning toward one hell of an explosion. Again and again she told herself that as soon as she found Brian, she would stop relying on Luke, stop depending on anyone except herself.

But maybe this trouble reaching him was an indication that the time had come already. With the calendar spinning toward her hearing before the school board, what choice did she have but to start using her own skills?

Entering through the French door, she stepped into what her sister called the great room, an expansive space dominated by a huge stone fireplace, oversized furniture in distressed leather, and tastefully decorated bookcases. Atop the gleaming wood floor, an Oriental rug pulled the room together with its warmth and color. Carol had acquired some expensive tastes during her tenure selling real estate in the Bay Area. No wonder she had been strapped for cash when their mother had her stroke last winter.

Not that Carol would have admitted such a thing. But now that she and James had settled into the home they'd purchased the previous November and Carol had begun earning huge commissions on expensive commercial properties, she had suddenly grown generous with her money.

"You look exhausted, Susan. Why don't you sleep late tomorrow and help yourself to some espresso when you're ready?" she'd suggested the night before, apparently forgetting that both her younger sister and her mother preferred tea. "If Mom's up to it, I plan to take her to tour this *fabulous* community we've found. I'm just dying to show her the services they offer."

She'd explained to Susan on the sly that the place was an upscale retirement community she and James had found. The residence included not only the finest dining and recreational opportunities available, but access to an exclusive rehabilitation center. And a fabulous salon, Carol had added pointedly, referring to their mother's pinkish-orange "California 'do." Susan had the uncomfortable feeling that, to the upscale childless, extravagance on behalf of an aged parent was almost as good as spoiling a son or daughter beyond reason. Better, perhaps, since they could casually allude to their own saintliness at cocktail parties.

Not that the Maggie Dalton she knew would be sucked in by any of it, Susan thought as she searched in vain for tea bags. Her mother might have allowed Larinda to coax her into trying a shade of red not existing in nature, but at heart, she was as down-to-earth and unaffected as any woman Susan had ever known. There was no way Maggie would choose a pretty view and the trappings of success over the town she had known for a lifetime and the friends she had loved almost as long.

There was no way she would pick Carol over Susan.

Susan blinked in surprise at her own thoughts. As she attempted to figure out the fancy European coffeemaker, she wondered, was she competing with her sister for her mother's heart, as they had competed for attention when the two of them were growing up?

Susan liked to think she'd gotten past all that. Maybe she *had* at one point, but the devastating turns her life had taken had caused her to regress. At the thought, she made a face, but wasted no time on self-loathing. After what she'd been through, who wouldn't want some mothering?

Abandoning her attempt to make sense of the coffeemaker from hell, Susan retrieved the scrap of paper she'd tucked inside a pocket of her wheeled carry-on suitcase. She then picked up the phone and called her sister's cell phone.

"Mom's *loving* this place," Carol confided. "The director's taken her to the masseuse right now. And a bit later, we're invited to have lunch in the dining room. They have a new five-star chef they're just *dying* to show off. Would you like me to swing by and pick you up so you can join us? I don't mind a bit."

Susan would rather have her toenails pulled out with rusty pliers than sit through the hoity-toity hard sell she suspected would come next. "Uh, no thanks," she said. "Since my flight's this afternoon, I thought I'd do a little shopping before I leave civilization."

Carol should have spotted the lie immediately. Susan hadn't willingly entered a mall in years. Besides, she was closing in on broke, and then some. But since her older sister's strongest religious convictions involved the healing powers of retail therapy, she swallowed it, hook, line, and sinker.

"Sounds like a great plan. I hope you won't be too cramped driving the T-bird. If I'd thought about it, I would have asked James to take it and leave you the Escalade today."

Susan rolled her eyes. The Thunderbird, a sleek and retro mint-green two-seater, was James and Carol's "fun" car. The other two were serious—as in seriously pretentious. "I'll have plenty of space for what I'm after," Susan said. "I appreciate your trusting me with the sex-appeal-mobile."

Carol laughed at her description. "It's no trouble at all. And there's a city map in my office, in that stack of papers on the file cabinet. Take it so you won't get lost—and have fun, Susan. You certainly deserve it."

Though having fun wasn't on the day's agenda, Susan was secretly delighted with the chance to drive the sports car. Placing the map on the impractical white leather seat beside her, she revved the engine and grinned at the power in its purr.

And nearly backed into someone who had just stepped out of a taxi and onto the driveway.

She gave the mirrors a double take before shifting out of gear and engaging the brake. Relief flooding her, she jumped out of the car. "Luke—what are you doing here? Hey, are you all right?"

He didn't *look* all right, but she couldn't put her finger on the problem. Though he needed a shave, he was handsome as ever, especially when he flashed a smile of recognition. Yet both Luke's smile and his hazel eyes looked strained. There was something odd, too, in the way he held himself, as if he were recovering from surgery or an injury.

Instead of answering, he hugged her. Without letting go, he said, "I got myself into some trouble after I left you the other day."

"What happened?" She pulled away so she could read his face. "I called your mother, but . . . well, she pulled the old 'he doesn't want to speak to you' routine. Before she hung up on me, that is."

He made a face. "Where were you going? I don't want to freak out anyone inside, but I'd really like to sit down while we talk. It's been a long couple of days."

"Nobody's home right now, but let's find out if those legs of yours will fit inside this car. We can go and grab some coffee, maybe breakfast if you haven't eaten yet. From the looks of things inside the kitchen, my sister and her husband live on frozen yogurt and espresso."

"Breakfast sounds great," he said and slung his travel bag into the trunk she had popped open. To her surprise, he fit inside the two-seater, though there was little room to spare.

While she headed toward an intersection where she recalled seeing several chain restaurants, he explained, "I decided to drive over to Rocky Rim once I left your place. I thought if I paid off this Boone character, I could talk him into parting with whatever was left of Brian's mail. Only . . . well, I don't know how to say this except straight out. I found the guy dead—or at least I'm pretty sure he was."

The car glided to the shoulder, seemingly of its own volition, as Susan struggled to absorb what he had said. "What happened to him, and what do you mean you're 'pretty sure' he's dead?"

"There was a lot of blood, and . . . let's just say he looked the wrong shade of gray to still be breathing. But when I squatted down to check, something . . . something must have happened. I guess someone hit me, because I have one hell of a lump on the back of my head."

"Oh, God." Panic jolted through her, and her own wound gave a little throb of sympathy. "So you were knocked out? Did anyone show up and help you?"

"I don't think you could call it helping. When I came to, I was lying in the desert by my pickup, out of sight of town. It was early the next morning, and whoever'd dumped me there had taken both my cash and keys. Probably would've taken the truck, too, if it was running worth a damn."

"A thief? Did you see him?"

"I guess so, and no, I didn't."

"You were out cold all night long? That sounds really serious. I hope you saw a doctor—but how did you get out of there if you didn't have your keys?"

"I hot-wired the truck." He gave a shrug. "At least my misspent youth came in handy for something. And yes, I saw someone. I'm not quite as stubborn as you are."

"And he said?"

"*She*—I went to Dr. Elbertson. I have some bumps and bruises, but that's not what kept me unconscious."

"What was it?"

"According to my blood work, I was drugged. The doctor says it's some kind of sedative they use in Mexico that's made its way onto the streets all over. Causes some short-term memory loss, along with one hell of a hangover."

"You mean one of the date-rape drugs you hear about?"

"Something like that, only it was probably injected."

"God, Luke, are you all right?" She felt sick thinking of what had happened, and what more could have happened to him. Abruptly, she wished she'd never gone to him for help.

Almost imperceptibly, he nodded. "I'm getting there, but I can tell you, I'd like to find the bastard who put me out."

After what seemed an endless wait for some kind soul to let her in, Susan rejoined the flow of traffic. She loved the Thunderbird, but city driving made her edgy. Or edgier than normal, anyway. Besides that, she felt hemmed in by the closeness of the buildings and smothered by the carefully maintained plantings so bright they hurt her eyes. The Bay Area had a lot to recommend it, but apparently, she was more cut out for the subtle flow of untamed landscapes that ranged from bronze to dun.

"Does your mother know you came here? She'd be frantic if you just disappeared."

"I would never do that, especially not with Brian missing. I made sure she had my cell-phone number and told her I had business on the West Coast. And I do, with you. I found out more about David Spencer. Some stuff I think we ought to check out while we're here."

"Hold that thought for a moment. I wanted to know,

did you ever hear any more about this Boone guy? The one you thought was dead."

"Not a word, but I never called the sheriff's office. For one thing, I wasn't too eager to explain why I'd gone there in the first place. If someone, maybe Ramirez, made the wrong connections, he might think you and I were somehow involved. Involved with the guy's death, that is."

"Point taken." She pulled into the parking lot of a chain restaurant famous for its breakfasts. "Is this okay? I'm sure there are fancier places, but I don't know my way around here all that well."

"This is good."

The two of them went inside and ordered, Susan opting for hot tea and a whole-grain bagel and Luke going for coffee and the full complement of eggs, bacon, and biscuits. She was relieved to see he still had an appetite, after what he'd been through.

"So tell me what you found out about Spencer," she asked.

After taking a long draw from his black coffee, Luke said, "He's pretty well-off for a supposedly dead man. Over two hundred thousand in various accounts. And that's only what my, uh, associate's found so far. There has to be more, especially considering what Brian borrowed from Hal's bank."

"For a rich man, he sure jumped at your utility refund line in a hurry."

Luke shrugged. "If you dropped a ten in front of Bill Gates, I'll bet he'd still bend down to pick it up."

She smiled over the warm pool of her milky tea. "Or have one of his people do it for him. But how did you find out about the money? I know there's lots of info floating around out there, but—"

He gave his head a quick shake and answered quietly, "You don't want to know that. But you'd probably be interested to hear that Social Security has no record of Spencer's death."

"So the guy on the telephone *was* him, right? Or at least he lied about Spencer being dead."

"Here's the rub," Luke said. "I plugged the name into a search engine and came up with a memorial donation in his name. To a foundation that does hospice care for patients in the Bay Area, mostly guys dying of AIDS. It looks like a man named David Spencer did die two weeks before Brian's disappearance."

"Could you get Spencer's address from that source?"

Luke waited for the waitress to set down their meals and refill his coffee. Once she had bustled off, he shook his head. "Afraid not. So there's nothing to do but go after the man we spoke to on the phone."

For several minutes they worked on the food. After eating half her bagel, Susan poured herself a refill from the small silver teapot the waitress had left. "You could have called to tell me this, Luke. You didn't need to come here, especially after you were hurt."

Luke swallowed another mouthful of his breakfast. "I know what you promised, but I know *you*, too. You would have gone to talk to him. I couldn't let you do that alone."

"But I—" she began.

"You were about to head that way when I showed up, right?"

His lack of faith annoyed her, despite the fact he was correct. "How do you know I wasn't running out for tampons?"

The dreaded T-word would have embarrassed Brian right off topic. He'd always had a phobia about anything too female. Though she'd been groggy from the anesthesia and numb with grief, she remembered how he'd acted like a regular fool when the doctor had tried to talk to him about her D and C after the miscarriage.

Since she hadn't indulged in a while, she dragged out Voodoo Brian and cut him in half with sharpened shears. Starting at the intersection of his floppy little legs.

If Luke was bothered by her question, he gave no sign of it. "I know because the map was open on the passenger seat when I climbed in the car. When I went to move it, I could see you had it folded back to that guy's part of town."

She winced and thought of what her students would have surely told her. *You're busted, Mrs. Maddox.* Luke had her dead to rights.

"So you're a decent judge of character," she conceded. "You want a gold star on your forehead?"

He grinned, channeling the smart-ass he'd been as a kid. "No, but I'll let you stick it on my—"

"Let's not go there, Luke."

"Fine," he said, sobering abruptly. "I'm finished eating. So how about we go and look up that address instead?"

After an hour-and-a-half drive into the most remote corner of Ocotillo County, Sheriff Hector Abbott decided he should have waited and sent Forrester and Lopez out here when they came in this afternoon. As much as Hector hated to admit it, he was getting too damned old to enjoy running down every half-assed anonymous tip that came into the station. Especially with this shit-for-shocks patrol car shaking his bladder to pieces on this sorry excuse for a park road, the only one that led to the canyon just beyond the park's borders.

As he tapped the brakes and waited for a roadrunner to strut across the road, his mind wandered once again to the loose rein he kept on his people. Now and then he might step in with some advice or clarify the way he wanted something handled, but he'd long believed that folks worked harder, better, and more honestly without bosses breathing fire down their necks. Besides, it never occurred to him that anyone would want to give anything less than his best on the job, especially one as important as protecting lives and property.

That was one reason why he'd found it so upsetting when he'd figured out Ramirez hadn't logged the items they had taken from the Maddox house last winter, as he had claimed. Hector might never have discovered it, except he'd gone looking for the inventory after the break-in at Susan's home. He'd hoped that something on the list would jump out, maybe strike him as the sort of item the intruders might have wanted.

When no such record turned up, Ramirez had been out of radio contact—the county had a load of dead spots, with all its rocky outcroppings and ravines—so Hector had phoned the state lab to check on the status of the items they were analyzing. He'd been at first perplexed and then dismayed to learn the state boys had no record of receiving any items from the Maddox house.

Hector might have written off the whole business as a bookkeeping snafu, except for the matter of the boots. The same custom-made, full-quill ostrich boots that Manuel was rarely seen without since he'd bought them last winter. The boots had been the object of much admiration and discussion around the office, especially after Deputy Forrester had gotten himself a quote from the bootmaker and found they went for something like a grand a pair. There had been a truck as well, around the same time, a shiny white Ford pickup only two years old. Leather interior, too, and one of those fancy stereo systems for the Tex-Mex music Manuel favored.

Forrester had made some offhand joke that he hoped he wouldn't have to bust Manuel for being on the take. But what Hector recalled most clearly was Manuel's reaction. Like his half brother, Lupe, Ramirez had always been something of a hothead, but that day he'd gotten right in Forrester's face and threatened him with nine kinds of ass-kicking if he ever again implied such a thing. An even-tempered veteran, big-bellied Forrester had laughed the outburst off as so much bullshit, but Hector had pulled Manuel aside for a chat about his temper.

That afternoon, Manuel had claimed he'd only been kidding around, so Hector let it go. Afterward, he'd thought it likely his deputy was playing peacock for pretty Grace, who'd come to work at the jail around that time. But in light of what Hector knew now, he wondered, had Forrester's gibe been on the right track?

As the car rolled forward over the rutted road, Hector pondered how to handle what could well turn out to be an explosive—and poorly timed—situation. If Myers, his opponent, convinced the area's other newcomers that the sheriff's department was not only outdated but corrupt, the transplanted suburbanites would lap up the story like a cat on cream, and that Dallas upstart would soon have his ass parked behind Hector's desk. And Hector would find himself nothing but a mild curiosity, like one of the worn-out wagon wheels or rusty branding irons he sometimes saw in gift shops. Not quite an antique, and not quite junk yet either; just another curious relic of a bygone day.

"The hell I will," he muttered and clenched his jaw so hard his teeth ached with each bump.

A couple of minutes later, he squinted at his dashboard, but it was no good. He had to pull over and dig out his drugstore glasses to read the numbers on his odometer. Leaving on the flat-topped half-lenses, he rolled forward another two-tenths of a mile into a low area nearly overgrown with scrub trees. After checking the notes he'd jotted down this morning, he turned to the right and followed a smaller, even rougher track.

He stopped and opened a gate with a rusting placard that read "Private Property—No Trespassing" just below a faded "For Sale" sign. Once upon a time, some idiot from Dallas had bought about a hundred acres out here to use for hunting, but after getting snakebit the first time he'd used it, he had never come back. The land had been for sale for the past ten years, and the lock had been removed to allow interested parties to take a look.

Mostly, however, hikers and climbers and the occasional pair of lovers used it as a private retreat. And there was Cactus Annie, too, a crazy old woman who wandered all around the park area with a gigantic, shaggy mongrel by her side. She was more or less a permanent fixture, since she apparently had no other home or any belongings besides that mutt, a ratty backpack stuffed with junk, and an ancient army jacket. About a year ago, when Hector had tried to run her off for trespassing, she'd started ranting about the lunacy of people thinking they could own Mother Earth, could cut her into little squares and fence her off from others, until he'd wanted to haul her in to calm down for a while. But then that black-and-white dog had bared its teeth and started growling, and he couldn't bring himself to shoot the only thing she loved.

So he'd thanked his lucky stars the landowner wasn't around to raise a stink, and had let her be. After all, he didn't have the manpower—and God knew he didn't have the patience—to chase after trespassers in every godforsaken nook and cranny of the county.

The solitary track led into a narrow canyon, more a crack between two halves of a broken loaf of mesa. When the front end of his cruiser smacked the ground as it waddled through a muddy rut, he shifted into Park. According to his park map, Shotgun Canyon went back only about a mile and a half, and his source had led him to believe he wouldn't have nearly that far to walk.

Reluctantly he climbed out of his air-conditioned vehicle and surveyed the deteriorating path ahead. One thing was certain. Anyone who'd driven back here, as the caller claimed the woman he'd seen had, would have needed four-wheel drive. Especially considering the amount of rain the area had had around the date in question.

Though he had to admit the black-and-white photographs Susan had taken last December had their own stark brand of beauty, Hector was still hard-pressed to understand the attraction of this particular canyon. Personally, he detested the way the almost sheer walls towered high above him. Their bulbous, rust-brown massiveness closed in on him, planting an irrational fear that they would collapse and crush him. He hated, too, the way deep shadow had taken him from blazing midday into what must be perpetual dusk. Though the canyon should have been cool, heat hung heavily, trapped between the looming walls. Within minutes, Hector's shirt was soaked with sweat, and he was calling his informant every vile word he'd ever learned.

He cursed himself for a damned fool, too, as he struggled to free his feet from a tangle of puncture vine. The Creator must have been in a foul humor the day He'd made the vicious stuff, which Hector had seen cripple horses, deflate tires, and tear the hide off crawling babies' chubby knees.

Finally extricating himself, he made his way toward the thin rivulet of water the caller had described. There was only enough moisture to make a stinking mud hole dotted with a string of puddles, most of which were colonized by spiny grasses and ill-tempered, biting flies.

"If I ever get my hands on the son of a bitch that called this morning, I'll shoot him on the spot," Hector swore after falling in a patch of slime-green muck. As he pushed himself onto all fours, he noticed the piglike tracks of javelinas and, beside them, the larger and infinitely more frightening print of a big cat.

Cougar, he decided. Nothing else could be that size.

The pungent odor of animal filled his nostrils, and the coarse white hairs rose on his arms. For here he was in the cougar's hunting ground, its home court, and the lions were no respecters of the law. Hector had his gun, of course, but with all these scattered rocks to hide it, the damned thing could be on him before he could reach his holster.

He thought of turning to go home. He was getting to be an old man, almost sixty-nine now, and he'd taken a bad spill. The heat was stifling, too, and the rookie, Lopez, needed this experience. He and Forrester could ride together, keep an eye out for each other and—

Hector pictured some greasy-haired punk laughing at the thought of making him traipse through this horseshit, laughing at the big, bad sheriff who was about to lose his mud over a tumble and a paw print.

"Like hell," Hector bellowed. His voice echoed through the canyon and startled a doe out of some nearby tall grass. She bounded past him, toward the canyon's mouth.

Hector stood stock-still, heart thumping, and listened to the clatter of the deer's hooves echo in the canyon before dying away. Taking a deep breath to steady himself, he recalled the muffled words on the telephone this morning.

"You'll find what you've been looking for ten feet to the left of the fifth pool of water," he'd said, and there it was, with the oddly stacked trio of squared-off boulders just where he'd described it.

Would something be behind those man-sized boulders, something Susan Maddox—with her four-wheel-drive Jeep—had left there, back in December of last year, the same day she'd supposedly been out taking pictures? Hector felt apprehension prickling behind his neck and fresh perspiration breaking out across his brow at the thought.

As he lumbered toward the boulders, careful to avoid the thorns and slick spots, he tried to picture what he might find: The ashes of some evidence too damning for Susan to leave inside the house? Some clue that Susan knew of her husband's and Jessica Beecher's affair? Even, Hector thought darkly, his own ambush and death in the crosshairs of his anonymous "informant's" gun?

If he did die here—if this whole thing had been some kind of setup—would his men find him before the cougars, javelinas, and coyotes picked his carcass clean?

After a moment's hesitation, Hector dismissed this last thought, as he did most things that bothered him. More than likely, he'd find nothing in the deeper shadows of the boulders, nothing but more rust-brown rock and slime-green algae and . . .

The thought trailed off as he glimpsed not color but its absence. The starkly unexpected glow that could only be the white of naked bone.

Chapter Fifteen

Luke navigated while Susan drove the T-bird over the Oakland Bay Bridge into San Francisco. Not that he could see much of anything. Fog surrounded them, deadening sound as well as obscuring their surroundings.

He was struck with the sensation that they were soaring through a cloudbank in a glider plane. It felt strangely intimate, as if they were alone in a world of their own choosing. A world where she could be his lover, not just his brother's wife.

He hadn't wanted to face how much he needed Susan, hadn't wanted to admit to such impossible desire. As he'd rested on the red-eye flight from Texas, his mind whispered a thousand warnings of what would happen if he made Susan his. Their mothers would both be hurt and furious. The law would be suspicious and the gossip brutal. Brutal enough that Susan would never again teach in Ocotillo County.

He swore to himself he cared too much for Susan to risk hurting her that way. But the moment she'd stepped out of the Thunderbird and met him on the driveway, he'd known damned well that all the reasons in the world meant nothing to his heart. So for the time being, he relished the illusion that the world had shrunk down to nothing more than the two of them.

A car horn intruded on his fantasy. Blinking at the sound, he groped for words in the hope that normal conversation would bring him down to earth. "Nice view, huh?"

Susan leaned over the steering wheel, her gaze fixed on the road ahead. "Just keep an eye out for taillights—and our turn. I can't see a damned thing."

They ended up missing it the first time, but eventually they reached a residential street in the Pacific Heights area. The visibility was better here, and Luke could make out older single-family dwellings tucked between more modern brick apartment buildings.

Despite the large bank accounts attached to David Spencer's name, Luke had envisioned the man's home as an anonymous-looking apartment or a derelict old cottage, something that spoke of frequent moves and subterfuge. He was surprised when Susan parked in front of an Italianate row house instead.

"Nice digs," she said.

She wasn't kidding. Painted in tasteful shades of gray, lavender, and white with gilded trim, the row house and its neighbors looked like the sort of show-places that senior citizens visited on bus tours.

"Think he'll be here?" Susan asked.

Luke glanced down at his wrist and frowned at the reminder that his watch was missing. His gaze flicked to the car's clock instead. Almost eleven-thirty. "Not if he works days," he said.

Susan stared at the house and drew in a deep

breath. "So what now? I mean, even if he *is* home, if we say what we're after, what's to keep him from slamming the door in our faces?"

Luke thought about it for a moment. "Let's not both go, for one thing. That way, if one of us tips him off, the other can try something different later."

She stopped chewing on her lower lip. "I've got it. Why don't I say I have a delivery for David Spencer? That way I can see if he's the guy."

"First of all, we don't have a package. And even if he says he's the man, then what? You'll jump all over him demanding answers?"

She had the good grace to look abashed, for they both knew that was exactly what she'd do. "Maybe you'd do better. I noticed when you called him earlier, you were Johnny-on-the-spot with the quick lie. I'm not sure whether to love you or hate you for that particular talent."

She smiled to show she'd meant the statement as a joke, but in the confined space of the small car, the air vibrated with the potential in her words. *I'm not sure whether to love you* . . . Hope constricted painfully in his chest.

His first instinct was to duck behind a cocky comeback, tell her he had other talents he knew she'd love for sure. But he couldn't bring himself to say it, couldn't bear to see her roll her eyes and turn away that gorgeous face. Instead, he said, "I've had some on-the-job experience catching corporate saboteurs and hackers. I'll handle this guy the same way—and try to forget he has anything to do with Brian. I want you to wait here."

It was an indication of her nervousness that she didn't argue. Instead, she did the very last thing he expected. She leaned over the gearshift and softly kissed his mouth.

Her lips felt like warm velvet, so inviting that he wanted to sink into them, to lose himself inside her. But before he could deepen the kiss, she pulled away from him.

"Thank you," she said quietly. "I was all set to take care of this myself. But now that you're here, I can't imagine going it alone."

He brushed a stray hair from her cheek, his fingertips tingling at the feather-light contact. "You don't have to. Ever, because we're going to see this through together."

He had to turn away and leave the car then, before he passed the point of no return.

Susan backed up the Thunderbird so it would not be visible to anyone answering the door. Though remaining out of sight made perfect sense, she hated not being able to keep an eye on Luke.

The longer she waited, the more nervous she became. One by one, frightening scenarios unfolded in her imagination. What if Luke said something wrong and this man called the police? How could Luke possibly explain his presence? Or maybe the stranger would pull a gun and force Luke inside. Or what if, instead of the stranger she and Luke had both expected, Brian himself opened the door?

What if Brian *was* this David Spencer? She thought of all the money hidden in Spencer's accounts. Could it be the funds siphoned from the dealership and their own savings? And there had been the loans Brian had stolen from Hal's bank, too. Had Brian assumed a new identity here instead of running to a foreign country?

At the thought, her mouth went ash-dry and her stomach turned to gurgling liquid. She'd grown so accustomed to thinking of Brian in the abstract—a sort of caricature of the philandering husband, raising toasts to her ignorance in some tropical paradise— that she'd stopped considering Brian as the man, the husband, he had been. If he were really here and if she got the chance to face him, what in God's name would she have to say?

The old hurt rippled through her like shock waves from a faraway explosion. Faraway, because she'd chosen to distance herself from the pain, to use whatever it took to get her to a place where she could survive. And if what it took was anger, so be it.

She climbed out of the car, her mind focused on only one thing: dragging that scheming bastard back to Clementine so she could have her life back. If she had to wrestle him into Carol's car and drive him all the way back, she would damned well do it.

Luke met her on the walkway and gestured for her to get back in the car. Eager to hear what he had to say, she lost no time in doing as he asked.

"Was he in there?" she blurted as soon as his car door closed.

Luke shook his head. "No, but his neighbor stuck her head out. Their doors are right next to each other, and she thought I was there for her. Or so she said. She's an older lady, uses an oxygen tank to breathe and probably doesn't get around well. So maybe she just wanted a little conversation."

"Did you ask about who lived there?"

"Would I miss a chance like that? I chatted her up a little to begin with, told her I was an old college friend of David Spencer's and I wanted to surprise him."

"What did she say?"

"At first, she seemed confused, and she started to tell me she'd never heard of him. Then, all of a sudden, something clicked in place. She looked upset, but I finally got her to tell me that Spencer never lived there, just his friend. But there was something in the way she said it, as if she meant *friend* some other way."

"A lover?" Susan guessed. This wasn't at all what she'd expected.

Luke nodded. "Could have been. Anyway, she said David Spencer was the name of Mr. Petit's friend, the one who'd died last year. Spencer didn't have any family, so Mr. Petit's handling his estate."

"But if Spencer's dead, why would this Petit guy ask you to send his check?"

Luke's breath fogged the windshield, so Susan started up the car for ventilation.

"Maybe," Luke said, "he can apply the money to any of Spencer's outstanding bills, since he's executor."

"Is he really? Didn't you tell me that Social Security doesn't have Spencer listed as dead?"

"That's a good point. Could be he's just greedy and he wants the money for himself. He might feel like he's entitled to it for some reason. People can be strange that way."

"So what's next?" she asked. "Did the neighbor tell you where we might find Petit?"

"She couldn't tell me where he works. Only that it has to do with the theater. Set design or something. I guess the guy's some sort of artist out of Atlanta or maybe Charleston, she wasn't sure which. After I get into a hotel room, I'll check theatrical companies' Web sites and see if I can find any mention of him."

"Do you want to find a room now, or did you have something else in mind?"

Luke pulled a PDA from his laptop case and looked up something on its small screen. "I have an address here—directions, too—to the hospice that supposedly took care of David Spencer. Want to see if we can find out anything there?"

"You're the navigator," she said. "Just point me in the right direction. But keep in mind, I need to get back in a couple of hours if I'm going to make my flight."

At Luke's prompting, they drove toward a location about two miles away. While they waited out a light, he said, "Why don't you call your airline and let them know your plans have changed? You can reschedule your return flight once we see where this thing with Petit leads."

"I'm worried, Luke. I'm scared it's all leading nowhere, that this is going to turn out to be nothing but a wild-goose chase. I mean, what could Brian have to do with some dead person who may or may not have been involved in a relationship with a San Francisco set designer and may or may not have died of AIDS . . ."

"Light's green, Susan," Luke said.

She didn't move until a couple of car horns behind her prompted her to push the accelerator. As soon as possible afterward, she swung the T-bird into a vacant space in front of a closed florist's shop. An oversized Ram pickup was parallel-parked several spaces back, but she paid it no heed.

"A year or two back—I don't remember when exactly—Brian and I saw this show on TV, one of the prime-time news magazines he liked," she said. "It was about these investors who were buying up life insurance policies of people who were dying, mostly men with AIDS. The investor gave the dying man a lump sum, let's say it was fifty cents on the dollar, so he could pay medical bills and take care of debts that would have to be assumed by his life partner or his family. Then later, when he died, the guy's life insurance payoff went to the investor."

"I remember hearing something about that. Sounds like sort of a sick way to make money, waiting around for your investments to die off."

"I thought so, too, but the thing was, Brian saw it differently. I remember him asking who it's hurting, since the dying guy needed the money while he was still alive."

"So what are you thinking?"

"I'm thinking maybe that show gave Brian an idea. And maybe there's a reason David Spencer isn't officially among the dead."

Comprehension dawned in Luke's expression. "Because Brian paid him off before he died—"

"And because Brian's using his identity to stay in the country undetected. And living off the bank accounts he set up in Spencer's name."

"It sounds . . . it sounds entirely possible," Luke admitted.

Susan nodded, her heart beating faster and faster as more pieces fell into place. "And it explains the mail I saw addressed to Brian's storage unit, too. If Brian was assuming someone's identity, it would make sense for him to check out the person's background to be sure he wasn't buying a criminal record. He might prefer, too, to find someone who was physically similar to him, so the guy wouldn't be listed in some government database as being of a different race from him, say, or twenty years older. And once he found the right person, he'd probably want to see if that name could get credit, too."

"If you ever want to come to work for me, I'd hire you in a minute. You have a great mind for computer forensics."

"I don't give a damn about tracking down your hackers and corporate saboteurs," she told him. "The only thing I care about is finding Brian Maddox and dragging his sorry ass to Texas—and to jail."

"Amen to that," Luke said. "We'll still check out the hospice, just in case there's something. But afterward, let's head for a hotel. Because if you're right—and I think you probably are—we won't find Brian by hassling Spencer's lover. We'll find him by following the money trail."

As Hector Abbott drove toward the Maddox ranch with the bad news, he still found it hard to believe that Susan had fooled him all these months. Between her pestering about the investigation and her Oscar-worthy portrayal of a wronged woman, he'd never in a hundred years have figured her for the murders.

Yet it wasn't only her behavior following her husband's and Jessica Beecher's disappearances that had convinced him of her innocence. He'd been hearing about Susan—and felt as if he'd known her personally—for years.

For one thing, in the days her mother had been waiting tables, she had spoken often of her daughters. Hector had spent a lot of mornings with Maggie Dalton, had eaten a lot of her boss's half-burnt breakfasts trying to get to know the woman better. Before he'd gotten so set in his ways, he'd often thought of asking her to see him outside of the coffee shop, but somehow, the timing had never seemed exactly right.

In more recent years, Hector had heard of Susan's work, too, especially what she'd done to turn around some of the roughest kids this county had to offer. She couldn't save the hard-core criminals, but he'd been impressed by the changes he'd witnessed in those who had teetered on the edge. He knew for a fact that she'd helped find college scholarships for at least a handful.

But she could have been a saint and it wouldn't have made one bit of difference. Because she'd clearly snapped, maybe when she'd learned her husband was about to run off with all the money he could steal. Or had she somehow learned that Jessica was carrying Brian's child? It hardly mattered how it had happened, only that she'd killed them and dumped the bodies out in Shotgun Canyon for the cougars and coyotes.

But the scavengers had left traces, the way they always did. They might have scattered bones and hair and scraps of desiccated flesh and clothing, but they'd left enough to make identifying the corpses a simple matter, the kind of formality fit for the county's half-blind coroner.

And they'd left behind enough of the larger, presumably male, head for one of Hector's deputies to find a woman's wedding band jammed halfway down its leathery throat.

The ring was a perfect match, right down to the three diamonds and the inscribed date, to the man's band the sheriff had locked inside his desk drawer only days before.

Chapter Sixteen

According to the notes pinned to the memorial quilt hanging outside of the bereavement center, David Spencer had been a good friend, a gentle lover, and a talented costume designer.

Susan's fingertips caressed the edges of a small photo of a painfully thin man in a wheelchair. His face was somewhat blurred; Luke thought it was because he had been laughing when the shot was taken. He found himself hoping it was true, that Spencer, though a stranger, had found something joyful in the last days of his life.

"I wonder if Brian feels strange about stealing this man's life," said Susan.

Along with the sadness in her voice, Luke heard fear as well. Was she afraid they wouldn't find her husband, or that he would pop up unexpectedly around some corner?

Shaking his head, he answered, "I doubt he's worrying about anything or anyone beyond himself. As usual."

Colleen Thompson

He wondered, though, if his brother now had a child to think of, too. He knew he should say something to prepare Susan for the possibility, knew she would be furious to think he had kept such a thing from her. So far, he'd excused his lapse by telling himself that Jessica Beecher's pregnancy had only been a rumor. But his mother's subdued reaction to that news still had him wondering. Had Brian confessed to her that Beecher's wife was carrying his child? Luke could easily imagine Brian blaming Susan for his missteps, convincing their mother he never would have cheated if he hadn't wanted children of his own so desperately. And it was no stretch to envision their mother swallowing his story in its entirety, with the painstaking precision of a snake unhinging its jaws to swallow an egg whole.

He would tell Susan today, he promised himself, as soon as they were somewhere private. When he touched her shoulder, she glanced at him, a question in her eyes.

"Later," he said as a grandmotherly woman bearing a remarkable resemblance to Barbara Bush approached them. Her name tag identified her as Irene Hildebrandt, and she introduced herself as the center's executive director.

When she offered them a tour and an overview of the hospice's services, Luke got the idea she'd pegged them as potential donors or maybe volunteers. She answered their questions about the center enthusiastically—until Luke brought up David Spencer's name.

"We were wondering," he said, "about the way he . . . about how he was able to afford care, at the end."

"You didn't really know him, did you?" she asked,

her expression hardening like concrete. "You're another of those hideous reporters."

"Reporters?" Susan asked. "What do you mean?"

"I *mean* Bruce Sayres from the *Village Underground*.
He thinks he's doing the gay community a favor, letting
them in on a new option. I've been trying to make him
understand that this center doesn't condone illegal
acts. Nor do we need the publicity. We're here to bring
dignity to the last days of the dying, not to act as a
clearinghouse for criminals in the market for a new
identity. Since he started his series, you wouldn't believe the calls I'm getting."

So Susan had been right, Luke thought, though he
cursed his clumsy handling of the Barbara Bush clone.

"We're not reporters," Susan said. "We're interested in
helping out a friend, seeing to it that he doesn't have to
leave his family burdened with—"

The administrator threw up both her hands. "Get
out, both of you, or I'm calling the police. I told you, I
won't be a party to this disgusting traffic."

With that, she turned on her heel and strode back
through the arched doorway that led to the back office. Luke heard her tell the help desk volunteer to dial
9-1-1 if they weren't gone in thirty seconds.

Outside in the car, Luke said to Susan, "For what it
was worth, I thought you were pretty handy yourself
with that quick lie."

Susan made a face. "Too bad I picked the wrong
one."

"At least we have some inkling you were on the right
track about the identity thing. That'll help us locate
Brian."

"We're close now, aren't we?" With that pronouncement, her mood appeared to shift abruptly. A grin replaced her strained expression, and hope shone in her eyes. "I can feel it."

He wanted to warn her not to expect too much too soon, but she'd had so little cause for enthusiasm, he couldn't bear to do it. He returned her smile instead. "It's starting to look like it."

"Could I borrow your cell phone? I'd better let Carol know I'm putting off my flight."

Luke handed it to her and waited. When her call to Carol's cell phone didn't go through, she left a message telling her sister she'd decided to postpone her return home and make a day of her shopping expedition.

Once she hung up, he asked, "So what are you going to say when you show up empty-handed?"

"I'll tell her I had the stuff shipped to Clementine so I wouldn't have to pack it. Sounds like the sort of thing she'd do. So where to next, a hotel?"

He winked at her. "I thought you'd never ask."

But inside, he wasn't smiling. Because in his room, he meant to spoil her good mood, for he'd have the privacy to tell her what he should have earlier.

He thought back to how helpless he'd felt that day on the telephone after her last miscarriage. This conversation, he was certain, would be harder still.

The idea had him so distracted that he never noticed the silver pickup in the rearview mirror, the same one that had followed them from the Pacific Heights town house.

Susan was relieved when Luke's attention went to the hotel room's data port instead of the massive king-sized bed. As his laptop booted and connected to the

Internet, however, she was troubled by the way his gaze kept finding hers, then sliding away.

Something was bothering him. Perhaps it was the setting, for the beautifully appointed room seemed better suited to honeymooners than a pair of . . . a pair of what? What was she to him, anyway, and what would she be once this was over? Something less than family, and something more than friend. Probably just a painful memory, the way he'd be for her.

In spite of the burst of optimism she'd felt only a few minutes before, her eyes teared at the thought of losing what she sensed growing between them: the chance of happiness.

What an idiot she was, to imagine anything beyond the possibility of day-to-day survival. Funny, how resilient hope was, how it kept slipping up on her like an oft-kicked dog that couldn't help circling back for one more beating.

Forget Luke. Think instead of going back to Clementine, of going back to teaching and coming home to Mom and Peavy at the end of every day. Those things could really happen, and they *would,* once she saw Brian safely behind bars.

"This connection's horrible." Luke squinted at the screen. "Just downloading my e-mail's taking an eternity. Glare's bad, too."

He turned to close a pair of heavy curtains. Instantly the room was cast in shadow, as if it were evening and not a sunny afternoon.

She turned on a bedside lamp. "Is there something else wrong? You seem preoccupied."

"I, uh, there's something we need to talk about," he said. "I'm just not sure—"

His cell phone rang. Picking it up off the desk where

he had laid it, Luke glanced at the screen, then lifted his index finger toward Susan to indicate that she should wait.

Susan frowned to see him step into the bathroom and close the door to take the call. Who was on the phone, that he didn't want her hearing? Some girlfriend she hadn't heard about, or was it his mother? She wasn't certain which thought bothered her more.

She wiped the moisture from her eyes and told herself it probably *was* some woman he'd been dating. Ignoring the little stab of jealousy that followed, she sat on the bed and pulled her plane ticket from her purse. She used the hotel's phone to call the airline's toll-free number to postpone her departure.

By the time she'd finished, Luke was emerging from the bathroom, his expression bleak.

"Is something wrong?" She knew she shouldn't ask, that a few ill-advised kisses gave her no right to pry. But she couldn't stop wondering if what he'd been about to say was related to the call. "If you're trying to tell me you're involved with someone—"

"Why would you think that?" He had started walking toward the desk, where he'd set the laptop, but he changed course and sat beside her on the bed. With nothing except the San Francisco yellow pages as a buffer.

Move, right now, she told herself as awareness set her skin to prickling. *Being this close is a bad idea.*

But she only cleared her throat. "Well, it stands to reason, doesn't it? For as long as I can remember, there's always been some woman chasing after you. Usually more than one."

His lips twitched in obvious amusement. "I learned my lesson back in high school: only one woman at a time. And yes, the person on the phone was female. But I'm not involved with her, at least not in the way you're thinking. You remember the associate I mentioned?"

"The one who's looking into David Spencer's finances?"

Once more, his mouth flattened into a grim line.

"She had bad news," Susan ventured.

"Of a sort. She couldn't go into any detail, not on a cellular connection. But there's something strange about those accounts she tracked down. Brian—or David Spencer—hasn't touched them since making the original deposits back in late November."

Her heartbeat quickened, and she dug her nails into her palm. "That just means she'll have to find the other money, right? The money from Hal's loans."

He shook his head. "That's harder than it sounds. There are lots of institutions out there, thousands. Realistically, there's no way to check everywhere he might have put the money. And that's assuming he's still in the country. If he's using an offshore account . . ."

Hope slunk away once more, its tail between its legs. "So you mean . . . you mean . . ." She turned her face from him, unwilling to let him see the fresh tears pricking like hot needles at her eyes. "I thought . . . I was so sure we would find him soon. I was *counting* on it."

"I'll keep looking, Susan. If it takes me twenty years, I'm going to get that bastard."

"I don't *have* twenty years. Can't you understand that? If I'm not ready for the school board, if I can't show some sort of proof—"

"Let's call Bruce Sayres," he said. "Maybe he knows something."

"Who?" She hated the way her voice shook, the way her hands were shaking.

"You remember. That reporter with the *Village Underground.*"

He was grasping at straws, she realized, trying anything to keep her from having a major meltdown. Brian would have done it differently, bitching at her for having what he called a "female moment," or, worse yet, trying to shame her out of it.

Luke wasn't Brian, thank God, but even so, she did feel shame. While he flipped through the phone book, she bent forward, resting her elbows on her knees and her forehead in her hands. As she struggled to regroup, she heard him dial and, after a brief pause, leave his name and cell-phone number, along with a short message asking Sayres to call him back.

There was nothing she could do to stop the tears from rolling down and dripping from her nose. This was all too *much*, the gnawing fear and desperate hope and endless, endless setbacks.

"I'm sorry," she told Luke. "I'll be all right in a minute."

He moved the phone book to the nightstand, then surprised her by reaching down and pulling off her shoes. Next, he lifted her feet onto the bed. She let him lay her down then, as if she were a child.

"It's fine," he told her, settling himself next to her. He was lying on his side now, close enough that his breath stirred her hair. "*You're* fine. And you should never apologize for being human."

Opening her eyes, she saw him looking at her, his face less than a foot away. She had the strongest urge to touch his lips, to feel what he was saying as well as hear it.

Go over to the window, the voice of reason whispered. *Peek through the curtains and say something nice about the view.* Three stories below, people would

234

be walking toward Fisherman's Wharf two blocks away: couples hand in hand, babies in their strollers, groups of singles out to ogle or be ogled.

She didn't move a muscle. "What were you going to tell me before that woman, your associate, called?"

His expression clouded for a moment; then he shook his head. "Nothing. It was nothing."

A lock of hair lay across her cheek, and he reached to tuck the strands behind her ear.

"My brother's a goddamned idiot," he told her. "I hope he rots in jail."

"You mean hell." She tried a smile. "Because that's where he's left me."

When he pulled her into his arms, she meant to resist. But the masculine scent of him, the solid weight and the strength that lay dormant in his muscles, bound and gagged her resolution.

Even so, she tried to ignore the warmth spreading through her. Tried to quiet her body's tingling awareness of the slow rhythm of his fingertips as they stroked her back.

"Then stop letting him define your life," he said. "Let me help you move on."

In the taut silence that stretched between them, Susan could swear she heard the crackling of a fuse. The tingling heated a place beneath her stomach, and she felt herself begin to melt like candle wax.

When his mouth dropped to take hers, she told herself, *One kiss*. Then she would stop the long, slow detonation that had already begun.

The explosion blossomed where their mouths merged, lips melding, tongues tasting with an unquenchable hunger. She pulled him closer so she could feel the muscles working in his back as he slid a hand beneath her sweater and cupped her throbbing breast.

Just this, she told herself, her will scrabbling for purchase. This and nothing more, because it felt so good, so completely right, a salve against all the frustration and the hurt.

When his hand slid beneath her to loosen the constriction of her bra, she tried to protest, but the only thing that came out was the low moan of her need. Then he was kissing her again, his stubbled cheeks rough against her neck, his lips and tongue hot against her ear. His fingertips toyed deftly with her nipples, and a jolt of pure pleasure arced downward, setting off a throbbing hunger.

"I need you, Susan. Need to taste you soon."

His words blew like a desert wind, spawning a damp, answering heat in the cleft between her legs—a heat that made her forget she'd ever known his brother.

Luke slid to his knees beside the bed and helped her pull off her sweater and bra. He gazed at the fullness of her breasts with a worshipful attention that made her burn for his touch.

"Oh, God," she whispered, her body trembling. She'd forgotten what it was to be looked at this way, had forgotten how it felt to see desire shining in his eyes.

"I have to see you first," he said as he undid the closure of her jeans. "Have to look at all of you."

She helped him remove her jeans. The panties remained, a thin, moist barricade of silky blue. He laid the heel of one hand on her hipbone and toyed with the elastic.

Her exhalation quivered, and she had to struggle

not to beg him to finish stripping her, though he remained completely clothed.

Instead, he climbed back on the bed again and started kissing her, kisses that soon slid from mouth to neck to breasts. His whiskers abraded hardened nipples, but before she could cry out, he soothed them with his tongue. All the while, his fingertips tormented, sliding over and around the edges of her panties, sometimes dipping cunningly beneath the lacy band.

Until he moved to pull it downward with his teeth. Once he had her naked, he began removing his own clothing. Slowly, purposefully, without ever taking his eyes off her body.

"My God, you're beautiful," he said, "even more beautiful than I remember."

"Funny." Her voice sounded strange and husky, even to her own ears. "I was thinking the same thing."

His body had lived up to its youthful promise, broadening through the shoulders, filling out long limbs with muscles that quivered in anticipation. A dusting of dark hair covered his chest, then gathered in a furrow that pointed toward his erection.

He sat beside her flexed knees, kissed them, then trailed more kisses up the insides of her thighs and to the core of her. Her body arched with the damp heat of his questing mouth, the impossible pleasure coiling deep inside her, increasing and increasing like a watch wound far too tight. When he thrust a finger deep inside her, her world suddenly splintered into shards of blinding light.

Her cry had not yet ended when he shifted position to drive high and hard inside her. When she could see again, his face came into focus, wild and exultant as he hovered over her. The pleasure built as their bodies took up a long-forgotten rhythm, but it was his kiss, so hot and feral and tasting of her passion, that threw them both over the final precipice.

As with every fatal fall, this felt like flying for a time.

Chapter Seventeen

They made love again that afternoon, neither of them daring to mention the future or the past. As if he understood that they had nothing but the present, Luke lingered over each caress and every kiss, each scent and sight and taste of her, until his body burned like liquid fire beneath the cell-thin surface of his skin.

It was not until afterward, when both were smiling and sated, that his exhaustion, along with the lingering effects of the tranquilizer he'd been given, finally caught up with him. With her head cradled on his shoulder and her arm draped across his chest, the only things keeping him awake were the words clamoring for release.

"You are an amazing woman," he said. "Do you have any idea?"

She responded with a murmur of contentment and a nuzzled kiss against his neck.

"I know the timing's rotten—hell, the timing's always been wrong for us, but it doesn't matter," he said. "I want you to know I love you. I've loved you for as long as I can remember. That's one of the reasons—the main reason—I had to hightail it out of West Texas after you and Brian married. I could never stand to watch . . ."

His words trailed off as he became aware that she was snoring softly. "A man works for sixteen years on a proper declaration, and you go and sleep through it."

Smiling, he kissed her temple, then drifted into a sleep so deep that some time later he didn't hear his phone ring.

Something—it was Susan—shook his shoulder. "That could be Sayres," she said.

At that moment, Luke didn't remember who Sayres *was*. He reached for her to pull her back against him, but she climbed over him and said, "I'll get it."

Already half asleep again, he let her.

He was out cold, never realizing what his mistake would cost him.

Smiling at Luke's sprawled form, Susan followed his earlier example by taking the telephone into the bathroom so she would not disturb him.

"Sayres here, from the *Underground*," the male caller said. "I'm calling for Luke Maddox."

She closed the door behind her. "He can't come to the phone now, but this is Susan Maddox. We were hoping we could meet with you—about that story you did on the purchase of identities."

Though his voice was clearly male, his laughter sounded feminine. "Can't help you make a connection, dear heart . . ."

Static overtook his words, and she said, "Hello?"

"Sorry. I'm in the car. I lost you for a sec. Listen, Miss Thing, even if I knew how to help people like yourself, the cops have been looking for a reason to bust our paper for an age. We're not about to hand them an excuse."

"Oh, no. It's not that." She spoke quickly, eager to convince him before he hung up on her—no matter that he *had* called her "Miss Thing.""I need some information from you about David Spencer."

"And I should help you with this *because* . . . ?"

She forced herself to ignore his sarcasm. "You should help me because I'm David Spencer's wife."

"Oh, sweetie. If you'd bothered to read the article, you'd know that Mr. Spencer was really G-A-Y."

She rolled her eyes at the sarcastic space between the letters. Jerk. "My husband's real name is Brian Maddox. But it seems he's living large as David Spencer now—on other people's money. A chunk of it is mine."

That merited a high-pitched "Oh" of surprise. In the background, she heard what sounded like a large truck rushing past his vehicle. "I'm still listening," he half sang.

Happy to have his attention, she said, "I thought you'd like to hear from one of the victims of your 'victimless' crime. And maybe help me flush the bastard out. He wasn't doing Spencer a favor. He was exploiting Spencer's good name, credit history, all that. Maybe you'd like to do a follow-up story?"

"I'd be *very* interested in seeing you, Ms. Maddox. Just tell me when and where."

"I can meet you in the Fisherman's Wharf area in half an hour. You name the place."

He chose a dockside restaurant she'd seen advertised, famous for its seafood stews, served with sourdough bread baked on the premises.

"Can you give me the address?" she asked, despite her lifelong aversion to both the smell and taste of fish.

His next words were lost in static, but this time he didn't come back on the line. As soon as she broke the connection, the cell phone rang again. Certain that Sayres was calling back, she didn't bother looking at the screen for the ID.

"Susan?" The single word was deeply feminine—and just as deeply shocked.

Susan's heart sank. Virginia Maddox's voice—or at least the fury in it—was instantly recognizable. "Oh . . . hello."

"My God," her mother-in-law said. "How could you?"

When Susan glanced in the mirror and caught sight of the whisker burns marking her neck and breasts, a denial died on her lips. "Would you . . . would you like to speak to Luke?" she asked lamely.

"I swear to you," Virginia hissed, "I'll pull in every favor owed this family, every string I can grasp, to make sure you pay for what you've done. I'll see you dead for it."

Shock reverberated through Susan's system, and her heart thudded at the pure vitriol—and rising hysteria—in her mother-in-law's voice. Certainly the woman had disliked her before, even blamed her unfairly after Brian's disappearance, but now Virginia sounded as if she'd like to pour herself into the phone line and slash Susan's throat in person.

"What's happened?" Susan managed. Surely Virginia understood that her sons were both grown men, more than capable of making their own decisions.

Her mother-in-law went on as if she hadn't heard. "You couldn't stand it that Jessica was giving him a child, could you? You didn't want children of your own, or maybe you'd decided you weren't capable of having any, but when Brian had a chance of happiness—"

"Jessica was *pregnant*?" Susan braced herself against the counter, so strong was the wave of dizziness and nausea that washed over her. "Jessica was carrying Br-Brian's baby?"

"Don't pretend you didn't find out. That was what set you off, wasn't it, why you had to—"

"I don't know what you're talking about, but if you're blaming me because your son—my husband—knocked up another man's wife, you need to stop by my classroom for some basic lessons in biology."

"What choice did you leave him? You betrayed him by going on the pill behind his back. I told Luke how it hurt your brother, how that was surely the reason he turned to Mrs. Beecher."

"So Luke knew," Susan said flatly. "He knew Jessica was pregnant."

"Everyone knows," his mother shot back, "Luke included. But now, there'll never be a child because of you, you . . . you horr-horrible—"

Her words splintered into fractured sobs, frightening in their intensity.

Her fingers shaking, Susan randomly punched buttons until she broke the connection. Slamming the phone down on the counter, she turned and vomited into the sink, her hand sweeping her hair back from her face.

As she rinsed her mouth and the basin, she tried to tell herself it wasn't true, tried to convince herself her mother-in-law had merely lied to hurt her. But the idea wouldn't fly. For one thing, Virginia would surely find the idea of a Maddox bastard too distasteful to invent, especially since it would further tarnish her precious firstborn's reputation. But what convinced Susan completely was the way the words resonated with her memories of the last few arguments she'd had with Brian—over her unwillingness to jump back into another pregnancy after her last miscarriage.

Now she believed utterly that Jessica had been pregnant when she'd disappeared. Pregnant with Brian's child. A child that, unlike those Susan had carried, was likely to be born. *Had* been born by now, assuredly.

She retched again to imagine such a topic bandied about in Ocotillo County circles, spread to every living soul except Hal Beecher and herself and perhaps her mother. No one would risk telling a woman already recovering from one stroke.

Everyone knows, Virginia had said. *Luke included.*

Susan wondered how long he had known and why, why, *why* he hadn't seen fit to share the truth with her.

As quickly as possible, she washed up and dressed. After another glance in the bathroom mirror, she dragged a comb through her tangled hair, then applied a little lipstick to counteract her sudden pallor. Not that she gave a damn what Sayres thought of her appearance, but she didn't want to frighten him off.

Striding through the bedroom, she didn't even spare Luke one last look. As she left, however, she slammed the door behind her hard enough to wake the dead.

Luke jumped at the sound, imagining his house had been struck by a lightning bolt from one of the thunderstorms that periodically ripped through Central Texas. It took him only a split second to realize he was far from Austin.

A moment later he remembered where he was . . . and what he had done with Susan. He couldn't help smiling.

"Drop something?" he called toward the open bathroom door. He couldn't see inside, but the light was on.

When Susan didn't answer, his smile faded, and worry replaced the plot he'd been hatching to lure her back to bed. Rising in an instant, he went to check.

"Susan?" But she wasn't there.

He couldn't find her clothing either, so he decided she must have gone for ice and accidentally slammed the door behind her. Until he spotted the empty bucket on the dresser.

Alarmed, he realized that her purse was missing, too. Rushing to the window, he was just in time to see the mint-green T-bird tear around a corner, its tires squealing as it passed a silver Ram truck parked along the street.

What the hell?

His cell phone rang, triggering a memory. It had rung before, while he'd been asleep. Susan had told him she would get it.

He answered, "Maddox here."

"Luke Maddox?" the male caller asked. "Is Susan still there? I wanted to make sure she had the directions straight. This is Bruce Sayres—I tried to call back after we were disconnected, but your number was busy."

"Let me jot down those directions," Luke said as he switched on a light. "She can't get to the phone right now."

As soon as Sayres gave the name and address of the restaurant, Luke said, "I'll find it. We'll be there shortly."

When Sayres hung up, Luke went to the phone's call log. Who else had spoken to Susan, and what had the caller told her that prompted her to leave without a word?

He groaned aloud at the sight of his mother's number. He could only imagine what she'd said when Susan had picked up instead of him. But he couldn't fathom that a tongue-lashing—no matter how ugly— would send her fleeing in such haste. After what the two of them had shared today, the connection they'd reforged, wouldn't she simply sit down and discuss it with him?

Unless . . . What if his mother had been so upset by what she would surely—and correctly—have perceived as an affair that she'd bludgeoned Susan with the one piece of information she'd held back, the news of Jessica Beecher's pregnancy? Even worse, what if his mother had told Susan *he* had known? In a twisted way, it made sense. His mother wanted desperately to drive a wedge between the two of them, and whatever scruples she might have had about disclosing such a hurtful secret would have dissolved in a red haze at the sound of Susan's voice.

In record time, Luke dressed and shoved his feet into his shoes. Grabbing the room key and his cell phone, he ran for the stairs, for he had no intention of waiting for the elevator.

In the hope that the busy tourist area would have plenty of taxis, he blew through the lobby door and tried to catch one. The first two cabbies shot him an appraising look, then veered around and sped away. Swearing under his breath, Luke finger-combed his hair and tried to calm himself by dragging in deep breaths. No one would stop for him if he looked like a man fleeing the scene of a violent crime.

Yet he felt almost as desperate, for the thought of Susan suffering made him wild to get to her. He was furious with his mother, too, but catching up with Susan was his first priority.

He'd decided to forget the cab and head for the restaurant on foot when a beat-up taxi, painted a startling shade of purple, stopped. As he climbed into the backseat, the driver pulled off his earphones and grinned at him, displaying gold-capped teeth and Rasta braids, an unlikely combination in a green-eyed, blond, white guy.

"Where to, mahn?" he asked in a Caribbean accent that sounded as real as the dusting of freckles on his face.

When Luke named the restaurant, the driver nodded and sped off, then replaced the earphones on his head. His head and upper body jerked in rhythm to the music Luke could just make out.

Unfortunately, the Wharf was especially crowded and they had to sit in traffic. Luke used the delay to phone his mother.

As soon as she picked up, he demanded, "Did you tell Susan about Jessica? Did you tell her I knew?"

His mother's weeping spun him into confusion. He'd expected anger, even threats, but tears were so out of character, he didn't know how to respond.

"He . . . he's dead," she sobbed. "All this time, dead. They haven't . . . they haven't officially identi-identified the body yet, but I *know* it's him. There was another one, too. They think it was a woman."

"Wait," said Luke, trying to make sense of what she was telling him. "Do you mean Brian? And Jessica Beecher?"

"Hec-Hector Abbott found the bodies in that . . . that canyon by the park, the one where Susan told them she'd gone hiking. Don't you see? She killed your brother! That horrible, horrible woman murdered both of them."

The shock of her words vibrated through him, worsened by their sheer impossibility. He wanted to explain that Brian couldn't be dead, that he and Susan had just linked him to another identity in San Francisco, along with money he and Jessica could live on for a long, long time.

Except his brother hadn't touched that money, had he? Wasn't that what Sibyl had said?

Was it because Brian and Jessica had been killed before they'd had the chance to vanish? Killed by—

He wouldn't believe it had been Susan.

"There's no way she could have done it," he told his weeping mother.

But she only answered, "Please come home, Luke. Come home *now*."

Chapter Eighteen

If she hadn't been driving like an idiot, Susan might have noticed the huge pickup following in her wake. As distracted as she was, she didn't give the truck a second thought until she heard a squeal of brakes behind her. Glancing in her rearview mirror, she saw that the truck had run a red light and cut off a purple taxi, but was picking up speed again.

Recognition penetrated the fog that had settled over her mind. She'd seen that silver truck before, earlier today. Seen it following her and Luke as they had left the hospice center.

Her heartbeat pounding and her mouth dust-dry, she made several quick turns in succession. Her route took her into an area off the tourist track, where she saw only warehouses and a few delivery trucks—and the enormous pickup, gaining on her in the mirror.

She might not have lost her pursuer, but she'd succeeded in disorienting herself. She turned her head, desperate to find her way out of this thinly peopled area. When she caught a glimpse of blue, she hung a left, which put the bay back on her right. If she kept driving in this direction, she thought she'd run back into the Fisherman's Wharf area. Surely she'd be safe there, with all those pedestrians milling about—and the officers that regularly patrolled the area.

A light changed ahead of her, and several cars and trucks stopped. Boxed in, she slowed to do the same, then watched the truck pull into the lane at her left. As it crept up beside her, someone rolled down the passenger-side window and motioned for her to put down hers. From her low-slung vantage, she couldn't see the person's face, couldn't make out anything except a decidedly male hand, its knuckles sprinkled with dark hairs.

The disembodied fingers flipped open a small leather wallet, and a silver badge winked in the afternoon light.

Despite the fact that she was probably about to get half a dozen tickets for the traffic laws she'd broken, Susan felt hot relief flood through her limbs. She would gladly accept the fines, her sister's scolding for misusing her "fun" car—*anything* except the panicked certainty that trouble had followed her here from Ocotillo County. And once the officer finished handing out citations, she promised herself she would drive straight back to see Luke. Instead of blasting off like a maniac, as she had before, she was going to take a deep breath and ask him why he hadn't talked to her about the rumors. She hoped for his sake he had a damned good explanation.

The officer waved her into an empty parking lot near a warehouse built on a wide concrete pier. Probably some sort of shipping concern that had gone belly-up, judging from the realty sign on the building's side.

Still almost giddy with relief, she grinned up toward the officer. "You scared me half to death. I was sure you were a—"

She stopped dead, recognizing the scarred face in the truck's window at the same instant she registered the pistol in his hand. It was Manuel Ramirez—both out of uniform and one hell of a long way out of his jurisdiction.

She didn't take her eyes off him. But her hand groped for the gearshift, and her right foot stamped down hard.

The cabdriver had long since pulled off his earphones, but they dangled from his head still, caught on a wheat-gold braid.

"Your lady friend," he said to Luke; "she in some kind of hurry."

"That truck's tailing her," Luke answered.

"An' now we tail that truck." The taxi blew through a yellow light, its loose-sprung body nearly taking flight as a tire caught a curb.

While Luke slammed hard against the side of the backseat, the cabbie laughed like a maniac. "Next time you buckle up, mahn."

Luke paid him no heed, for his attention was completely focused on the truck's passenger, who had just stuck something out his window as his and Susan's vehicles were stopped at another light.

After putting on her indicator signal, Susan turned right into a bayside warehouse parking lot. The oversized pickup followed closely before pulling up beside her.

"I think your lady got cop troubles," the driver told him as he pulled up to the curve. "I don't want no part of that."

Probably not, thought Luke, considering his driving these past few minutes. After thrusting two twenties into the man's hand, Luke climbed out . . .

In time to see the Thunderbird speed away from the pickup and race along the water's edge.

Immediately the driver threw the truck in gear and roared after her, turning its wheels in an attempt to cut her off. Susan, Luke could see, was going to try to shoot in front of it, to zip past and then head for the street.

She never made it.

The pickup caught the edge of the front bumper and struck the left front end hard, deflecting the small car's forward movement—sending it rocketing over the pier's edge and into the bay six feet below.

The impact drove the breath from her lungs and made her world explode into a silvery-white haze.

She had no idea how long she sat there, dazed, before she realized the air bags had deployed, covering her with fine white powder that stung her eyes and made her cough. The sack softened slowly, as if the air were leaking from it.

Trying to see past the dust and the deflating air bags, she felt the car shifting. Cold water began pouring through the open window.

She had to get out of there. Her first impulse, to throw open the door, proved fruitless. She fought to climb out the window, but something held her back.

The seat belt. Desperately she fumbled with it as the water level in the car approached her waist.

She shrieked with the realization she couldn't make the thing release. Struggling, she tried to tear it off—until she heard a voice, as clear as if it came from the seat beside her.

Calm. Down. Now. You can't afford to panic.

Luke's voice, she realized, tears flooding her eyes. Pissed as she'd been that he hadn't told her about Jessica, Susan was struck by the fact that her mind had conjured him.

Because she loved him.

Whether he was real or imagined, his *advice*, at least, was solid. She took a deep breath to steady herself, then slowly and deliberately unbuckled her seat belt.

A fraction of a second late, for the car suddenly nosed deep and glided like a dolphin beneath the murky water.

Luke heard tires squealing in the street behind him, heard someone shouting, "My God, call nine-one-one!"

But he was running too fast to do it himself. Racing toward the spot where Susan's car had flown over the pier's edge, he was terrified that if his attention faltered for a moment—whether to glance down at his cell phone or look to see which way the silver pickup truck had gone—he would lose track of the place he'd heard the splash.

Panting with effort, he reached the edge, just in time to see the Thunderbird tip forward and begin its plunge. In the second before the hardtop roof disappeared beneath the surface, he thought he made out movement inside the window.

She had survived the crash, then—or at least he prayed that was the meaning of what he'd seen. Kicking off his shoes, he heard a man behind him shouting, "Don't go in—it's dangerous. Wait for the rescuers. They'll be here any minute."

In time to pull her body free, but not the living woman. Luke understood this as surely as he knew he didn't want to face a life without her.

So he made a shallow dive—into water so damned cold it tore his breath away.

Susan had time to suck in a lungful of air before she was submerged completely. Which left her only a minute, maybe a couple, to get herself out of the car.

She felt the passing seconds, felt them fleeing with the panicked pounding of her heart. Felt—thank God—the car's nose bump the bottom, leaving her to hope the water wasn't all that deep.

Not that that would matter if she couldn't get out. Blind in the murky water, she struggled to pull her heels onto the seat's edge, to try to get leverage to push herself free of the half-deflated air bag and the steering wheel.

Though she no longer had to fight the cascade pouring through the open window, there was no way she would be able to push herself out that way. The cramped confines of the sports-car cabin and her own long legs made it impossible.

She tried the driver's-side door again, but something—either the weight of water or damage from the accident—left it frozen stubbornly in place. Even if there was a way to get the removable hard top off from inside the convertible, she'd never be able to figure it out in time.

In time . . . in time . . . in time. The refrain echoed in the thunder of her pulse, the aching pressure in her lungs. There had to be some way out.

Feeling her back wrench with the contortion, she shoved her way over the center console, then past the deflated passenger's-side air bag—and was shocked when she felt the top of her head break though what felt like the water's surface.

An air pocket. Tilting back her head instinctively, she pushed her mouth toward blessed oxygen and released the stale air in her lungs.

The trapped bubble of air was barely large enough for her to snatch a few more breaths, but finding it gave her the strength to try the passenger-side door.

Please, God, please, her mind screamed, while in the background, something whispered, *No atheists in submerged cars either, are there?*

The door swung open, her own private miracle, and she pushed herself free from the car. Or almost free, for she jerked to a stop as her right leg tangled in something—the passenger-side seat belt?

Startled, she sucked in saltwater—water that sent her lungs into shocked spasms.

A child of the desert, she was going to drown. The irony mocked her, along with the realization that she would never have a chance to tell Luke that she understood why he'd kept silent about Jessica Beecher's pregnancy.

It's because he loves you. He's loved you all along.

The dimness grew even darker as something blotted out the weak light from above. Something that disentangled her from the seat belt and dragged her higher, higher, toward the sun's glow . . . and every possibility she had just dismissed.

Chapter Nineteen

Though two days had passed since he'd pulled her limp body from the bay, Luke still couldn't take his eyes off of her. Some part of him was afraid he'd dreamed the aftermath, that if he looked away even for a second, the mirage she was would vanish. That she had truly died that nightmare afternoon.

"It *was* Manuel Ramirez," Susan repeated, as she had told the detectives time and time again. "His scar looked . . . it looked angry, red around the edges, maybe because his face was flushed."

He must have been excited at the prospect of killing her. Luke shuddered, though moments before, he'd thought the plane too warm for comfort. He prayed the California Highway Patrol would find the pickup, which turned out to be a stolen vehicle when the officers traced the license number a witness had reported. He prayed, too, that Manuel and the driver would be in it, that both of them would be arrested soon—or maybe shot trying to escape. He could live without ever knowing why Manuel had meant to kill her, could swallow all his questions if that was what it took to keep her safe.

"How're you feeling?" he asked, focusing on the raw abrasion on her cheekbone from the air bag. She should have spent another day in the hospital, no matter what the insurance company's guidelines or the doctors said. He'd offered to pay for it himself, but once he'd told Susan that bodies had been recovered, she'd been hell-bent on getting back to Ocotillo County.

"My back and face are both a little sore, but otherwise I'm fine. Just the way I was when you asked five minutes ago."

Her patience was wearing thin; he knew that. Still, he couldn't help himself. "You should take another muscle relaxer or a pain pill or maybe put some more ointment on those scrapes."

She pressed her lips together until the color bled out of them. Another image overlaid what he was seeing: that same face, only stark white; those same lips, only blue. He felt the bottom drop out of his stomach at the memory.

She took his hand in hers and squeezed it. Through her bones, he felt the deep thrum of the jet's engines. "You're going to have to stop this."

"Stop what?" he asked, though he knew very well.

"The hovering and staring. First of all, you're starting to seriously creep me out. I can hardly sneak off for a pee without you—"

"You're not the one who had to watch it," he erupted. "Not the one who had to see it happening without being able to do a damn thing to stop it."

Her brows rose. "No, I had to *live* it, Luke, and you did do something. You kept me from drowning. You stayed with me in the ambulance and the ER. And you stopped Carol from finishing what Manuel started when she found out about her car."

He knew Susan wasn't serious about her sister, but he couldn't help being contrary. "Carol was just grateful you weren't hurt worse. Or killed."

That was what she'd *said,* at any rate. *It's only a car,* she'd told them. *We have plenty of insurance.*

Yet there had been an unmistakable subtext, the intimation that Susan had brought her distasteful problems to California to soil Carol's pristine life and further compromise their mother's health. As if anyone could have predicted that Manuel Ramirez—and probably his half brother, Lupe, too, from the witness's description—would follow Susan here and try to kill her.

"Even if they do catch Manuel," Susan said, "the sheriff and the others will be watching us. No matter who those bodies turn out to be, we'll need to be careful."

In spite of both the detectives' and the doctors' advice, Susan had been eager—almost frantic—to return home. Yet she refused to entertain, even for a moment, the idea that Brian and Jessica had been dead for all these months. Luke understood that she'd constructed a scenario she could live with, a way she could feel about Brian's treachery. It wouldn't fit with the idea that he'd been murdered, that he might have become, at least in part, a victim.

For now, Luke didn't force the possibility on her. If it were true, if Brian and Jessica were both dead, she'd have time enough to face it as she could.

"Do you think she's had that baby yet?" asked Susan. "The one you decided not to mention?"

Luke winced at the confirmation that, as he had feared, his mother had bludgeoned Susan with the

Colleen Thompson

hardest club at her disposal. "I didn't hear it 'til a couple of days before we left. But there were lots of rumors. That one might not be true."

"It will be. He did it on purpose, to pay me back for going on the pill."

He took her hand and squeezed it. "You changed your mind after the last miscarriage, about having a child?"

"I changed my mind," she said, "not about kids but about having one with *him*. At first, I didn't know if I could take another disappointment so soon. I'd really had my hopes up. I—I felt that baby move inside me, fluttering like moth's wings. I carried her that long."

Her nose reddened, and she reached for a tissue from her purse. "I tried to explain to Brian, but he didn't—he simply *wouldn't*—understand, especially after the doctor told us there was a new medication that would probably allow me to carry to term. And then my mother had her stroke. But even before, there were things we needed to work out in the marriage, things that needed fixing before a baby came along."

"You don't have to tell me," Luke said, but she went on as if she hadn't heard him.

"I asked him—begged him, really—to come with me to counseling, but he blew off all the appointments. He kept saying it was just my hormones fluctuating and I was making too big a deal about the . . . about losing the . . . He seemed to think that pregnancy was like one of the horses. If you were thrown, you had to climb right back up into the saddle."

Luke frowned. "I don't think it was ever about children, just control. He's always been like that. I've never understood it. But then, I've given up trying to comprehend why he would throw away a life a lot of men

260

would kill for. Why he'd throw away a woman I'd give everything I've ever had to—"

"Stop it, Luke. Just stop." She jerked her hand away as one of the flight attendants stopped his cart beside them. Susan took bottled water while Luke asked for Dr Pepper, though something harder sounded tempting. Unlike Susan, he couldn't escape the thought that his brother had been lying in a remote canyon all these months with the scavengers tearing at his carcass, that he'd been furious all these months with a dead man.

The brother he'd grown up with, who shared his memories. The brother he had cursed so often over these past months. The brother he'd betrayed when he had seduced Susan . . .

The very woman his mother was so certain had killed Brian.

Guilt welled at the thought, like blood in a fresh wound. Even though Luke still couldn't buy his mother's theory. For starters, why would Susan have come to him in secret with such a desperate desire to find Brian if she'd known him to be dead? For another thing, Luke's gut told him she was no actress; every ounce of anger and frustration he'd seen in her rang true. She wanted Brian brought to justice far too fervently for Luke to believe she'd already dealt out her own brand. Besides, his heart told him she wasn't capable of such a thing, no matter how his brother had hurt her, no matter what he'd done.

"I still can't make sense of it," said Susan. "Why would Ramirez come to California after me?"

Luke shook his head. They'd rehashed this topic a dozen times, but neither of them had come any closer to an answer. "All I can think is that he wanted to stop you from tracing Brian for some reason."

"What if Brian paid him to keep anyone off his track? Or maybe Brian's still paying him now."

"I suppose it's possible, but I can't believe he'd risk his career and prison over a little payola. What if"—Luke hated bringing this up, but the idea wouldn't go away—"what if Manuel killed Brian, maybe for the money we haven't been able to trace? Since he's probably the one who stole the mail from your Jeep, he could have figured you were getting too close to the truth."

She shook her head. "Brian isn't dead. He can't be. What about the witness who saw him and Jessica at that gas station in New Mexico?"

"Eyewitnesses are wrong sometimes. The man could have seen another couple, or he could have made up the whole thing for attention. Ask any cop; it happens all the time."

"So explain the tape, then," Susan challenged. "Jessica called her house and left a message on her answering machine. Have you heard it? She was saying good-bye and she was sorry—and the time and date on the machine said it was left the day after Brian's car was found burnt."

"Those machines' dates and times can get messed up," Luke explained. "Mine has to be reset after every power outage. Or they can be faked, I would imagine."

"You're wrong," she snapped, clearly not appreciating his contradiction, "and this seat's killing my back. As soon as that cart's out of the way, I'm going to walk up and down the aisle a couple of times."

When she did, he moved to the aisle seat so he could keep an eye on her. He knew Manuel Ramirez and Lupe weren't aboard—he'd assured himself of that before the plane took off. Still, if Luke had his way, he'd never let her out of his sight again.

And he didn't, until that choice was taken from him later on that very day.

Sheriff Hector Abbott waited in his car along the ranch road leading from the interstate to Clementine. He'd been sitting there for hours, arrest warrant in hand, ever since an old buddy of his with the El Paso P.D. had called to tell him that Susan Maddox's red Jeep had left the airport parking lot.

The call had been strictly unofficial, for Hector had given other law-enforcement agencies a wide berth. As far as he was concerned, it made sense, for doing it his way, not only would justice be served in the matter of two murders, but the Ocotillo County taxpayers would keep an experienced sheriff on the job.

He scrubbed at his mustache and thought how that might not happen if the Texas Rangers, the FBI, or even the California authorities became involved. Sure as shit, the FBI and Rangers would start digging into Ramirez's involvement, then focus more on "ir- regularities" in his office than on the murders. The San Francisco detectives, on the other hand, would be concerned only with getting to the bottom of the crime that took place within their jurisdiction, whether or not Susan's near-miss had anything to do with her misdeeds.

Hector couldn't afford to take the focus off those killings, couldn't afford to leave his constituents to wonder how one small community could have three unsolved murders. Not that anyone gave a damn about an aging hippie with a criminal record, but when the news broke—as it would within a day—that the bodies found in Shotgun Canyon had been identified as those of a former football star turned auto dealer and the wife of the county's most prominent banker, folks would demand a quick arrest. Even if the charges didn't stick—and despite his own certainty, he'd need either stronger evidence or an out-and-out confession to avoid that possibility—the public would blame the DA and the courts instead of him.

Unless the citizens were treated to a drawn-out investigation into the actions of a deputy-turned-vigilante. That was the best explanation Hector had come up with for the man's behavior. From the start, Ramirez had been vocal about his suspicions.

"You honestly believe that this woman with the sick mama and the missing husband would all of a sudden decide to drive out to the armpit of the county for a little quiet time with nature? It's a bullshit story. Bullshit."

The rookie, Lopez, saw it differently. As a high-school junior, he'd been one of Susan's students when she'd been new to the classroom. *"Of course she'd go there when things got tough,"* he'd argued. *"If you knew her, it would make perfect sense."*

But her impromptu trip made even more sense if she'd been getting rid of bodies. Weird that she'd commemorate the event by taking pictures, but criminals so often did strange things. Hector had long since given up on trying to make sense of most of them.

One thing was for damned sure. He'd never understand what had driven the hardworking, if temperamental, Ramirez to take the law into his own hands. Was he simply frustrated by a criminal justice system that freed as many criminals as it punished, or did he have something personal against Susan? Possible, he thought. She was a fine-looking specimen, and Grace Morton wasn't the only married woman whose skirts Manuel had sniffed.

The more he thought on it, the more Hector figured some kind of obsession was in play. Why else would Ramirez steal the evidence from her home? Why else would he—if what that detective from San Francisco told him was the case—chase Susan all the way to California and steal a truck, then knock her in the bay?

Hector hoped like hell that instead of getting his ass busted on the West Coast, Ramirez and his trouble-making half brother would quietly disappear. Lupe, it was said, had connections down in Juarez. Maybe the two of them would head across the border for a while. Then Hector could quietly fire his AWOL deputy and no one around here would have to know anything more.

And Hector wouldn't have to arrest the brothers for breaking into Susan's house, as he was now certain they had done. On a hunch, he'd pulled out Manuel's employment record and compared his prints to those found on Susan's filing cabinet, her CD cases, and the office closet door. Hector was no expert, but a few minutes with a magnifying glass convinced him Manuel had come back after his earlier, official visit. Surprisingly, none of the prints matched Lupe's, but with his B&E record, he'd probably had the good sense to wear gloves.

Hector put down the lukewarm dregs of the Coke he'd been sipping and watched the tiny red dot that had crested the hill. His heart galloping under the combined assault of caffeine and anticipation, he waited until he could be sure that it was her Jeep, waited until she passed him.

Though she was talking to a passenger, she glanced toward Hector, then rippled her fingers in a friendly wave.

Ignoring the uncomfortable feeling the gesture gave him, Hector flipped on his lights and siren and pulled out behind her. No matter how he felt about the woman, it was time to bring in a murderer.

Single-handedly, of course, because that would look even better in the paper.

Chapter Twenty

They'd given Susan her own cell at the old stone jail-house, isolated from the other two women in custody: a hot-check writer and a prostitute, both frequent guests of Ocotillo County.

Because a murderess is worse, thought Susan. *Because they think a murderess might hurt those other women.*

From the interview that night to the arraignment the next morning, this was almost the only coherent thought she'd had, that they'd decided she was not only a criminal, but one of the very worst.

Were they right?

"You're under arrest," Hector Abbott had said in his official voice, *"for the murders of Brian Maddox and Jessica Beecher."*

She wound her arms around her middle and began to tremble, as she had off and on throughout the night. Hadn't she murdered both of them a thousand times inside her mind? She'd made an effigy of Brian, one she'd burned and cut and stuck with pins until he bristled like a porcupine. She'd turned Jessica into a paper doll, one she'd crumpled up or torn or shredded for her part in the plot.

While they'd been dead the whole while, lying in a canyon where Susan loved to hike.

Hands trembling like a drunkard's, she asked herself, had she walked by them that day in December? Had her camera focused on the walls that loomed above their makeshift grave? Or had she passed some scavenger feeding on the bodies—or even the killer on his way out of the park?

She couldn't remember any of it, couldn't recall a thing except her grief and fury after she returned home and learned that Brian had not been alone. She'd been so upset, so damned near torn wide open, she hadn't trusted herself to sit beside her mother's hospital bed without wailing, and the idea of sitting around her house, *Brian's* house, had been unthinkable. She'd taken an emergency leave of absence after her husband's disappearance, so she hadn't even had the comfort of her school routine.

If coherent thought was difficult inside her cell, sleep was impossible, so hour after hour she sat on the rough bench, her back braced against the cool, uneven stones. Occasionally she picked a stray hair or imaginary lint from the simple white uniform they'd given her, or sniffed at the rank blend of musty basement, ancient sweat, and institutional disinfectant. But mostly she stared down the empty corridor, her mind struggling to make sense of a view sliced into vertical strips by iron bars.

Better get used to it, her mind warned. *This is all you'll be seeing for a long, long time.*

From somewhere unseen, she heard the sound of a

door with hinges in need of greasing, then the echoing tap of hard soles on a concrete floor. A busty young woman in a brown uniform walked into view with a brisk, aggressive stride. A fried-looking platinum curl dangled from her tightly clipped hair but failed to soften the square jaw. Her plump cheeks, bright with blush, and the blue slicks of eye makeup were the only spots of color Susan had seen in hours. She found herself staring at them instead of paying attention to what the guard was saying.

"Attorney's here. Come see'm." Despite the dark roots visible along her hair's part, she was good-looking in a tough way, the kind of female who invariably attracted the wrong sort of man.

When Susan failed to react, the guard dragged some kind of short club along the bars. Susan put her hands over her ears to block the harsh, metallic sounds. Still, she heard the next terse order.

"Up and out, or we'll send his ass straight back to Austin."

Austin? That made no sense. Her public defender, Dan Ryder, was as local as he was uninterested in hearing what Susan had to say.

Still, she unfolded her stiff limbs to stand, mostly to keep the guard from making any more loud noises. But as she started down the corridor, she began to wonder, had someone called her family in spite of her request to leave them out of this, and were they wasting money on an expensive criminal defense?

"Suicide watch, my ass," the guard muttered. "Stone-cold killer's more like it."

Susan blinked at her. Was that how they saw her, because she hadn't broken down? Did they think she was some kind of merry widow, off vacationing with her lover while her husband and his paramour lay rotting in a canyon?

"It wasn't like that," she tried to explain, forgetting Ryder's bored advice to watch what she said here. She stopped walking, whirling toward the guard as if her understanding was the only thing that mattered. Glancing at her name tag, Susan said, "I didn't kill them, Ms. Morton."

The guard wasn't nearly as tall as Susan, but that didn't stop her from grabbing her prisoner by the arm and digging her fingers in with bruising force. "Don't recognize me, do you? You don't know who you're fuckin' with, *Miz* Maddox."

Her words had a sneering quality that gave Susan her first inkling. Even under better circumstances, she would not have known the woman otherwise. The younger version, the one who had twice failed basic science, had been a chunky girl with mouse-brown hair and the meanest mouth at the consolidated high school. Though boys had whispered even then that she was an easy lay, she'd clearly set out to enhance the total package with store-bought blond and whatever antigravity device she was using to push up her breasts.

"Grace Cato, right?" asked Susan, thinking how it figured she'd found the young woman here, inside a cage. The only wonder of it was that it was Grace, and not she, who could leave at will.

"Grace Morton now," the guard corrected, a venomous smile spreading across her face. Clearly, she was pleased that her younger self had made an impression. "Tables have turned now, haven't they?"

Susan knew better, but she was too exhausted, too

emotionally scraped raw, to keep her mouth shut. "So you're assigning homework these days?"

"Shut the fuck up." Grace chuffed an ugly laugh. "You don't know how long I been waitin' to say that. Since you made me do summer school, at least. You know I graduated two months behind my class? Because of *you*, bitch. You."

Susan remembered Grace's failure to turn in assignments, show up for classes, or come in for the extra help she'd been offered.

Susan glanced at her, trying to judge whether it was safe to resume walking.

"Did I fuckin' tell you you could look at me?" Grace clamped a hand behind Susan's neck. "Did I tell you you could stare?"

Susan froze, more confused than frightened. Though she hadn't recognized the voice, that rock-hard grip on her neck registered. She'd felt it before, could see evidence of it in the dark spots that still marked her flesh. Grace's fingers, Susan was certain, had left those print-shaped bruises.

Susan's heart lurched with the realization that Grace had been one of the pair inside her house last week. This young woman, who worked for the sheriff's department, had been the one who'd grabbed her and smashed her head against the door frame. Was Grace Cato—or Morton or whatever her name was now— somehow involved with Ramirez? And if she was, how many others within the department were as well?

Terror curled in Susan's stomach and licked along her spine. Was Grace retaliating for far more than a failed class? Did she know that Susan had identified her cohort to the authorities in San Francisco? Or—

worse yet—did the guard mean to finish what Ramirez had started?

Glaring savagely, Grace raised her nightstick and pressed the end against Susan's throat. "I asked you a question, bitch. Or do we need another strip search?"

Terrified by the promise of violence in the younger woman's eyes, Susan dropped her gaze. And flinched at a loud noise, certain the guard was about to smash her windpipe.

A split second later, she realized the sound had been that of the door opening. A male voice followed. "Morton, get your ass in my office, *now*."

Grace's fingers on her arm dug deeper, promising she'd make Susan pay for witnessing her disgrace. And pay even more dearly if Susan dared to complain about her treatment.

"I was just taking this prisoner upstairs to see her attorney when she started resisting, sir," Morton said. "Isn't that right, Maddox?"

Susan's mouth opened, but she couldn't force an answer past the knot of terror that tightened in her throat.

A tall black man stepped into view. "I'll escort Ms. Maddox to the interview room. And you'll be waiting in my office when I return."

Making a sound of pure disgust, Grace pushed Susan away and stalked down the corridor, her footsteps pounding out a rhythm of frustration.

Susan breathed again. She distinctly remembered Bernard Fielding from a parent conference, when he'd asked her to keep an eye on his son. The younger Fielding had been a good student and quite popular, but he'd gotten several threatening calls after he'd begun dating a white girl. Fortunately, the calls had stopped and Ocotillo Consolidated had lumbered one step closer to the twenty-first century.

"H-how's Jason?" she managed. Her face burned with the awkwardness of falling back on normal niceties in such an abnormal situation.

"He's doing well at Texas Tech. In his junior year already."

"Engineering major, right?" she asked, absurdly desperate to recall this snippet from her normal life. A life, she realized now, that she never would reclaim. Should a band of angels float down from on high to sing odes to her innocence, the fine taxpayers of Ocotillo County would never tolerate a teacher who had been charged with such crimes.

The realization felt like a cold blade to her heart.

Fielding smiled and nodded. "You always took an interest. The kids liked that about you."

They did, she remembered. They hadn't all been like Grace Cato. Susan felt so grateful, she couldn't stop the tears from leaking down her face. "I didn't do it." Her voice sounded so high-pitched and strained she barely recognized it as her own. "I swear to you, I didn't."

"I'm not here to worry about that," he said. "I'm not here to judge you. Now let's go and see your lawyer, and you can tell him all about it."

When Fielding took her arm, she flinched, though the pressure was gentle. Pausing, he pulled up the white sleeve of her top. Fingerprints were clearly visible, a crimson row that Susan knew would soon turn dark, to match those behind her neck.

She heard the harsh rasp of his exhalation.

"This won't happen again." He pulled the sleeve back down to cover the offending marks. "I'll see to it she straightens out her attitude."

Though his words had the weight and gravity of a promise, Susan said nothing about her suspicions regarding the break-in at her house. How could she make such an accusation with so little evidence to offer? Besides, as much as she wanted to trust Fielding, she didn't know him well enough to bet her life that he was not somehow involved. If he meant to seriously discipline the guard, wouldn't he mention taking pictures of the bruises?

He took her upstairs to the building's ground floor and left her in a tiny, pale green room, where a bookish-looking man with a beaky nose and a shock of red-blond hair pumped her hand energetically and introduced himself as Buster Hardy.

Under other circumstances, she might have laughed, the name ran so counter to the wiry man's appearance. "I'm sorry," she said, "but I thought the judge appointed Mr. Ryder as my attorney."

"You can keep him if you'd like, but Luke Maddox hired me," he said. "I'm better."

His matter-of-fact claim barely registered, for the mention of Luke stung like a plague of wasps.

"But I thought . . ." she started, sinking into the metal folding chair across from the attorney's. A scratched and dented table stood between them. "I was sure he . . ."

All through the night, she'd been too shocked to cry, incoherent with her misery. Now she couldn't stop the tears from coming. Luke had heard, he'd *heard* Hector say she was under arrest for the murder of his brother. Even as the sheriff mumbled his way through her rights, Luke had tried to tell her he didn't buy it for a second, that he'd stand by her until this thing was

274

straightened out. In fact, he'd shouted at Hector until the sheriff threatened to arrest him, too.

Yet she had been dead certain he would back away from her. How could he not, with his mother grieving, his brother's body lying in some morgue? If blood was thicker than water, wouldn't spilled blood form the strongest glue of all?

"He made me promise to tell you that he loves you," Hardy said quietly, "and that he doesn't believe one word the sheriff said. Luke will come and see you as soon as he's been cleared for visitation."

"They're saying Brian's dead," she told the lawyer, her eyes filling with tears. "All this time, he's been dead."

"That seems to be the case."

"I don't even know what killed him—what killed either of them."

Hardy shook his head. "I'm not certain anyone does right now. The bod—they were in pretty bad shape, from what I've heard. There was enough left for dental records, though. That's how they were ID'd so quickly."

How could she explain that this changed everything? That Brian had been dead while she had blamed him? He'd been *dead*, while she'd been sleeping with his brother. She couldn't get past the shock of it, couldn't think of how to feel. About Brian or herself. About Luke, either.

Would it be fair to allow the newspapers and the gossips to tear Luke all to pieces when she wasn't certain she could stand to look at him again? Would it be right to let him sever his last ties to a widowed mother who now had no one else?

The selfish part of her shrieked, *Hell, yes*. If Luke didn't care about his reputation, why should she? And as for Virginia Maddox, maybe it was time the woman learned that her family name and political connections couldn't buy her everything.

But even as Susan thought these things, she knew that both were wrong. Luke might not lose his job over local gossip, but he couldn't comprehend the other costs as she did. If he chose her over his family, he would never again be welcome in his hometown, would never be able to think of it—or her—without bitterness. And Susan understood as well that mothers made mistakes the same as anyone else, only theirs so often came out of myopic love and wounded pride. As had her own mother's when she'd refused to acknowledge Susan's marriage.

"I won't see Luke," Susan told the lawyer. Rising from her seat, she said, "I'm sorry you had to make the trip out here for nothing."

The attorney shook his head, then brushed thick, coppery bangs out of his eyes. "Luke Maddox has been a friend of mine since he moved to Austin a few years back. We play racquetball a couple of times a month, meet for beer and barbecue almost as often. I know him well enough to say unequivocally that my services aren't contingent on your seeing him. He wants you taken care of, no matter what else happens."

She shook her head, remembering the shocking bills she'd received for legal advice after Brian's disappearance. She knew those would be nothing, nothing at all, compared to this. She'd heard that people sold their houses to pay for criminal defenses. And that often even that was not enough. "It's far too much money, too big a debt to—"

Hardy smiled. "First of all, Luke Maddox can afford it. Easily. Secondly, from what I understand, your Podunk sheriff has a shit case that any decent judge'll toss out in a heartbeat."

For the first time since she'd been arrested, hope fluttered inside her. But almost immediately it was stilled, suffocated by the thought that, however experienced and competent this Austin attorney might be, he knew nothing of the secret machinations of Ocotillo County, where sheriff's deputies were killers and jailers were housebreakers, where a band of conservative ladies-who-lunch ran the elections, and a washed-up teacher in a hundred-year-old jail could be silenced before she ever went to trial.

"Susan doesn't want to see you," Buster Hardy told Luke on the phone. "She tried to refuse my services, too."

Luke glanced over his shoulder at his mother's bedroom door and breathed a sigh of relief when it remained securely closed. Even with the sedative the doctor had prescribed, she'd fought sleep long and hard before she'd finally surrendered. Her good friend, Ellie Gomez, who had driven in from Midland to be with her, was resting in the guestroom, so she would be awake and ready when Virginia needed her again.

Confident he wouldn't be overheard, Luke carried the cordless phone into the family room. "You said she *tried* to refuse your services," he noted. "I hope you talked her out of it. Everyone around here knows a Dan Ryder defense is no defense at all. The guy hasn't gotten anybody off in twenty years."

"Wouldn't want to piss off his racquetball amigos?" Hardy asked. "Or is it golf instead?"

"Roping buddies," Luke corrected, "the West Texas equivalent. These guys like to cowboy on the weekends."

To keep from pacing, he sat on the sofa.

"That's a new twist," Hardy said. "But yes, I did talk her out of it. I *am* a lawyer, and right now, she's in no shape to argue."

"How *is* she?" Luke asked.

"Scared, exhausted. I'd say she hasn't slept or eaten. She looked pretty banged up, too, but she told me the marks I saw were from the break-in and the accident that you described."

Luke tried not to picture her in jail garb, tried not to imagine the abrasions and the bruises standing out against the pallor of exhaustion. But it was useless. She'd filled his mind to overflowing so that every time he closed his eyes, images of her suffering spilled over. And yet she didn't want him to come and visit her.

"Did she say why she won't see me?" Tail swaying eagerly, Duke padded over and rubbed his ear against Luke's hand. Absently Luke ruffled the dark fur.

"She doesn't want anyone right now, doesn't even want her family notified," said Buster. "That's not as unusual as you might think, in these circumstances. People get confused, embarrassed—"

"She doesn't have one thing to be ashamed of. If anyone should hang his head, it's Abbott, imagining she's a murderer when one of his own damned deputies tried to kill her. What he's thinking, I can't—"

"You're preaching to the choir, Maddox," Hardy assured him. "But maybe your sheriff doesn't need a conviction. Only an arrest. It's nearly August, right? Just a few months short of an election. Didn't you tell me that up 'til now, Hector Abbott hasn't had an opponent in decades? When I was with the state attorney general, I saw elected officials do some crazy things to keep jobs they thought they owned."

Luke agreed that Hardy could be right. But instead of easing his mind, the possibility made him more determined than ever. "You've got to get her out of there as fast as possible. If this is nothing but some bullshit political ploy, I'm going to the papers with everything I know."

"You let me do this my way, or I won't be involved," said Hardy. "As your attorney, I'm not about to let you incriminate yourself, and if we want real action, we're going to go through legal channels, maybe the A.G.'s office or the Texas Rangers. But let's hold that back for right now, use it if we have to. Given a long enough lever, a man can move the world."

"What do you mean, Buster?"

"I mean, let me see what I can do."

Luke didn't ask him to elaborate. If his friend was hinting that coercion would loosen the system's grip on Susan, it wouldn't do to make him spell it out. Buster was a good man, smart and levelheaded. Luke's gut told him he could trust the studious-looking lawyer with his life.

But in some ways, it was far harder to trust the man with Susan's.

The watcher's hands shook so hard, the piece of paper trembled. He laid the paper down on the table and smoothed its tattered edges, hoping it wouldn't look as damning from that angle. Hoping it wouldn't fit together with the puzzle pieces in his brain.

Blood dripped off his fingers, dotting and obscuring but not erasing a single damning word. *BIG REWARD*, the photocopied filer screamed in crude block lettering, *FOR INFORMATION LEADING TO THE ARREST OF THE MURDERING PIECE OF FILTH WHO RAN OVER MY BEST FRIEND!!!*

Colleen Thompson

A string of profanity followed, each expletive under-scored with angry double lines. Below this was a photo of a hairy black-and-white dog, along with the date, December eighth of last year, and a description of the vehicle.

A description that jibed perfectly with the hubcap he had found that day and the vehicle he'd seen parked beside *her* house only days ago.

More blood, hot and slick, dripped onto the last lines of the flier: *CONTACT CACTUS ANNIE. THE RANGERS HERE KNOW WHERE TO FIND ME.*

Yet if the rangers had had their way, he never would have found the flier, never would have understood the terrible mistakes he'd made. When the ranger had spotted him staring at the paper on the bulletin board near the campground, he'd strode over, torn the thing down, and tossed it in a trash basket.

"She's a sad old woman," the ranger had said, shaking his head, his green eyes sympathetic. "I take down maybe a dozen of these every week. Wish I knew who keeps making copies for her. We can't have her plastering this sort of language all over, scaring off our visitors."

"Anybody know what really happened that day?" the watcher had asked carefully. Though he usually didn't speak to the park personnel, he came to the park often enough that they knew him by sight. Some might even feel sorry for him, a speculation that made him feel like breaking something. This day, however, familiarity had prompted the graying ranger to speak more freely than he ever had before.

"Way I understand it, some Ranger Rick-wannabe pushed his overpriced wheels too fast around a curve, ran right off onto the opposite shoulder and knocked poor Annie's mutt twenty feet into the brush. It was

280

stone dead when we found it. If Annie'd been walking a little closer, he would have killed her, too."

"So how come you didn't catch him?" Though his heart was pounding, the watcher had kept his question light and curious. He'd never been much good with people, but he'd figured out they clammed up if they felt criticized.

The ranger had shaken his head. "We sure would have liked to. Cantankerous as she is, we sort of keep an eye on Annie, help her out as much as she'll let us. But no one else saw the accident, and she didn't get the license number, didn't even see if it was from Texas. And this yahoo didn't sign in at the ranger station like he should have. He must've slipped past when our guy stepped in the rest room. Could be he was just cutting through this end of the park on his way to Shotgun Canyon. We really try to discourage that, you know."

The ranger had raised his thick brows, implying that he knew his visitor went there often. But he didn't lecture—and it was a damned good thing, because by that time, the icy crystals had started forming in the watcher's veins.

Veins that even now were leaking over a table in the house he'd broken into after snatching the flier from the trash basket. But despite the gray dots swimming in his vision, the watcher decided that his punishment wasn't coming fast enough. After arranging all his special photographs around the flier, he picked up the blood-streaked shard of glass and dug into his wrist deeper, until the pain shot through his bones.

He could never undo his phone call, could never make up for failing to comprehend that everything, from *her* journey to the canyon to what he now knew had been a family member's innocent kiss, had been a test to see if he was worthy. Had the watcher passed the test, they could have been together, exactly as she'd promised that night she'd left her ring for him to find.

Instead, he had failed so utterly that she would never see him as more than a fucking loser, a vindictive shit who'd struck out at her like a toddler in a tantrum. Screaming with rage at the thought, he swept the photos and the papers off the table, his wrist smearing a bloody arc across its cool tiled surface.

It looked almost like a sunset, he thought in the last moments before his intolerable existence flickered and went out.

Chapter Twenty-one

Luke pulled into the driveway at Susan's house behind a dented green Dodge and the camouflaged El Dorado, which resurrected more memories every time he saw it. If he got hold of that wreck, he'd get rid of that god-awful paint job, replace the broken windshield, lay the chrome on thick, and—

"Sorry to bug you, man, but I didn't know who else to call," Marcus said as Luke climbed off his motorcycle. "When I saw his dad's heap here, I started pounding on the door, thinking maybe he's done something stupid. Then I saw that broken window and got scared. I ran over to the neighbor's and borrowed his phone book. You were the only other Maddox in the listings."

Luke clipped the chin strap on his helmet and hung it over the handlebar. The bike's windshield remained a cracked reminder of his run-in with the hawk, for he hadn't yet had time to order a replacement.

"You should have called the sheriff," he said.

Marcus shook his head. "It's breaking and entering to come here, right? I wouldn't want him getting into trouble. He's . . . he's had this thing for Mrs. Maddox for a long time, and we're all upset about her getting busted. But you've got a key, right?"

Marcus had been the cocky one earlier, bragging about how he and Jimmy would steal the contents of Brian's storage unit. Had something spooked him since then, perhaps something that had happened with the aging hippie, Boone?

But instinct warned Luke that this wasn't the time to ask about that. Right now, they needed to find Jimmy before the neighbors got nervous enough to call the authorities themselves.

Luke had never had a key, wasn't even certain Susan was still the house's owner, but when he spotted drops of blood on a bedroom window's broken glass, he didn't stop to worry about technicalities. After using a rock from the desert garden to smash out the remaining shards, he reached through to unlock the window and slide it open.

Climbing through, he glanced back at Marcus. "Come on. Your friend might need help."

Marcus hesitated, but finally the shaggy black-gold head nodded.

This must be the master bedroom, Luke decided after glancing at the furnishings. Instead of the mess he'd expected to see, neat rows of labeled boxes stacked along one wall and well-swept floors bespoke a cleaning crew's attention. Since he and Marcus didn't see Jimmy, they split up, racing from room to room as they shouted the boy's name.

It was Luke who found him, slumped over the kitchen table. Blood—a great deal of it—was everywhere, smeared across the table and pooled on the tiled floor beneath Jimmy's dangling hand.

"Oh, shit," said Luke a second before Marcus's harsh cry echoed through the room.

"Is he . . . is he—? Damn you, Jimmy, if you're dead, I'm gonna, gonna . . ." The teen's words disintegrated into harsh sobs.

Jimmy certainly *looked* dead, his flesh so waxy, his head canted so unnaturally to the side. Luke's mind filled with the sight of the dead hippie, the smell of his spilled blood. So strong was his sense of déjà vu, Luke raised his arm reflexively and glanced over his shoulder, preparing for the blow that had struck him from behind five days before.

Shaking off his shock, Luke rushed forward and pressed his fingers to Jimmy's still-warm neck. He dug deeper, trying several positions, praying he would find a pulse. There it was, weak and thready, but unmistakable. Jimmy lived—at least for now.

Grabbing Marcus's big hand, Luke thrust it toward Jimmy's slashed wrist. "Elevate it, and keep pressure on the wound. And hold the other wrist, too. I'm calling for help, but we can't let him bleed out before they get here."

Moisture streamed from Marcus's eyes and nose. Against his sudden pallor, pimples stood out like dark welts. "I'm sorry . . . so sorry I went along with it. Sorry that I helped him."

Helped with what? Had Jimmy and Marcus killed the hippie when he'd caught them stealing Brian's mail? Luke didn't stop to ask, for he was too intent on snatching up the kitchen phone and praying it was still connected. He lost his footing on the blood-slick tile and went down on one knee. Rising, he ignored the splash of crimson soaking into the left leg of his jeans and grabbed the receiver.

The dial tone was one of the most welcome sounds he'd ever heard. When the 9-1-1 operator answered, he asked for an ambulance and gave the address.

"Hurry, please," he said, "before this kid bleeds to death."

If he hadn't already. Though the dispatcher would have kept him on the line, Luke hung up to look for linens to make bandages. A minute later, he was tearing a bedsheet into strips while Marcus kept up a steady stream of *"Don't die, don't die, don't die,"* in the voice of a small boy.

"Keep hold of the other arm while I wrap this one," Luke said.

Marcus watched Luke's every move, but still, he couldn't seem to keep himself from babbling. "Shouldn't've done it. Never should have got involved with any of this stuff."

Luke started to ask him what, but his gaze had fallen on the photographs littering the floor. They were all of Susan, many of them identical shots that looked as if they'd been torn loose. From yearbooks, he decided. One appeared to be a candid of her leaning over Jimmy's lab table and pointing out some part of a frog he'd dissected.

All the photos were smeared and spotted with the boy's blood.

"Jesus," Luke breathed, then fell silent as he turned his attention back to Jimmy's wrists. When he had finished, he told Marcus, "Keep the pressure on. The bleeding's slowed a lot, but it still might help."

Luke hoped the diminished flow didn't mean the kid had exhausted his supply, but he seemed to be breathing. Yet when he called Jimmy's name and shook his shoulder, the boy still didn't stir.

Marcus's palms made bloody prints as he gripped the bandaged wrists. "Maybe we should lay him on the floor now, put his feet up. I . . . that's what I remember from my health class, for shock."

"Good idea," Luke said, and carefully they followed the suggestion. As they laid him down, Luke noticed a crumpled paper with a picture of a dog, but he paid it little heed.

"Not much to do but wait now," Luke said. "You want to tell me what's been going on?"

Marcus shifted to wipe his streaming nose against the shoulder of his T-shirt. For the first time, he seemed to notice the pictures strewn across the floor. "Oh, shit," he said. "Shit, Jimmy. I never knew it was so bad."

"What was so bad?"

Marcus sighed, sounding more like an old man than a kid. "He didn't realize I knew about it, how he liked to watch her. I'd see his dad's beater parked on Old Hale Road, you know, other side of the hill here? So I followed him one day and caught him watching with a pair of old binoculars."

"What did you say?"

"Nothin', man. It's not something you just bring up with your best friend, like, 'Hey, Jimbo, I see you like to look at our biology teacher while you whack off.' "

Luke winced at the image. "Little awkward, I guess. But stuff like that gets serious. There are stalking laws for a reason, Marcus. People end up getting hurt." Glancing toward Jimmy's limp form, he added, "People end up getting killed, and I don't mean only him."

Luke knew something about stalkers; one of his employees had dated a woman so thoroughly terrorized by her ex-boyfriend, she'd ended up moving out of state and going to the courts to have her name changed. In most cases, the person who ended up hurt was the victim, when she didn't live up to the stalker's warped imaginings. But in this case, had Jimmy's obsession led him to kill those he perceived as impediments to Susan's happiness? Boone, when he'd stood between her and the items she had wanted? And maybe even—and this suspicion froze him to the marrow—maybe even Jessica and Brian, if the kid had somehow learned of their affair?

"He didn't hurt nobody," Marcus insisted. "Well, nobody except you."

"*Me?*" Luke echoed, but it made sense, didn't it? Jimmy lived on Rocky Rim. He could have had the opportunity, especially if he and Marcus had been returning to break into Brian's unit again. "He's the one who hit me?" Had Jimmy drugged him, too? And if so, why? Had the boy perceived Luke as a rival?

Marcus hesitated, looking so thoroughly miserable, Luke almost felt sorry for him. "I . . . I'm not sure, not for certain anyway. When I came in, he was standing over you. There was this big rock in his hand, and Boone was . . . Boone was . . ."

Luke nodded. "He was dead. I saw him, just before someone hit me from behind. If Jimmy would hurt me, what makes you think he didn't kill Boone?"

"Because he said it was that cop—he saw him leaving."

"Which one?" Luke asked, although he knew the answer even before Marcus said it.

"That one with the scar, you know? Right along his forehead. Some Mexican name."

"Ramirez," Luke said grimly. "But I still don't understand what you did. Maybe if you tell me—"

"I helped Jimmy drop you in the desert so the cops

wouldn't find you with Boone's body and start asking questions about Miz Maddox. We figured you'd get yourself home when you came to."

"Nice of you to take my keys."

Marcus's gaze dropped. "Sorry, man. I accidentally left them in my pocket when we drove off. I'll get 'em back to you, I swear it."

Luke had no such hope for his cash, so he didn't bring it up.

But Marcus wasn't finished. "I don't know why I let him talk me into helping. My mom's gonna kill me when she hears about all this. I mean, I've done some dumb things before, but Boone got *murdered*. We should've just told what we knew."

Luke thought of his own stupidity at seventeen and how it had cost him Susan and damn near cost Ramirez everything the night they'd had their race. Luke thought, too, of the mercy Hector Abbott had offered him, how he'd used that second chance to build a better kind of life.

"The ambulance will be here soon," Luke said. "And probably someone from the sheriff's department, too. Why don't you make yourself scarce before they turn up?"

Marcus glanced down at his friend's face. "How can I leave Jimmy? He's been my best friend since the fourth grade."

"I think the Jimmy you remember left you a while back. This one's going to need a lot of help. He's sick, Marcus, very sick, but that doesn't mean you have to let him wreck your future. Here, you can let go of his wrists now. I'll take care of him."

The tears restarted, washing down Marcus's chalky face. "But I . . . I can't just—"

"Don't screw this up, Marcus. Susan—Mrs. Maddox—has more confidence in you than that. She'd want you to get straight, to finish school and make a good life for yourself. So get the hell out of here right now. That way, you can be the friend Jimmy needs when he gets better."

Marcus stared at him wide-eyed behind the screen of greasy bangs. After a moment's hesitation, he jerked a nod.

Without another word, the boy unlocked the patio door and took off toward his beat-up El Dorado. Moments later, Luke heard wheels backing down the drive.

"You're welcome," he said dryly. And prayed the ambulance would arrive soon.

As Luke knelt beside Jimmy, he heard a low groan.

Jimmy was trying to pull the bandage from his left wrist. His eyes were cracked open, and his fingers fumbled weakly at the knot.

He swore under his breath. "Failed . . . failed her. Let me die."

Luke gently restrained the boy's efforts to unwrap the bandages. "Help will be here any second. You need rest. Don't try to talk."

But in the three minutes before the rescue crew arrived, Jimmy Archer did talk.

And Luke Maddox listened carefully to every chilling word.

When the phone rang at 1:45 a.m., Grace Morton grabbed it on the first ring.

"Who's callin'?" she snapped. Though she'd been dead to the world a moment before, she darted an instinctive glance toward her husband's side of their swaybacked double bed.

Moonlight slashed through bent mini-blinds across a flat expanse of colorless chenille. He wasn't home yet from the bar, Grace realized as she released a pent-up breath. Last time someone had called at this hour, he'd been so sure it had been a boyfriend that he'd whaled the shit out of her, split her lip and everything. He'd been right, of course, about the lover, but it wasn't as if the bastard hadn't known from the get-go how she was. The two of them had started running around together back when she was nineteen and married to her first old man.

The line crackled with the static of a poor connection, so she didn't immediately make out the words. But some quality in the voice made her heart do a wild little skip beneath her breast.

"Manuel? What the hell are you doing, calling here? The last time, the fat prick knocked the snot out of me." Self-preservation dictated the reminder, but she was glad enough to hear from her latest lover. A few months back, she'd been getting bored with him, had been almost ready to move on to a long-haul trucker she'd met at the bar, when Manuel had cut her in on some real action. Her blood thrummed in her ears at the thought of the things they'd done together since then.

"I need a favor, baby," Manuel said, his words now clearer.

"Don't you always?" Fact was, she didn't mind. For her, risk had always honed sex to a keen edge, one she'd do damned near anything to keep experiencing. The two of them had screwed right on the floor in Susan Maddox's living room the night they'd broken in, and she'd nearly come again when she had knocked the bitch's head into the doorjamb. Violence, she'd discovered, was an even better aphrodisiac than fucking in the rest room of the fat prick's bar, or letting a male prisoner have a quick taste in a jail cell. Better even than screwing her cousin in her grandfather's tack room while the ignorant old man groomed his mustang just outside.

"Where the hell are you, anyhow?" she added. "I hear they've got you down as AWOL from work."

"What else do you know?" he asked.

"Plenty, but nothing about you. Abbott's busted Susan Maddox for the murders, did you know that? They ID'd those stiffs he found the other day."

"I heard that part," he said. "That's where my favor comes in."

"What favor's that? Could be I'm fresh out, far as you're concerned." The fact was, Grace had a short attention span. Eyeball-popping as the sex had been, the memory was already fading to an itch another cock could scratch just as well.

"I need you to get rid of *her*, and I need you to do it right now."

"You're nuts. That's one line I ain't crossing." She might get off on danger, but she wasn't suicidal. "Not for you, not for anybody. If I end up doin' hard time with some of them fine individuals I've shepherded through our jail, they'll freakin' break my neck."

"Things didn't go so well here. There's cops everywhere; we can't get out of the area. If I get caught, she'll make me, and I swear to you, I'll take you both with me."

Her bowels turned slick and icy. She didn't know the

identity of the other party and didn't give a rat's ass, but there was no way she was paying for whatever he and Manuel had cooked up. "What the hell are you trying to say?"

"I'm saying I need you, same as you needed me to help get Fielding off your back before."

She didn't want to think about that, didn't want to wonder what Ramirez had on her boss that had so far kept her from being fired. "Are you threatening me, asshole? You're the one who—"

"You loved every minute of it. You said you liked it dirty. Well, you're up to your fucking eyeteeth in this now. And who's to say who killed that hippie? You were sure as hell there. I could tell the jury how you got off on it, let them hear you—" He gave a rough imitation of a woman coming. "Sick bitch like you, you won't have to worry about jail time. They'll go for the needle, don't you think?"

A powerful cramp twisted in her belly, and she was more certain than ever that she was going to lose it. "But I can't do it," she pleaded. "If something happens to Susan, Fielding's going to know for sure it was me. He caught me earlier givin' her a hard time."

"Don't worry about Fielding." Manuel snorted laughter. "He might make noises, but it's all bark—I promise you. Remember, I used to work over at the jail, too, back when he was still a guard. With what I got on him, he won't dare push."

"But I can't. There's just no way to—"

"Sure you can do it, Gracie." His voice was slick as grease, his words silken as a serpent's. "You can do it easy. Let me tell you how."

She listened to his plan and had to admit it was a good one. No one would be all that shocked to find that a woman accused of double homicide had found a way to off herself; plenty of prisoners managed it, no matter how carefully they were watched. But still, it was a huge risk, one Grace weighed against the possibility of turning state's evidence and spilling her guts to the D.A.

Until Manuel added, "There's more money than I told you earlier. A whole hell of a lot more." He named a jaw-dropping figure. "Do this for me, Gracie, and we'll split it fifty-fifty and take off for Acapulco, or the Caribbean or Belize, anywhere you like."

She pictured icy drinks with bright parasols, swaying palms and blue waves, sand as white as sugar and the money to enjoy it all. And the fat prick and his big fists a thousand miles away, sweating out his life in a bar that stank of spilled beer, piss, and cigarette smoke.

The tight knot of fear eased into a smile. "Well, honey," she told her lover, "why the hell didn't you say so in the first place?"

Chapter Twenty-two

Luke was waiting in the dark house when his quarry came home from God knew where, maybe from some woman's, or maybe from some other secret he was living. Luke didn't care what, except that the delay had given him time to snoop through the PC's files. If the computer had been connected to a home network, he might have been able to do the job from anywhere, but his target was using dial-up, and, worse yet, the PC had been turned off.

At first, Luke found none of the files he'd sought, but he knew from experience that didn't necessarily mean they weren't there—they could have been erased. With time and a lot of painstaking effort, he might be able to reconstruct what was needed from remnants remaining on the hard drive's unallocated space. He'd attached his disk-cloning device to the computer's hard drive and set it to work making a copy he could use for his forensic work. While waiting out the process, he'd started going through the home office, desperate to unearth something—anything—that would more quickly bring this situation to an end.

Finally he found a plastic case of CDs inside the locked file cabinet he'd pried open. Inside were silver disks, each marked with the name of a month. There were only twelve, indicating that the user rotated the disks each year, copying over the previous year's file.

Luke thanked the cyber-gods that at least one person in the universe had a solid backup routine—and prayed his target hadn't remembered to erase any incriminating files. Plucking the CDs marked "October" and "November," he'd popped the first inside the laptop he had brought and thoroughly, systematically invaded his quarry's privacy.

Not that Luke gave a damn about that any more than he cared that he was breaking and entering. Armed with what Jimmy had told him before being taken to the hospital, Luke wasn't about to let a little thing like a locked door—or even the security system he'd encountered—stop him from getting what he needed to set Susan free.

"Hurry up, you murdering son of a bitch," he said when the door connecting garage to kitchen did not immediately open.

He fought to still the trembling of the pistol in his hand. He'd never liked guns in the first place, but when he'd found it in the desk drawer, he'd had sense enough to know he ought to take it. Even though he'd rather use his hands to take the man apart.

When the door finally opened, it sounded like a crack of thunder to Luke's ears. The house's owner stepped inside and reached for the light switch on the kitchen wall.

"Stop right there and put your hands up," Luke ordered. His eyes had long since grown accustomed to the moonlight streaming through the windows. Besides, the darkness left his prey at a disadvantage.

The man gave a little shout and lurched, prompting Luke to grab a muscular arm and haul him inside, then spin him around and slam his face into the wall. A plate displayed in a decorative hanger rolled off its perch and shattered on the hardwood floor near the men's feet.

"I said put your hands up and keep still," Luke repeated and used his thumb to flip back the gun's hammer. The click seemed unreal, a sound effect from a B movie—until he realized that it might have been the last thing his brother had ever heard. And that this gun might have been the one to kill him.

This time, the man complied. "For—for God's sake, don't kill me. I'll give you money, anything, just don't hurt me."

Luke's sense of unreality grew stronger, the feeling that he had stepped outside himself. Sure, he'd bent, even broken, laws in his business, but he had his own inviolate sense of right and wrong. One that would never before have allowed him to break into houses or make a man plead for his life. Nausea looped serpent's coils around his insides, squeezing until he felt sure he would be sick.

He reminded himself he didn't have that luxury. Brian and Jessica might be beyond saving, but Susan wasn't. And right now, she was the only one who mattered. Not this groveling piece of filth, and not even Luke's own future. He would right this wrong whether Susan wanted him to or not.

"I don't want your goddamned money," he growled through gritted teeth. "I just want to hear it from you.

Why'd you do it, Beecher? Why did you kill my brother and your wife?"

Hal tried to look at him, but Luke shoved him hard against the wall once more. The banker yelped in fear, reminding Luke of the terror Susan must have felt when she'd been slammed into that doorjamb. Luke's grip on Beecher tightened like a vise.

"Is that you, Maddox? Luke?" Hal asked. "I . . . I don't know where you got such an idea, but I didn't . . . I could never hurt my Jessie."

"Save your bullshit." Luke pushed the gun's muzzle into the back of Hal's neck, then cheered silently and savagely as the banker screeched in terror. Until Luke wondered if his brother had been as scared, if he had begged and lied, too, telling Hal he'd never really meant to run off with Jessica. In spite of all the evidence to the contrary, evidence that, though deleted, remained ghosted onto Hal's computer's hard drive and carelessly left among his backup files. And if that wasn't proof enough that Beecher knew, the unheard message Luke had found on Hal's answering machine would be—a message from Ramirez demanding more money to keep him from going to the cops and cutting his own deal.

"You *knew*," Luke told him. "You knew what they were planning. Jessica should have kept it to herself, but she couldn't resist e-mailing her best friend about the new life she'd be starting, how she and Brian planned to use the money from the dealership—"

"If I knew that, don't you think I would have stopped her—"

"And she was so excited over the new baby, gushing, really. I read what she wrote: 'It's a sign from God, how He wants a second chance for me away from all these terrible memories. Away from Hal trying to put Alyssa's name on a clinic where I'll have to drive past it, away from having to look at his and Robby's faces and remember every single day.' "

Hal's body sagged at his wife's words. "How could she say such a thing? Robby's . . . Robby's our firstborn, our *son*." His voice shook with anguish; his shoulders shook with sobs. "How could . . . how could she do that to our child, our family? How could the bitch betray Alyssa's memory like that?"

"So you murdered them, both Jessica and my brother."

"I never meant to do it. It was an accident, I swear it. Yes, I drove back from El Paso in time to catch them at the house before they left town. I admit it. I'd read her e-mails, but I was certain I could talk her out of leaving."

"She was pregnant with my brother's child." Luke relaxed his grip, though he kept the gun trained on Hal.

Slowly, cautiously, the banker turned to face him. "It didn't . . . it didn't matter to me. I would have taken her back. Robby needed her so much, and . . . and I thought, maybe an abortion. Or we could have kept the baby, could have just gone on like it was mine. I told her, told them both that. I . . . I begged her not to leave me. I told Bri . . . I told your brother I'd give him anything . . . anything he wanted . . . to go away and leave my wife alone."

He sounded so pathetic, Luke had to remind himself the man had lived with murder for eight months. Two murders he had gone to great lengths to disguise. "And when they wouldn't listen, what did you do then, Hal? Did you shoot them? Did you kill them with this pistol?"

"It was an accident," Hal repeated. "Br . . . Bri . . . He

just shook his head and put his arm around her, as if he had some right. They turned away and started walking. But I hadn't finished talking yet. I was still telling Jessica how I loved her when the thing went off. Not that one, the other pistol, the one I left out in the desert."

"Who was it, Hal? Which one did you kill first?" The barrel of the weapon in Luke's hand shook anew.

"It was . . . it was your brother."

"His *name* was Brian Maddox," Luke shouted. "You can damned well say it when you mention him."

"Brian. It was Brian Maddox I shot first. The bullet went straight through his back, and it came out right here."

Even in the dim light, Luke saw him touch the left side of his chest.

"He never moved and never shouted, never groaned or anything," Hal said. "He just dropped like a stone, right here on this kitchen floor."

Luke's stomach lurched at the realization that he might be standing on the same spot where his brother had died. Thrusting the thought aside, Luke focused on the rest: that Brian had died instantly, shot from behind, that maybe he'd never even seen the gun before Hal used it. If Hal was telling the truth, it certainly didn't sound as if Brian had been terrified, as if he'd pleaded for his life. It wasn't much, but it was something, some tiny mote of comfort floating on this hell-wind.

"I thought it would be all right then," Hal went on. "I thought Jessica would finally listen. But instead, she screamed and screamed, and then the gun—"

"Don't tell me. The gun went off again. And then you had an idea, didn't you, to take money from your bank? A half million you claimed Brian took when he skipped town. That was why I couldn't find it when I located the accounts he'd set up earlier."

"You don't understand," Hal pleaded. "I had . . . I had taken it already."

"*You* embezzled from your bank? Why would you do that?"

"It wasn't what you think. I didn't . . . I would never take the money for myself. It was . . . I did it for Alyssa, for the clinic. So her memory would stay alive forever, so poor people could find help, so other parents wouldn't have to watch their children die."

"It never occurred to you that you'd be caught?"

"At first, I didn't really think about it. I just thought about the clinic, how it would look, all new and shining off of Main Street, how it would do such good for years and years. And then, when I started to realize that people might not understand, I hoped . . . I thought I could find some way to pay it back. I trusted that the Lord would provide."

Luke was struck by the fact that both Hal and his late wife had a strange take on religion—one was certain that God would help him with a cover-up, the other imagined that He'd blessed adultery.

"When you found out about your wife and Brian, that was when you thought of blaming him," Luke said. "That was when you forged loan applications, wasn't it? You planned to kill him from that moment, didn't you?"

"No. I swear I didn't. It was only later, after they were dead, that I . . . I couldn't let my son lose both his parents."

Luke had his doubts about the selflessness of Hal's motives, but another question troubled him more. "So how did you manage that answering-machine message? The one from Jessica."

"She . . . she'd tried to walk out on me six months before she . . . before the end. She left that message and ran off to her friend's in Amarillo with Robby. I drove there and got her back, but I recorded the message and saved it in case she took off again. I wanted something, some proof of her history, if she fought for custody. After . . . afterward, I just played back the old message into the machine. Then I destroyed the first one. But I swear to you, I only did it for my son."

Luke's throat tightened. "You conniving bastard. You had every step planned, didn't you? So where does Ramirez come in? I know he's in this with you. I know all about that old man he killed on Rocky Rim, and how he stole evidence from Susan's Jeep, too."

When Hal said nothing, Luke pressed the muzzle of the gun to the tender flesh below his left eye.

"No. Don't do it, please," Hal begged. "Ra-Ramirez caught me leaving the park. I'd just left the . . . their bodies, and I was driving as fast as I could to get back to El Paso for my meeting. I'd hit . . . I'd hit this dog, too, and . . . Well, Ramirez pulled me over. There was . . . there was blood on my face, on my hands, from Jessica and your br . . . from Brian Maddox. And my SUV was . . . I'd used a shower curtain and some old sheets, but it was a mess. I . . . I couldn't go to jail. My son—"

"Quit using that poor kid as an excuse. You were scared shitless and you know it. So what did you do? Offer Ramirez a payoff? Then hire him to do your dirty work?"

In the silence that followed, Luke heard the ticking clock. Hal didn't answer him, in spite of the gun's presence.

"Did you pay him to kill Susan to keep her from getting too close to the truth?" Luke demanded. "And did you cut in the sheriff, too, to get him to arrest her when that failed?"

"What? Oh, no, not Abbott. Just . . . just Ramirez. And then I had to give him more, to keep anyone from finding out. But I couldn't get Susan, couldn't make her trust me. I knew she'd found something, but she never would say what."

"Smart woman. I ought to head-shoot you for what you've done to her, and my brother and your wife, too. Not to mention my mother. Do you know what she's gone through?"

"Ou-ought to? You mean . . . you mean you aren't going to kill me?"

Luke shook his head. "I'd rather see you rotting in prison, watching out for convicts armed with shivs and praying you won't get raped in the shower. I've already called the Texas Rangers while I was waiting for you. We're going to get this sorted out tonight."

At least that was what he'd been telling himself, that he'd have Susan out of jail and in his arms before the sun rose. Part of him knew it might take longer, that already the night had dragged on far too long, but still, Luke held on to the possibility.

The phone began to ring. Luke did nothing, waiting for the answering machine on the kitchen counter to pick up. Moments later, Ramirez came on the line. "Don't sweat our little problem, Beecher. She'll be committing suicide tonight, with a bit of help. But it's gonna cost you big time. Another hundred grand. I'll call back in the morning, and we'll make the arrangements."

It was all Luke could do not to snatch up the receiver and scream at Ramirez to take it back, all he could do not to squeeze the trigger and leave Hal dead, so he could drive off without delay.

Because Luke knew beyond all doubt that Susan was the "little problem" the deputy referred to and that the so-called suicide he'd mentioned was meant to silence her for good.

Chapter Twenty-three

It was frightening how quickly Susan's focus shifted to survival. She remembered from her educational psychology classes a pyramid of human needs, recalled how as long as a person felt unsafe, she couldn't think of learning, love, or achieving personal goals.

Just as well, since she'd lost all hope of any of those things. For now she could concentrate on little more than the effort to lift her plastic utensils to her lips, then chew and swallow the unidentifiable food on her Styrofoam tray. (*Filet d'Naugahyde,* some perverse corner of her brain guessed. *Powdered potatoes au gratin. Lime-green gelatin containing bits of what was either fruit or insect parts.*)

She tried hard not to taste it, tried not to feel the slimy coolness as it slipped down her throat or to gag when she moved the next bite to her mouth. Her body demanded nourishment, even as her spirit went without.

The food might have been tasteless, but a full stomach finally allowed her the release of sleep. Though she'd feared nightmares, her exhaustion was so complete that she dropped into a black fragment of oblivion.

The nightmare would come later, when she woke.

People were such freaking idiots, Grace Morton decided as she waved good-bye to the women's guard who worked the graveyard shift. Or maybe it was only that most were happy to swallow any lie that benefited them.

Take Janice Stiles, for example. When Grace had shown up after three a.m. with some bullshit story about how she and the fat prick had had a fight and she had nowhere else to go, the vastly pregnant forty-year-old had only nodded tiredly and made a couple of sympathetic noises. When Grace had offered to finish her shift for her so she could go home and put her feet up, Janice had tucked her romance novel under one arm and disappeared faster than longnecks at a barbecue.

Which gave Grace the perfect opportunity to get cracking on the next part of her plan. Presently, the only female isolation cell was housed below ground in a basement used mainly for storage. After some flea-bitten whore had whined about a guard copping a freebie last year, Sheriff Abbott had forbidden male employees from going downstairs when a woman was locked up there. The rule was a pain in the ass, forcing whichever female guard was on duty to trot up and down stairs all day retrieving this or that. Tonight, though, it would guarantee that none of the men on duty would come down and interrupt her.

Perching on the edge of a beat-up desk in one of the supply rooms, she tore a white prisoner's uniform into thin strips. Making the cloth into a rope was nowhere near as easy as Manuel had made it sound. Acutely aware of the passing time, Grace cursed when her first few efforts came to pieces as soon as she pulled on them. How the hell did suicidal prisoners manage it anyway?

Then a memory resurfaced, of her half-Comanche grandfather leaning against the hitching post outside the barn, his age-spotted hands patiently twisting horsehairs from wiry manes and tails into strands, then methodically winding those strands into rope. The old fart had always had to do everything the hard way, but if the memory served her, she swore she'd light a candle in his memory.

The recollection of his patience worked even better than his methods, and before long she had a workable rope, not nearly as good as her grandfather's but plenty strong enough.

Now all she needed was some way to render Susan Maddox more cooperative. Manuel had been sketchy on the details, only suggesting that Grace should be careful not to leave marks. She figured a few might be all right, though, since the bitch still bore bruises from their late-night encounter in her house last week, along with fresher bumps and scrapes from a car wreck a few days later. Drugs would be easier, but Maddox had no history of using them, and afterward, the coroner would surely test her blood. Forcing her at gunpoint seemed like a good plan, but the more Grace thought on it, the more she doubted it would work. Her old teacher might be depressed—who wouldn't be, in her situation?—but instinct warned Grace she'd still fight like a wildcat if backed into a corner. If Maddox forced Grace to use the automatic she'd smuggled in under her shirt, the shot would surely bring others running from upstairs. Maybe Grace would be able to talk her way out of a murder charge and maybe she wouldn't, but she decided she damned well didn't want to find out.

A prisoner suicide would be far better, and Grace grinned as an idea came to her that would guarantee the plan's success.

Hector Abbott floored the accelerator of the patrol car he kept parked at his house, but he didn't bother flipping on the lights or siren. For one thing, he wasn't likely to encounter any traffic during the six-block drive at four a.m. For another, he didn't want anyone, even his own people, to hear him coming.

Luke Maddox's call had roused him in the dead of night, and what he'd said had raised chill bumps on Hector's flesh. Ramirez was planning to have Susan killed tonight in jail. If Hector's suspicions were correct, Grace Morton might even be murdering her now.

Luke wouldn't tell how he knew, wouldn't do anything but demand that Hector get his ass downtown and do his job. He wished he could have told Maddox to quit bothering him, wished he could have dismissed him as just another riled family member, but the unmistakable authority in the younger man's voice put Hector in mind of old George Maddox, Luke's father. George had been one hell of a man, never a braggart or even the kind of fellow to let folks know the considerable good he did in the community, but more than man enough to handle Virginia Hale, who'd had enough pride for any six grown women from the time she was in pigtails.

However Luke knew about Ramirez's plan, Hector would bet his pension the younger Maddox brother wasn't going off half-cocked. As Hector sped past darkened homes and businesses, he was equally certain that he'd only have about five minutes' lead time before Luke reached the jail, and there would be hell to pay if anything had happened to his brother's widow.

Since he'd learned that the two had been together in San Francisco, Hector had figured Luke and Susan's relationship was more than one of in-laws. Even before the trip, they'd been seen together several times of late. Something was going on there, Hector reasoned, and wondered if it could have extended back to when Susan and Brian had been married. Could Luke, too, have been involved in his brother's and Jessica Beecher's murders, or had Ramirez been the guilty party all along?

As he pulled up in front of the old jail, Hector figured he would know by the time he got downstairs—if he found Susan's corpse in her cell.

Hard, cold metal poked into Susan's hip. Two points, like prongs, shifted with her as she tried to move away, even in her sleep.

Intuition jerked her awake a split second before pain ripped through her, white-hot agony that sent every muscle into spasm. She would have screamed, but the message never made it from her overloaded brain to her clenched throat; would have flailed or struck or run to escape, but no part of her body could break free of convulsion.

It seemed to last forever, though she had no frame of reference to tell her whether her torment went on for a few seconds or an hour. Her thoughts were so scrambled that by the time it finally ended, her long limbs curled reflexively, like those of a spider blasted by a squirt of pesticide.

Though her eyes remained open, some time passed before she could make sense of what she saw. Grace Morton was standing over her, her unpainted face lit with a demonic smile. She was swinging something around—some kind of black baton with metal fangs. Grace's mouth was moving, Susan realized as her own heart thumped frantically and the garbled sounds in her ears resolved into harsh words.

". . . wish I'd had one of these bad boys back in high school. Then we'd damn sure see if you'd flunk me 'cause of in-fuckin'-vertebrates."

Rolling onto her side, Susan struggled to keep the moving stick in sight. What the hell *was* that thing anyway?

Grace shoved it under Susan's chin, pressed it hard into the skin when she tried to jerk away. "Don't move without my say-so or I'll zap you 'til your goddamned brains boil out your ears."

Susan froze, fearing the baton's bite—by this time she'd figured it must be some sort of stun gun—more than the pistol in Grace's holster.

The guard's grin widened, contrasting sharply with the cruel glee in her eyes. "I knew you'd see it my way. Now I'll need you to take off your clothes and throw them over there, back in the corner."

The terror jolting through Susan overrode her caution. "No!" she shrieked, spinning away from Grace as she looked for some avenue of escape.

Even had one existed, her weakened muscles were far slower than the snake strike of the stun baton and the impact of its venom. She dropped to the floor, helpless to escape the agony flowing through her left arm into her body.

This time, tears streamed down her face by the

time the shock ended. In spite of her damp face, Susan leveled the harshest glare she could manage on her tormentor.

"I . . . I don't know and I don't want to know what sort of sick ideas you've come up with, but I'm not taking off my clothes," Susan said. "And if you . . . if you think you can bully me into keeping my mouth shut about this, you're even dumber than you were in high school."

Instead of shocking her again, as Susan fully expected, Grace shrugged indifferently. "Have it your way, then. I'll just cut 'em off after."

After. The way she said it sent a different kind of jolt through Susan's nervous system, as did Grace's lack of concern about the threat to report what she was doing.

Because she means to kill me, Susan realized, her skin crawling.

Her gaze flicked to something—some sort of rope, she thought—wrapped among the bars with a long loop drooping above her cot, and the bitter taste of bile filled her mouth. Because she knew then, absolutely *knew*, what Grace meant to do and why she needed Susan naked.

The guard had fashioned the rope of prison clothes to make Susan's death look like a self-inflicted hanging. She thought of Luke and her mother hearing of the "suicide." As Susan imagined their bottomless grief, her rage rose like a hot, red tide. Her body trembled, not with pain or terror, but with a lethal rage she'd never guessed she possessed. She would kill this woman— *kill* the vicious bitch—to keep Luke and her mother from suffering such anguish.

She was so afraid Grace would read her thoughts that Susan willed her eyes to close and her body to go completely limp.

Grace punished her with a sharp kick to the thigh. "Get up."

When Susan didn't move, still-warm prongs pressed against her temple. Revulsion crawled around the pit of her stomach, but she concentrated on giving Grace nothing to work with but deadweight.

At Grace's string of cursing, Susan braced herself for another taste of lightning. Instead, she heard knees popping as the woman squatted over her and shook her shoulder. "Still with me, bitch? If you think I'm hauling your ass up on that cot myself, you're fu—"

Susan exploded into motion, the heel of her right hand striking Grace's sternum hard enough to set her on her rear. With her other hand, Susan clamped down on Grace's wrist in an attempt to keep her from raising the baton. She threw her whole weight into pinning the struggling, screaming guard, even as Grace's free hand groped for the gun stuck in her waistband.

Eschewing both his motorcycle and Hal's Hummer, Luke tore through town in a late-model Buick that had once been Jessica Beecher's. As he fishtailed around a corner, he ignored the odd sounds from the trunk, the thumping and pounding that assured him Beecher was very much alive back there. It had taken Luke only a few moments to disable the emergency trunk release and pull out the tools Hal might have used to free himself, and an even shorter time to convince the banker that the alternative to climbing inside was a bullet to the head.

Luke ignored the muffled shout behind him as he slammed on the brakes in front of the jail and bailed out, leaving the door open. He was far past caring about anything—especially Hal's condition—except getting to Susan in time to save her.

He'd taken a hell of a chance calling Hector Abbott and demanding the old man get to the jail, but Luke had felt he'd had no choice. For one thing, the ten extra minutes it would take Luke to drive from Hal's subdivision outside of town might have been ten minutes Susan didn't have. And Luke had believed Hal's denial that the sheriff was involved. Besides, it wasn't as if Luke could break into the jail himself and stop whatever might be happening. If he'd tried, especially in his desperate state, some trigger-happy desk officer would have probably panicked and shot him.

Even so, as Luke's feet pounded up the building's front steps, he wondered if he should have followed his first instinct and told Abbott the Texas Rangers were on the way. Would the old man have been more careful to safeguard Susan if he'd known his actions would be scrutinized, or would he—as Luke had feared when he had called—have been happier to see her dead, figuring a closed case would not draw as many questions?

As he pushed open the front door and stepped into an antiquated-looking entry area, Luke fought his need to shout or move too quickly—until he caught sight of a tall black man talking to another, older uniformed guard behind a counter.

"Have you seen Ab . . . have you seen the sheriff?" Luke demanded.

Both men looked up at him, suspicion written on their faces. How much did they know? Neither appeared armed, but Luke imagined they would have weapons within reach. The thought made him acutely conscious of the gun he'd left behind in Beecher's garage.

"I'm Luke Maddox," he continued, gambling on his professional experience, which told him a conspiracy could only range so far. "Has Sheriff Abbott come in yet? I called him about some trouble with a prisoner. It's important that I see him right awa—"

At what sounded like a distant crack of thunder, all three men turned toward a closed door along a corridor to their right. Both guards ran to a locker behind the counter and pulled out rifles. Weapons in hand, they raced to flank the door.

The taller man paused, his hand on the door pull, his dark gaze boring holes into Luke's face. "What sort of trouble? Are you talking jailbreak?"

Though his entire body shook with the need to push past both men, Luke forced himself to stillness. Forced himself to take another chance. "A killing. Someone means to murder Susan Maddox and make it look like suicide."

"Who's down there?" asked the black man, worry etched in his strong features. "Isn't Janice Stiles on tonight?"

The second guard, a thin man with oiled gray hair combed straight back from his forehead, shook his head. "I saw her leave a while back. She said the seven-to-three guard came in early and relieved her."

"Grace Morton—oh, *goddammit.*" With that, the black man flung open the door and raced downstairs, his weapon at the ready.

"Captain Fielding," shouted the second guard. "Wait, Bernard. We need to call for backup—Jesus!"

When his superior didn't listen, the older man followed in his wake.

Both guards were too preoccupied to know or care that Luke came after them, entering a dank concrete basement corridor lined with closed doors and lit with flickering fluorescent lights.

They found Hector Abbott lying beside the third, closed door, his shaking hand pressed to a splash of crimson on his left shoulder. Though his face was ashen and pain had pinched his features, his blue eyes were clear and focused as he looked up at his men. "It's Grace—you've got to stop her. She's working with Ramirez, tryin' to get rid of Susan Maddox."

Fielding turned to the older guard. "Call for help. I'm going in—"

"Not alone, and that's an order," Hector told him. "I'll last, but the prisoner won't."

Looking past them to Luke, he said, "We'll get your woman out of this, I swear it."

With his gaze focused on the blood oozing between Hector's fingers, Luke wondered if the lawmen could possibly deliver on that promise.

"Look what you made me do, you bitch," Grace screamed, fighting to swing the muzzle of the gun toward Susan's face.

The two struggled wildly on the unyielding floor, each desperate to gain control, neither hesitating to claw or gouge or do anything that might give her an advantage. Susan knew she'd cast the die the moment she'd jumped the younger woman. She'd given Grace no choice but to kill her, and now that the guard had fired on—and apparently hit—Sheriff Abbott, she wouldn't bother staging a suicide.

They rolled as one, Susan using her powerful legs to flip Grace beneath her. Though Susan was taller and more athletic, the guard still had the advantage of weapons, and of the adrenaline born of terror and sheer meanness. As Susan forced Grace's gun hand toward the concrete, the guard turned her head and sank sharp teeth into Susan's forearm.

With a shriek of pain and outrage, Susan lost her grip, and Grace's hand moved, in what seemed an exquisitely slow arc, to bring the muzzle up toward Susan's throat. With her other hand, Susan snatched up the stun baton and groped for some kind of switch, knowing she would never make it, certain Grace would pull the trigger first.

"Stop there or I'll shoot!" bellowed a deep voice from the corridor even as a second man yelled, "Halt!"

Grace hesitated for only a fraction of a second, but it was time enough for Susan to activate the stun baton. Time enough for her to push it into Grace's torso while uttering a fragmentary prayer that it wouldn't hurt too much when the other guards shot her to death.

The scene was something from a nightmare. More jailers pounding down the stairs with guns, Sheriff Abbott shouting orders, someone screaming for an ambulance, Grace shrieking when Fielding hit her once more with the stun baton as she reached for her dropped handgun.

Luke added his voice to the chaos, shouting, "Beecher did it! Hal Beecher was the one who killed them."

But Susan only blinked at him before sinking onto the bench in her now crowded cell. Her gaze lost focus as she stared into the middle distance, seemingly unaware of everything around her. Luke's heart lurched at the sight of what appeared to be a hand-made noose drooping just behind her, between the cell's bars. With a sickening jolt, the guard's plan came into focus.

As Grace was dragged out screaming curses, Luke pushed his way inside. Kneeling at Susan's feet, he laid his hands atop her thighs.

"Susan, are you hurt? Can you say something?"

When she failed to respond, he begged her, "Look at me. Did you hear what I said? It was *Beecher*. It was Beecher all along."

She blinked again and made eye contact. "Hal? Hal killed them?" she asked before throwing herself into Luke's arms and sobbing like a lost child.

Their reunion was cut short when arriving deputies dragged Luke away from her, their drawn guns pressed into his side.

An hour later, he stalked the interview room like an angry tiger, knocking one of the aluminum chairs out of his way as if it offended him, then spinning on his heel to glare at Buster Hardy.

"I *have* to see her now. I have to know she's all right. She was crying so hard, she couldn't even speak." If he'd only had more time with her, Luke was sure he could have coaxed her into talking. Could have prevented her from retreating to some silent corner inside herself, as she had when the deputies pulled him away. As Luke was hauled past the EMTs preparing Hector for transport, he'd shouted her name and struggled for one more look at her. Susan had been staring blankly at her feet as if she were surprised that they still anchored her to this world.

"When I tried to talk sense to the bastards, they said

to stop fighting or they'd shoot. All they cared about was goddamned Beecher. *Beecher*, after what that bastard did."

As his wiry attorney frowned at him, Luke's complaints wound down. He knew Buster well enough to realize his friend was losing patience, especially since he'd been rousted out of his motel bed by a five a.m. phone call.

Hardy righted the chair Luke had knocked over. The lawyer sat, his thick hair ruffled and his thin face washed out in the bright fluorescent light. He took a slug from a sweating soda, an off-brand cola he'd picked up from a machine. A second can sat unopened on the table.

"What did you expect?" Hardy asked, keeping his voice calm and steady. "You'd just charged in here with knowledge of a crime that was occurring in their own jailhouse. When they found out the sheriff had been shot, you're damned lucky they didn't blow your head off first and ask questions later. Law enforcement tends to get a little excitable under such circumstances."

"But I was the one who came to warn—"

"You were the one who had a *man*—"

"A murdering son of a bitch who'd killed my brother—"

"The local bank president," Buster corrected, "locked in the trunk of a car you'd taken from the house you'd entered, shall we say, without an invitation. Did you think of that, Luke? Did you take one second to think about the trouble you were getting into?"

"Susan's alive. That's all that matters. That and getting her out of this hole."

Buster grimaced. "That'll do you a whole hell of a lot of good if *she's* out and *you're* in. Now, if you'll listen

318

for one minute instead of shouting at me, I'll tell you what I found out on my caffeine hunt."

Luke lowered himself into the other chair, his attention riveted on his friend's face. He clamped his shaking hands between his knees.

"First of all, the EMTs checked over Susan. They took her to the hospital to be officially checked out, but it doesn't look like anything more serious than a human bite to the forearm."

"You're kidding. That woman—that guard—*bit* her?"

"So it seems. Maybe we can talk 'em into cutting off the head and sending it to the state lab for rabies testing."

The joke was wasted on Luke. "Was Susan talking? Is she all right? Are they going to let her out now?"

Hardy flashed a smile. "I'll check on her as soon as we get finished, but the good news is that your friend Beecher is in the next room spilling his guts. They made him wait for his attorney to hotfoot it over here, but I hear he's confessing to the murders as we speak."

Luke exhaled a pent-up breath and snapped the tab on the second cola. "Then they can't keep Susan."

Buster nodded. "That's the way it works. And maybe, if we play our cards right, it'll mean we can keep you out of jail, too, while we're at it."

Luke had faith he'd find some way to wriggle out of trouble. He only wished he felt as optimistic that freedom would include a future with the woman he loved, and that Susan, in her haste to put this ordeal behind her, wouldn't cut ties with all things Maddox and hit the ground at a dead run.

Chapter Twenty-four

Susan offered him no smile when she saw him standing at the entry to the apartment, but Luke counted it as a victory that she didn't close the door in his face. As soon as Peavy recognized him, the Chihuahua stopped his brain-rattling yapping and danced about on his hind legs.

Luke reached down and rubbed the little fuzz-ball behind his tasseled ears. His tail wagged almost hard enough to levitate his tiny rump.

"Luke. I thought we agreed you wouldn't come here." Susan turned away as she spoke, already reaching to take a framed print off the wall. The watercolor featured a small herd of Texas longhorns grazing in a field of bluebonnets. "I thought we decided that you wouldn't push."

From the looks of the boxes, she'd already made a big dent in the task of packing up her mom's apartment. Luke still couldn't believe that Maggie Dalton had decided to stay in California, so far from the town where she'd lived all her life. It reminded him that the only constant in this world was change, and that people changed as well as circumstances. Even his mother was at risk, making noises about selling the ranch that had been part of her family for generations, moving into a smaller place that would be easier to care for and closer to her friends. And Hector Abbott, who had been sheriff nearly as long as Luke had been alive, had announced from the hospital that he would be retiring to Colorado, where he planned to take up fly fishing and spoiling his grandchildren. Instead of being forced out in a cloud of suspicion, as Luke had supposed might happen, Hector was being hailed a hero for his part in thwarting Grace Morton and Manuel Ramirez's plan. The first Ocotillo County officer wounded in the line of duty in decades, Abbott was recovering in a room said to be filled with flowers, balloons, and handmade cards from local kids.

Luke, too, had made out better than he'd dared to hope. Despite the fact that only a few days earlier, he'd broken into Hal's home, terrorized the man, and locked him in a car trunk, the attorney general had referred the case to a grand jury without charges. By the time Buster Hardy had laid out the circumstances, the jurors, West Texans to the soles of their boots, had not only refused to indict Luke, but had made it clear that if they'd had the power, they would have given him a medal.

Grace Morton had no such luck. They'd not only indicted her for all the crimes the prosecutor had suggested, they'd supposedly sent a note to the judge asking if they could hammer her with a few more for good measure.

"*You* decided I should back off," Luke told Susan. "I don't recall agreeing."

"I'm grateful for what you did." She turned to look at him directly. "More grateful than I can ever tell you. I'll never forget it. But there's too much else I can't forget . . ." She waved a hand impatiently. "I can't go into this again. I'm sorry."

"Could I help you with that?" he ventured, waving at the boxes.

"Suit yourself." She shrugged, stiffly because of her bruises, and gestured toward a stack of newspapers. "You can start wrapping up the glasses in the kitchen."

He grabbed a handful of papers and carried them to the next room. And stopped, staring at the array of cakes, pies, and cookies stacked on every surface. "What's all this?"

She peered across the countertop that separated them. "Reparations, I guess. People have been stopping by all day. You should see the fridge."

Curious, he opened the door and found the cool interior crammed with casseroles of all descriptions, plates of sliced cold cuts and deviled eggs—the same sorts of offerings now littering his mother's kitchen. Ocotillo County's balm to salve all wounds, even the guilt of those who'd been spreading hurtful gossip far and wide.

Though he hadn't had much of an appetite the past few days, his stomach rumbled at the sight of such largesse. "I'll bet you haven't had dinner, have you? And you probably picked through lunch, too, if you even bothered. I'm making you a sandwich."

"I'm going to work on my mom's bedroom, get together the clothes she wants me to send. But you go ahead and help yourself." She spared him a fleeting smile. "There's a blue dish on the top shelf. I'm sure you'll like it. It's Roberta's tuna casserole."

·Standing at his feet, Peavy gave a plaintive whine.

"There's no need to get ugly," Luke said. Everyone in Clementine—including the dog, apparently—knew about Roberta's cooking. "I'm making you a sandwich, and you're damned well going to eat it."

"*You* decided that. I don't recall agreeing," Susan quoted over her shoulder on her way out of the living room.

"Your mistress is one mule-headed woman," Luke told the Chihuahua, "but I suppose you know that."

Peavy sat up on his hind legs and whined again. This time Luke succumbed, feeding him tiny scraps of cheese as he threw together a belated lunch. A few minutes later, Luke carried two plates with the sandwiches, a couple of deviled eggs, and brownies into the bedroom.

Unlike the front rooms, this one had not yet been packed. The antique dresser remained decorated with the inevitable doilies, a silver brush-and-mirror set, and a profusion of fussy perfume bottles. Family photos, including several of a pair of little girls Luke recognized as Susan and Carol, still hung on the walls, and a colorful quilt covered the carved oak bed. Susan stood in front of the small closet, her back to him, her shoulders shaking as she wept.

Luke set down the plates on top of a tall chest of drawers. Then slowly, cautiously, he crossed the room and wrapped his arms around her.

Instead of jerking away and cursing him as he more than half expected, she pressed her wet face to his shoulder. "Damn it, it's not fair," she railed. "Hal's confessed—the son of a bitch spilled every detail—and Manuel and his brother were both picked up at the border. And still I lose. Everything. My job. My friends. My mother. Every damned thing I thought mattered."

Her tight fist beat a rhythm of frustration against his chest, but he said nothing, sensed that doing so would make her turn away from him forever.

"And you know the worst of it?" she asked. "The very worst thing? I can't even hate Brian anymore. I . . . I . . . can't even hate him. He's even taken that from me by being dead."

For a long time Luke merely held her, stroking her back with his hands, pulling her closer when she finally gave herself over to her tears. "I'm having some of the same problems, about Brian. People stop by with their condolences, talk about how he was this great guy, and all the time I'm thinking I'm sorry that he's dead, you know? But that doesn't change what he did, what he meant to do."

Susan pulled back far enough to look into Luke's face, a look of wonder widening her eyes. Luke hoped she was realizing that the two of them were coping with a lot of the same feelings.

"He's cost my family, too," he added. "Cost us the business my dad spent his life working to establish. Cost my mother a considerable amount of pride, too, and we both know what a premium she puts on that."

Susan's smile, grim and fleeting, did nothing to dispel the sadness in her red-rimmed eyes.

"But there's one thing I won't let Brian ruin." Luke's hand touched her damp cheek. "It's the chance for you and me."

She turned away again, head shaking. "I can't, Luke. I've told you I can't."

He pressed his lips to her neck, a soft kiss to her ear. "Will you let him take *this* from you, too?"

Her neck arched as her head tipped backward. Her eyes closed, yet a tear dripped onto his face.

325

He moved around her and feathered light caresses onto her mouth, kisses that coaxed instead of plundered, invited rather than insisted.

"I won't," she whispered over and over, more and more insistently, until Luke drew back from her to stare at eyes as huge and luminous as a cat's by moonlight. "I can't do this, Luke."

His disappointment cut so deep, he couldn't speak past the thick lump in his throat. Brian—that self-centered asshole—had destroyed this with all the rest. He had poisoned the phoenix rising from the ashes of the past. Though Luke was certain Susan would eventually make a new life, he would never be a part of it.

As if she'd read his mind, she told him, "My old principal called, the one who took that assistant superintendent's job in Corpus Christi. She's heard about my problems, and she's offered me a job. It's not in the classroom. After everything that's happened, she thinks I need some time to 'get my head together,' or maybe she's just scared I'll break down in front of kids or parents. But it's a job, Luke, in a city where I can start fresh, forget all this ugliness."

"Why not Austin?" he asked, though she'd already explained when he'd proposed in the moments after her release. "I love you, Susan. Why not make a new beginning as my wife? I'd help you get a job there. I'll help you get past everyth—"

"I won't—I *can't*—let you fix my life," she insisted. "I couldn't live with Maddox money, Maddox influence buying my way out of hell. And then there are the memories, Luke."

"Don't you have any good ones?" he demanded. "Of me, of us?"

She raked her fingers through her hair, swept one

thick lock behind her ear. "I don't know. Maybe—I'm sure they're part of it. But I need some time to sort through what I feel, to come to some kind of peace with what I've—what *all* of us—have been through."

Her head jerked toward a knock at the apartment door. Luke cursed the interruption. He needed one more chance to make her remember how good, how right they'd been together, once upon a time.

"Don't answer it," he told her. "It'll just be a fresh round of casseroles."

But she only smiled sadly, then headed for the door.

As the knocking grew more insistent, Susan scooped up Peavy on her way to answer it.

"I'd ignore it," Susan said to Luke over her shoulder, "but I don't want them to start stacking plates and block the door."

"I can think of worse things than being barricaded in here with you," he said, his words so wistful that they set off a deep ache in her chest.

Unlike her other visitors, Marcus had come empty-handed. When she opened the door, he dropped his gaze, reminding her painfully of his best friend.

Peavy squirmed in her embrace, eager to greet the teen. Mindful of the dog's penchant for escape, she tightened her grasp.

"Is it . . . has something more happened with Jimmy?" The last she'd heard, his condition was stable, though he remained in the psychiatric ward.

Marcus shook his head. "Nothing really new. His dad came off his drunk long enough to sign the papers. He's letting the state take custody so Jimmy can go into that treatment facility on their dime. I . . . I'm really glad"— with an effort, he looked her in the face—"really grateful you talked that prosecutor out of pressing charges."

She nodded, still sad and disconcerted by the thought of Jimmy's dangerous obsession. Though she'd racked her brain for clues, she couldn't think of anything she'd said or done to make the boy believe she had romantic feelings for him. But to a child warped by neglect and probably abuse, perhaps a few scraps of attention had been all it took.

"I wish he didn't have to go away at all," she said. "I wish there was something I could do to . . ."

She stopped when Marcus shook his head.

"No, ma'am. No. Mr. Maddox was right when he said Jimmy's sick. Anybody who would take your ring and . . . and do what he did with it, anybody who would slash his wrists because he thought his teacher—his *teacher*, for God's sake—was going to marry him needs a lot of doctors. I mean, no offense, Miz Maddox, but you're like, what? Maybe thirty?"

Susan couldn't help herself. She laughed at the disbelief, the abject horror, in the teen's voice. "Two years past that," she said. "Practically in my dotage."

Marcus made a face that told her he hadn't a clue what "dotage" meant. And wouldn't ask her for a million bucks.

"Listen," he said, "I didn't really come here to tell you about Jimmy. I came . . . I'm s'posed to bring you over to the school-board meeting."

"The school-board meeting? What for? I was arrested, Marcus. Charged with murder, and my . . . my husband was . . . well, let's just say the family-values crowd won't soon forget this, especially with elections coming up."

"I think you'll want to see this."

She was all set to say no, but something about the directness of his gaze and the firmness of his voice made her hesitate. For one thing, going with Marcus would get her away from Luke, whose deft touches and soft words were tearing down her defenses faster than her common sense could shore them up. Besides, the more she thought about trading the wreckage of her life for a future counting the spines of mildewed textbooks in some windowless warehouse on the Gulf Coast, the more depressed she grew. She would do it— she would force herself to put the past behind her— but before she left here, she had one last lesson for the students she had taught.

She was going to let them see her go out fighting.

"Can you give me ten minutes?" she asked Marcus. "If I'm going to the school board, I'm going to dress the part."

"You look okay, Mrs. Maddox."

"For an old woman," she added, though she imagined that her careless dress and uncombed hair would have a different impact on the so-called "responsible" adults. "Five minutes, and I'll meet you by my Jeep."

"But I was going to drive you."

"No offense, Marcus, but I've seen your driving—and your car. I'm banged up enough already, thank you." She said the words lightly, trying to convince herself the old Cadillac meant no more to her than any other junker. She would never know for certain if it was the same one Luke had once owned, the same big old convertible where she had given herself over to the magic of the desert and the night. But she'd be damned if she would climb back in the thing again, damned if she would open the floodgates of the very memories she was struggling to hold back.

Marcus grinned. "Have it your way, then. I'll see you in five."

She passed Luke in the hallway on her way into the apartment's second bedroom.

"I didn't mean to listen in, but I heard the bit about the school-board meeting," he said. "So you're going? I thought you said you'd given up."

She opened the closet and reached for a pair of khaki slacks and a short-sleeved black linen blouse. "This way, at least the kids will see I tried. They'll understand I didn't choose to leave them."

"I'm coming, too," he said.

"They won't let you in. Personnel meetings are closed to the public."

"Let me drive you, then. I'll wait for you outside."

Susan thought of arguing, but she didn't have the strength. For one thing, she suspected that by the time she turned her back for the last time on her teaching career in Ocotillo County, she would be hard-pressed to see through the haze of her own tears.

As things turned out, it didn't take nearly so long for her to weep. From the moment they turned onto South Agave Avenue, her eyes filled with moisture, and she was relieved to have someone she trusted driving her and Marcus.

The squat, tan brick school-board meeting hall was surrounded by a sea of humanity. Hundreds of students carried signs and banners, every one of them with a lit candle in hand against the deepening dusk.

And it wasn't just the kids who had come. As she surveyed the crowd, she saw a number of her fellow teachers, along with former students and the parents of those she'd taught over the years.

"See the signs, Ms. Maddox?" Marcus asked from the backseat. "Can you read 'em?"

Not very well, between the pinkish streetlights and her own blurred vision. But she made out enough to get the gist. Signs such as *Justice for Susan Maddox, Bring Back the Best,* and *Fair Is Fair.* A dozen seniors standing by the front doors held posters that read, *We're 18 and We Vote!*

"There's one that ought to scare the snot out of them." Luke chuckled as he pointed out a large banner saying, *Write-in Your Vote—Susan Maddox for School Board.*

Despite the hot tears streaming down her face, Susan shook with laughter—then gaped like an idiot when the crowd spotted her red Jeep and started cheering.

Across the street, she noticed another tiny knot of citizens marching in a tight circle and carrying their own signs, with slogans such as *Morality in Our Schools* and *No Distractions!* Susan didn't recognize most of them, except for a couple of ultraconservative trouble-makers famous for protesting nearly everything.

She thought of mooning them as they drove past, but she quashed the impulse on the grounds that such an act would probably prove their point.

"Knock 'em dead in there, Mrs. Maddox," Marcus told her. To Luke, he explained, "We tried to make 'em let us in, but they made up some bull . . . some privacy rule. I think maybe we scared 'em."

"You were behind this, weren't you?" Susan asked, amazed to think of Marcus, one of the biggest screw-offs going, applying himself to anything, much less organizing a demonstration of this magnitude.

He looked away and shrugged, but she didn't miss the quick grin. "I had a lot of help. Caitlyn and Rolando, Shelby and V.C. all did lots. Some of the teachers, too, but they don't want the school board hearing about their part."

Susan couldn't blame them. If they faced retaliation, it wasn't as if there was anywhere else in the county they could teach. Most had families, and relocating would be far easier said than done.

People moved aside, leaving room for Luke to pull into the space closest to the front doors. She stared at those doors, at the hand-lettered *Closed Session* sign, and she began to shake, knowing that whatever went on behind them would forever change her life.

Luke grasped her hand and kissed the trembling knuckles. "I want you to remember, whatever happens in there, you have a future. And if you'll let me, I'll be part of it. No matter how long it takes you to come to your senses."

As she stared into his handsome face, she felt such a surge of emotion that her heart filled with the need to say how deeply she loved him, how if the time and circumstances had been different she would jump at the chance to wake up beside him every day. Only just in time, she clamped down on the impulse, convinced it would be unfair to give him hope. Still, she drank from the oasis of peace found in his smile, the comfort in the final squeeze he gave her hand.

With one last, deep breath to bolster her, she climbed out of the Jeep.

"Give 'em hell, girl!" Agnes shouted. Courtesy of Larinda's cutting-edge work, her hair bore a frightening resemblance to a certain hamburger-hawking clown's. Yet instead of hiding at home under a paper bag, she stood here, beside Roberta, the two of them wearing matching T-shirts with the slogan: *S.O.S.—Save Our Susan!*

Susan managed a tight smile, then walked up the steps and through the front door without a backward glance.

As Luke and Marcus climbed out of the Jeep, the teen dug in his pocket and produced the key to Luke's old pickup.

Flushing, Marcus said, "I'm really sorry, man. I wish I could go back and undo some of the things I got into. Y'know, I drove your truck that night, to leave it in the desert. I shouldn'ta let Jimmy talk me into that."

"You can't make the past better, only the future," Luke said. He palmed the key, twisted it around to look at the logo on the leather fob, then tucked it into his jeans.

"I guess." The teen glanced up, then flashed a sheepish grin. "Your truck was acting up and backfiring, scared me half to death. So I shot a little lubricant into the valves, fixed her right up."

"You like the old heaps, too," Luke said, thinking of Marcus's camo Cadillac.

The kid shrugged, and Luke saw the chance he had been waiting for. "I have a proposition for you."

Marcus looked up, puzzlement written in his features. "Yeah?"

When Luke made him the offer, the boy's eyes grew huge beneath the black-gold fringe of his bangs. "You gotta be kiddin', man. That's nuts."

Smart kid that he was, however, Marcus didn't turn down the proposal.

The school board didn't keep Susan waiting long; Luke would give them that. After fending off Marcus's thanks, Luke spent the next twenty minutes meeting some of Susan's most fervent supporters, many of whom impressed him by telling how she'd changed their lives.

Then he heard someone whisper urgently, "They're coming out now."

The message was repeated until the crowd grew silent to watch as Susan walked out the door, followed by a man Luke recognized as the superintendent, Dr. Winthrop, and the school board's president, who was up for reelection in November. Standing at the top of the steps with Susan between them, both men smiled and waved at the hundreds assembled. Susan glanced from face to face, her expression contorted by what Luke took to be an effort to fight off another round of tears.

He wanted to march up those steps and take her away from here, make her forget whatever hurts the bastards had dished out at that meeting.

But Winthrop was talking, raising his voice so it would carry as far as possible. A barrel-chested man who'd coached football before receiving his administrative degree, he needed no microphone to make himself heard.

"For once, the board and I are all of one mind on an issue," he said, then paused for a ripple of polite laughter at the reminder of their legendary budgetary battles. "What kind of message would it send to our students to punish a gifted teacher for crimes she clearly had no part in? Therefore, we have reinstated . . ."

A cheer rose from the crowd, obliterating his words and drowning out the tiny pocket of boos from the protesters. It took some time for things to settle enough for the superintendent and the school board to complete their speeches, in which they congratulated themselves at length for their fair-mindedness, as if they hadn't fired a woman over gossip in the first place. The listeners soon grew restless, and a few teens shouted for Susan to say something.

At last, the board president deferred to her. Even then, she stood silent for a long while, looking more dazed than relieved.

"Thank you," she finally managed. "Thank you, all of you, for being here this evening. I . . . I can't begin to tell you what this means to me . . . but I will say that any senior writing in my name on the November ballot will be risking detention."

This time, the laughter sounded genuine. She used the distraction to wave and then make for the safety of her Jeep. Luke climbed into the driver's side seconds later.

Considering the number of people eager to congratulate her, their escape was easy. Within minutes, they'd left the block dominated by the school administration building and Clementine Elementary's aging brick facade.

"I can't believe it," Susan said, so quietly that he could barely hear her. "I'm staying. I'm staying in my hometown, and I can keep my job. And with the money from the life insurance and your friend Mr. Hardy's help, I should even be able to fix the problems with the IRS. I'll get my life back, Luke. It's all I've ever wanted."

They rolled along little-used side streets for some time before Luke said, "I'm going to buy my mother's ranch. She wants to sell, and I'd like to keep it in the family."

"Will you lease it out," she asked, "or use it as a vacation place?"

"I'm going to live there, I think, scale back my involvement in P.O.M., and work online from home. My mother's going to need me, for one thing. And besides, I realize how much I've missed this place."

He felt her scrutiny, sensed the question in her stare. But he didn't come out and tell her he'd be waiting here for her to change her mind. He'd decided he would give her the time she needed—or at least as much of it as he could stand.

And then he'd take one last shot at resurrecting what his brother's murder had destroyed.

Chapter Twenty-five

Susan sat on the balcony of her new second-floor apartment, her feet propped on a plastic chair, the tests she'd spent the last few hours correcting tucked inside her grade book. Leaning to her left, she reached for the cold beer she'd promised herself once she had finished, the one she'd brought out ten minutes earlier in honor of this fine Friday evening and an October sunset so pure and clear its colors looked hand-painted against the backdrop of the sky.

She'd found a place on Clementine's outskirts and a balcony that overlooked an expanse of unclaimed desert to the west, just across the narrow side street where the dozen-odd residents parked their vehicles. The unit might be small and spartan, but the twilight displays and glimpses of wildlife more than made up for the lack of amenities.

By most people's standards, a single beer wasn't much of a celebration, but it had taken her more than three months to allow herself even that much of an indulgence. Three months in which she'd begun working her way toward normal, step by hard-won step. She wasn't there yet, not by a long shot, but this drink seemed like a move in the right direction.

"Damn it, Peavy," she snapped when her fingers touched a cool puddle and a paw. Sure enough, the little souse had knocked over the bottle and was greedily lapping up the spill.

When he glanced up at her, she could have sworn she saw him grin.

Grabbing him by the collar, she opened the patio door and shooed him inside. She'd long ago learned the hard way that Chihuahuas made mean drunks, and she wanted to grab something to clean up the mess he'd made.

As she reached for a couple of hand towels, she knocked a card off of her counter. She stooped to pick it up, smiling at the improvement in her mom's handwriting, which was now almost as legible as ever. Better yet, her mother's words convinced Susan she was happy in Oakland, where she'd made new friends and was moving toward independent living. Though Maggie hadn't brought up moving back, she'd mentioned coming for a visit around the holidays. It was something to look forward to.

And it would have to be enough, thought Susan, even as she tamped down another thought of Luke and waited out the hollow ache that always followed.

It was better this way, more sensible to avoid each other. After all, that was what she'd wanted. That was what she'd asked of him.

Her space. Her freedom. Time to put the past—and the Maddoxes—behind her once and for all.

So why, then, did it hurt still? Why, then, did she regret the way he'd acquiesced? She'd been burned before, too badly to waste night after night imagining him pounding down her door and demanding that she come to her senses, then throwing her over one of his broad shoulders. And carrying her off and ravishing her like some pirate of the desert . . . or a schoolgirl's fantasy.

Too late, she told herself. It had been too late from the day she'd married Brian, or maybe she had lost her chance when she'd still been a schoolgirl, when she had let her mother keep her from the boy she'd loved.

After wetting one of the towels in the sink, she made her way out to the balcony. She was surprised at how many stars had already come out of hiding, at how cold and empty the space between them seemed.

Headlights competed for attention as a big car swooped into a space along the street. Something about its shape nudged a memory, and she turned from her cleaning to take a closer look.

The Cadillac was long and sleek, just the way she remembered it. As he had all those years before, Luke Maddox slid out of the driver's seat and leaned against the newly painted blue door, his cocky grin competing with the pale light of a crescent moon. His jeans were too tight, his gaze too confident, and the Bruce Springsteen song playing on the radio too loud.

When she'd heard he'd traded Marcus his restored pickup for the wreck, she'd been afraid of something like this. Or afraid at first, then disappointed when months had passed without a word.

Now, her mouth began to water for something more than beer.

"Get a grip," she told herself. She had put together a nice life, a quiet life, without any Maddox interference or any Maddox help. She'd rocketed free of their orbit, even if she couldn't help recalling a more heavenly body than the one parked thirty feet away.

And yet, when Luke strode toward her, she felt the primal tug, undeniable as it was ancient. Turning, she went back into her apartment and locked herself behind the patio door.

But still she sensed him approaching, closing in on her like a predator that had scented blood. At the sound of a soft whine, she opened her mouth to shush Peavy before she realized the noise was rising from her own throat.

Outside her door, she heard Luke's footsteps, and she glanced down at the dog. "You can have the beer, boy. This girl is going for a ride."

She was too nervous to speak as the two of them walked into a night that smelled of mesquite and creosote . . . and the remembered scent of yucca blossoms from a springtime long ago.

He opened the car door for her, exactly as he had years before. Climbing into the driver's seat, he switched off the radio and turned to look at her with an intensity that made her breath catch in her throat and shivers of anticipation spark along her spine.

And then he asked the question, the very question so long emblazoned in her memory.

"Are you sure about this, Susan? Because there's still time to run home if you aren't."

She leaned into his arms and kissed him with a certainty in no way reminiscent of a sixteen-year-old virgin.

Because she was finished running from Luke Maddox . . . and determined not to waste this second chance.

CLAUDIA DAIN
DEE DAVIS
EVELYN ROGERS

SILENT NIGHT

Snow falls, but this is no ordinary white Christmas. There's no festive cheer, no carolers, no mistletoe. Three women are running for their lives: a college student home on break, the wife of a murdered DEA agent, a Denver widow. They're frightened and alone.

And Lindsay Gray, Jenny Fitzgerald and Tessa Hampton *are* in peril. A desperate snowmobile chase through the forest; a raspy, anonymous telephone call; a bloody stranger by the side of the road—every step seems to lead farther from safety . . . but toward what? Who waits in the darkness? Friends? Lovers? And on a cold, silent night, when do you call for help?

EVELYN ROGERS

More Than You Know

Toni Cavender was the toast of Hollywood. But when a sleazy producer is found brutally murdered, the paparazzi who once worshipped Toni are calling her the prime suspect. As a high-profile trial gets under way, Toni herself finds it hard to separate fact from fiction.

When an unmarked car tries to force Toni off a cliff-side road on a black, wet night, the desperate movie star hires detective Damon Bradley to find the truth. Someone is out to destroy her. Someone who knows the lies she's told . . . even the startling reality that lying in Damon's arms, she feels like the woman she was destined to be. Yet Toni can trust no one. For she has learned that hidden in the heart of every man and woman is . . . *More Than You Know*.

Dorchester Publishing Co., Inc.
P.O. Box 6640   _5215-6
Wayne, PA 19087-8640 $6.99 US/$8.99 CAN

Please add $2.50 for shipping and handling for the first book and $.75 for each additional book. NY and PA residents, add appropriate sales tax. No cash, stamps, or CODs. Canadian orders require an extra $2.00 for shipping and handling and must be paid in U.S. dollars. Prices and availability subject to change. **Payment must accompany all orders.**

Name: _____

Address:_____

City: _____ State: _____ Zip: _____

E-mail:_____

I have enclosed $_____ in payment for the checked book(s).

CHECK OUT OUR WEBSITE! www.dorchesterpub.com
____ Please send me a free catalog.

No More Lies
SUSAN SQUIRES

Dr. Holland Banks is head of the Century Psychiatric Hospital and president of the Schizophrenia Research Foundation . . . but is she going insane? The rest of the world seems to be. There's a sniper on the loose, she's being stalked, her father is conducting deadly experiments, and she's begun to hear voices: other people's thoughts. But a man was just admitted to her hospital—one who searched her out, whose touch can make her voices subside. Is he crazy, too, or a solution to her fears? A labyrinth of conspiracy is rising around her, and Holland's life is about to change forever. Very soon there will be . . . *No More Lies*.